The Incidental Murderer

By Andrew Tristem

For Rebecca and Toby

Table of Contents

Prologue

People debate whether it is nature or nurture that determines our characters. But to my eternal damnation I have discovered there is another far greater force which defines us. It is not linked to our genes or upbringing, yet is more profound than either. Sadly I came to understand this only after it was too late, after it had entrapped me. For I have learned through bitter personal experience that we are defined by the decisions we make and the actions we take. One moment of weakness and we are forever set on a course. A lie, a theft, a killing - once we have chosen a path there is no easy way back.

The process runs much deeper and wider than any of us could imagine. A person's character is cast the moment he gives up on the unforgiving minute of that distance run, haplessly destined to repeat the failure time and time again in all walks of life.

People aren't born or brought up to be good or evil, but become so through their very choices.

Chapter 1: The End

It was an act born out of frustration rather than anger, although that does not excuse it at all. And in that moment, the die was cast.

I clenched my left fist and with a short thrust of the arm, clouted the window. For a moment, the pane seemed to resonate harmlessly, silently. But milliseconds later, the whole shop front exploded with a loud bang into hundreds of shards of razor sharp glass, refracting a multitude of colours in the moonlight.

For just a moment revenge tasted sweet, until the full horror of what I had done dawned on me – surely, this would end my career in journalism?

Adrenaline pumped through my veins, my palms started to sweat profusely, throat dried. My eyes darted up and down the street to check for witnesses. Thank god, no one was there.

It was nearly midnight and Appleton village high street was empty of all life. Unless someone was hiding in the shadows, I had got away with my hideous act, temporarily at least. Guilt welled up inside me, but I pushed it to a dark place.

Jolting into action, I sprinted across the road to the car park where I'd left my dilapidated 20 year old rust bucket. It was a cold November evening and I was panting vapour clouds as I jumped inside and shut the door, quietly. I prayed that fortune would smile on me, and indeed, the old banger started first time. I slammed my foot on the accelerator and spun out of the car park, weaving my way through the thin country lanes as I drove back to my flat in Yeovil.

But I knew it would be a short reprieve. With no front page story for my edition of The Western Sentinel, I would be out the door just after midday the next day, five minutes after deadline. The editor had told me as much in my first week in the job. His words were whirling around my head as I motored home that night, "It's sink or swim at The Sentinel," he'd said smiling thinly, "and we've never had a blank page."

Councillor Tom Ripley, the man whose shop front I had smashed, was a very important person. He would tell you that himself. But for some unfathomable reason he despised the press and, in particular, he had a pathological hatred of the newspaper I worked for. In fact, I would go so as far to say that he had made the job impossible for me. Of course, a better reporter would have been okay, sniffing out all the quirky 'off diary' stories. But despite my 30 years, I was a cub reporter in my first few months of work, wet behind the ears, and in need of every bit of help I could get to fill the paper with stories, which meant relying heavily on local councils - and in particular Chairman of Appleton Council, Tom Ripley.

With a shock of jet black hair, never dyed despite his 52 years, which was combed upwards in a flattop style to give an extra inch or two of height, he was still barely pushing five feet tall. Some people called him Tiny Tom, but never to his face. That would be far too dangerous. He was stocky after years of weightlifting and well spoken, in the way of an air force colonel. Harrow educated and tough as old boots, Tom wanted two things – respect and money. And he wasn't going to let a small matter of the law stand in his way.

I had arrived at The Sentinel a few months earlier full of enthusiasm for my new career. After years of drudgery in a dull back office job at an information technology firm, I planned on being an important member of the community, respected by readers and councillors alike.

Naïve, yes, but I was relishing the prospect of being the 'eyes and ears of the people.'

My first day in the job should have given me a clear insight into things to come. One of Ripley's colleagues at Appleton council, Deputy Chairman Pat Cummings, collared me while I was drinking a pint in the Dancing Bear after my first public meeting.

Unshaven, with curly brown hair, a pencil moustache and a pot belly grown from decades of good living, his breath stank from a stomach full of Somerset cider.

"I don't envy you," he said in a whispered hiss. "The chairman, the council, is very wary of outsiders. You won't get an easy ride."

And he was as good as his word. I'd found out just what a prickly character Ripley was when I reported a burglary at one of his properties during my first week on the paper. He had his own way of seeking retribution and didn't want me to upset the way of things.

The burglary took place at a four bedroom detached house on Appleton High Street. A friendly contact in the police rang me with the story, so I telephoned Ripley to ask for a quote. It was our first conversation, and he told me to 'keep this one quiet.' I thought it was pretty arrogant of him, but I was so green that my response had been silence rather than a firm rebuttal, which he must have taken as passive agreement.

Being new to the job, I asked a colleague for his opinion on what to do. A fellow reporter, Don Bradley, asked me a simple question; who you are more frightened of, the councillor or the news editor? He was referring to Katie who ran the paper through total fear. I decided to run the story.

The morning the paper went to press, I had a call from a deeply irritated Ripley. I was expecting a mild rebuke, but the volley of unspeakable abuse yelled down the phone left me stunned, speechless even. It set the scene for our relationship over the next few months, although I would never use that as an excuse for smashing his shop window that night in Appleton.

Chapter 2: The Splash

As I strode despondently toward The Sentinel offices the next morning, I briefly flirted with the idea of turning around and driving back to London, without saying goodbye to anyone at the paper. But I knew that would have been an act of sheer cowardice that would have left me feeling even lower. So I decided to puff out my chest, and tell them straight; the job was not right for me. In short, I would resign.

At least I'd lasted longer than my predecessor at the Appleton and Longley edition of The Sentinel. He had fled in tears after one day. A former sub-editor at The Telegraph, he'd arrived bright eyed and bushy tailed, wanting to be a 'real journalist.' But he realised almost instantly, just how hard the job was going to be. That it would never improve. I, though, was blissfully ignorant of all its difficulties and delighted at getting stuck into the work. I didn't know I was doomed.

The Sentinel building was located near the bottom of the pedestrian zone, nestled between a stationery shop and an Italian restaurant. As I approached, my head still whirling with horrors of the night before, I saw a woman in her early twenties pacing up and down near the entrance to the newspaper. Spotting me, she scampered across in a state of near hysteria, and held out a hand. "My boyfriend's left for Bristol and I've got no money for the bus. Can you spare 20 pence?" she begged, tears streaming down both her cheeks.

I reached into my pocket and pulled out a few coins, passing them to her while looking briefly in her eyes.

"Thank you luv," she said before rushing towards a man five paces away, and repeating the plea.

I jogged up the set of stone steps, which led to the solid oak door entrance of the newspaper.

Jackie and Joan, the receptionists, greeted me with their usual friendly smiles from behind a glass shield, installed in case any disgruntled residents resorted to violence. It had happened more than once, so a panic button had been instated to press under duress. All ten of the paper's reporters were under instructions to rush down and deal with any threat. I was closest to the door, so was presumably expected to grapple with whoever was there.

On the way upstairs, I grabbed a copy of the local free paper, the Yeovil Gazette, which The Sentinel produced as giveaways at supermarkets to bump up readership figures. The stories were taken from the mid pages of The Sentinel's 'paid for' editions which covered eleven geographical areas, one of which was mine - Appleton and Longley.

On my left at the top of the stairs was the editor's office, and to ram home the importance "EDITOR" was painted in large gold letters across an oak panel on the dark brown Victorian door. On the right was the entrance to the newsroom. I pushed the door open and slunk quietly towards my desk, which was only five paces away.

As usual, the place was buzzing with the din of reporters bashing away at their computer keyboards, and making last minute calls before deadline. Of the ten reporters, just a two or three were 'seniors' and the rest were either 'junior reporters' or 'trainees,' like me and Sheffield, who sat opposite me. He was the only reporter we called by his surname, to distinguish him from me since we were both Simons.

It was the job of the news editor, Katie, and a chief reporter, Sofia, to whip the trainees or "cubs" into shape, although they weren't having much success with me or Sheffield. We weren't very good and they made it clear that we were a bit of a disappointment, occasionally roaring with laughter at our mistakes but more often holding their heads in despair.

It was Wednesday morning, which meant only pages one, called 'the splash', and two, 'the great unread', needed to be sent through to the newsdesk. Before sending stories to the subeditors, Sofia or Katie would scrutinise the copy and read the riot act to anyone who came up short. Everything had to be done and dusted by noon so the pages could be laid out by the subs, and sent to the printers in time for the paper to be distributed across south Somerset on Thursday morning.

Wednesday mornings were a tricky time for cub reporters, who were prone to being behind schedule, and were often frantically trying to make their stories 'stand up' after holes were spotted by the newsdesk. The old hands had an air of confidence, born out of years of experience, which was all the more frustrating for us. Despite the pressure, it was the buzz of the newsroom that first attracted me to The Sentinel. It created a dark humour which I enjoyed, perhaps a little too much.

Each reporter ran their own edition. Mine was by far the quietest, but I still needed to write seven 'lead' stories a week, for a patch with a population of just 5,000. It stretched ten miles long by five miles wide, with its main towns being Longley, Appleton and Bishopswood.

I barely had a chance to sit down when Katie beckoned me over with a curled index finger. It was generally a bad sign, as it invariably meant she'd spotted an embarrassing mistake. Sheffield and I called it the 'walk of shame,' because all the reporters would stop working to witness our frequent bollockings. Today was going to be more embarrassing than usual, though, because I was going to resign.

Tim, a senior reporter on the main Yeovil edition, with a reputation as a wind up merchant, rubbed his hands in glee as I strode the ten or so paces to Katie's seat. She was sitting in the middle of an 'A' shape of desks, which formed the newsroom. I composed myself as best I could because I wanted to look calm and dignified as I delivered my departing speech.

"A great story has just come in from your patch," she screeched, jabbing a pen against her notepad. "Someone has vandalised the Council Chairman's shop. It's the barometer shop on Appleton High. Know it?"

I must admit, the turn of events left me dumbstruck for a few moments, my resignation plans seemed in tatters. My inability to speak didn't please Katie.

"Do, you, know, of, it?" she yelled, her face turning instantly pink.

"Err, yes," I said finally.

"Get down there now. It's your splash," she said exasperated, shaking her head at my ineptitude. "Lord knows it's better than anything that's been in your edition lately. You'll need to type the quotes up by 11:50am, so get going. Go!"

I grabbed my reporter's note pad, which slotted perfectly into my jacket inside pocket and rushed out of the news room, crashing into the beggar girl as I left the building.

"My boyfriend has left me in…." she said. I rifled through by wallet and drew out a twenty pound note and shoved it into her hands.

"Thanks," she said, her eyes smiling as I rushed to my car, which was parked a few hundred metres up the hill.

I celebrated my good fortune by punching the air with delight as I sped along to Appleton. I parked in the same carpark I had used the night before, hoping no one's memory would be jogged. Its completion was the council's crowning achievement of the last decade, doubling the town's parking capacity to a hundred cars. That might seem a small thing, but Appleton Council wore the upgrade like a badge of honour. In their minds, no one could question the council's competence after that.

Ripley was speaking to two police officers outside the shop. Shockingly, it had been set on fire after I left, probably by the 'yobs' the council blamed for just about all the town's ills. Ripley was reluctant to allow photos of himself to be taken, but since our relationship had already broken down, I took the chance of snapping a couple of pictures of him standing outside the shop from inside my car. There was no point being polite and asking, as he would have said "no."

He spotted me as I got out and walked towards him, and looked down at his steel capped boots for a moment before meeting my gaze.

"Could I have a word?" I asked.

"I might have known that The Sentinel would be sticking its oar in."

"Do you mind if I ask a few questions about what happened to your shop?" I said doing my best to ignore the jibe.

"Tell your readers this if you must - I'll give a reward of £10,000 for information that leads to the arrest of those responsible," he said and fixed me with a hard stare.

"Can you estimate how much it will cost to replace the window?" I asked, feeling my first pang of guilt.

"A few grand maybe. But it's not the window that bothers me," he said. "Whoever did it also ruined all of the stock, including many antique barometers. That's what upsets me; some of them were priceless."

"Do you have any idea who may have done it? Could this have been a vendetta - someone who has a grudge against your business activities?" I asked, trying to pursue a news line that had popped into my head.

"What grudge - no one in this town has a grudge against me," he said emphatically. I knew it was a good quote because a big chunk of the town despised him. "I'd say it was mindless yobbos getting teenage kicks by smashing up other people's property," he added. "The police need look no further than the town's wayward youths for the culprits."

Police and firefighters were still checking the scene, and a cordon was in place on the pavement outside. I quickly moved on and asked one of the detectives if the 'vendetta attack' was a line of enquiry and was told that 'nothing was ruled out'. It was enough to 'stand up' the story, although I knew it would also mean upsetting Ripley, again.

As soon as I'd got some quotes from bystanders, I drove back to the office, arriving at around 11:40am.

"Copy in five minutes," Katie snapped as soon as I walked through the door.

There wasn't enough time to get everything down so I just typed up the 'intro' and the best five quotes and sent them through. Luckily, I heard nothing more from her after that, which meant there wasn't a huge hole in the story. Then, at 12:15pm, which was slightly later than usual, she told us the paper had been sent to the printers, and I breathed a huge sigh of relief. I'd survived another week.

I checked out the final version of the story before I left. Katie, Sofia and the subeditors had knocked my copy into shape. I thought the story was quite good for once.

'Vendetta' attack on civic leader's shop

By Simon Turner

A SHOP belonging to an Appleton civic leader was set on fire this week in a suspected vendetta attack.

Antiques worth tens of thousands of pounds were destroyed at a shop on the high street belonging to Appleton Chairman Tom Ripley.

Chairman Ripley denied that he had been targeted because of a grudge, saying the town's yobs are to blame.

He said: "No one in this town has a grudge against me. I'd say it was mindless yobbos getting teenage kicks by smashing up other people's property. The police need look no further than the town's wayward youth for the culprits."

Mr Ripley offered a reward of £10,000 for information leading to the arrest of those responsible.

He said: "Whoever did it ruined all of the stock, many antique barometers. That's what upsets me; some of them were priceless."

But police confirmed a vendetta attack against Chairman Ripley was a line of enquiry.

"Nothing is ruled out at this stage", revealed Inspector Barry Lane....

Chapter 3: Downshifting

I am what Americans call a downshifter. I gave up a well-paid but dull job fixing computers, to follow my dream of becoming a newspaper man. I would like to say I was inspired by Watergate or some Pulitzer Prize winning story. But the truth is my enthusiasm was sparked by a Thirties slapstick movie called "It Happened One Night". It's this tale of a down at heel newspaper reporter's chance encounter with a glamorous socialite which led me to believe that journalism could be the life of adventure I wanted. The reasoning was simple; if it's interesting to read, then it must be interesting to write. The lure was difficult to resist.

Certainly reporting would be an improvement on sorting out computer glitches. But I soon learned that while movie reporters get weeks to write up their stories, The Sentinel gave its staff minutes. To use a phase from the film, it really was 'a two bit sensation rag'. But it got into my blood anyway.

I liked the atmosphere of the newsroom right away. There was an obvious camaraderie. So even though my heart was set on being a national newspaper reporter, I jumped at the chance at working for The Sentinel. My plan was to work in Yeovil for a year before heading back to London to get a higher profile job there. The truth is, I had no other offers.

Cash strapped, I bought £50 car from a mate I'd met travelling around the world the year after leaving my job, and drove to Yeovil at a steady 50mph. I started work in mid-August and the weather was balmy. Everything seemed sweet. My keenness for the job spilled over into every conversation, which got under the skin of some of the more seasoned hacks, who thought they were being exploited by the paper.

Low pay and long hours having jaded their view of local newspaper journalism.

They joked that I must have been one of the oldest 'cub' reporters in the history of the paper - ten years older than the next one they hired, James Sheffield, aged 20, who became a great mate and a fellow suffering trainee.

I was freshly graduated from the easily accessible London Journalism School where I'd been awarded a post graduate diploma 'with distinction', although pretty much everyone was. The course was not recognised by the National College of Journalism Training, which is the closest thing to official training the trade has. But The Sentinel's editor, Peter Head, was sufficiently impressed with my keenness to offer me a job. Keenness being probably the most important asset for a trainee.

The bad news was I was given the quietest patch on the paper, with the highest attrition rate among reporters. The other journalists made that clear as soon as I started.

For the first few weeks I stayed in bed and breakfast accommodation, eating pot noodles and having to make do with my own company at night. I worked all hours to finish stories. Then I rented a room in a flat above a hairdressers at the top of Yeovil's pedestrian zone. The flat turned out to be pretty filthy, with plates of uneaten food left piled high overnight. The communal television disappeared one day, and the owner told me that one of my flatmates had stolen it. "Better lock your bedroom door," she warned. It was the best digs I could afford.

It was the first time I'd experienced missing meals because of work and my waistline shrank by two inches in the first six weeks in the job. I discovered that lunch time hunger pangs disappear by 4pm, and don't reappear again until dinner. I noticed that shrinkage around waistline lags a couple of weeks behind the cut in calories. And vice versa.

All the struggle was down to my own ineptitude as a reporter, of course. Many of the more experienced hands had time for a chat and a sandwich. It was just me and Sheffield that were always playing catch up.

Chapter 4: Drinks

In what was dubbed "le petite weekend," all the reporters headed off to the pub after Katie told us the paper had gone to press. Tim had come up with the name because the reporters were given Wednesday afternoons off every week after the paper was put to bed. We generally headed straight to the nearest and cheapest pub – Wetherspoon, which was just down the road from the office.

Simon was the only person who brought up my splash, although a couple of the old hands were kind enough to say my edition of the paper looked good that week.

"It is a lot better than the crap you usually come up with," Tim chimed in, in an attempt to wind me up, which he followed with "I'm only joking," and a slap on my back.

For some reason Tim had decided it was his job to be unpleasant to trainee reporters, and took pleasure at pointing out our fallibilities. Sheffield and I had to take it on the chin, because there was no denying that Tim was a far better reporter than either of us. That was hardly surprising though, since he had been at the paper for four years, so writing articles was second nature to him. He found it easy and he liked to remind us of that fact. He did have a weakness though: Sofia had told us that he hated being called Timmy, but I hadn't had the courage to test it out.

I decided it was best to ignore him, so I turned towards Sheffield who was standing in the huddle.

"Ripley won't like the headline though, so things could get interesting tomorrow," I said.

"Who cares; what can he do?" said Sheffield, which made me feel that I was being a wimp.

"He can make my life a misery at council meetings," I said.

"Yes but he can't stop you writing stories."

Sheffield was right of course. Some of the councillors tried to bully us reporters, but the editor would always back us up, even when we were in the wrong.

"Remember, we have an awfully big stick to hit them with," said Tim being a little more convivial for once. "Speak softly and carry a big stick, that's my advice."

Despite being broke, Sheffield bought a round for all the reporters who then sat in two distinct groups near a bay window. Reflecting the office set up, we instinctively divided into South Somerset and North Dorset. The Dorset reporters were huddled chatting about the stories at one end of the table, while the Somerset boys sat at the other end. It was generally accepted that the Somerset editions were more important because two thirds of the readers came from there. Everyone got on well individually but there was only the occasional chat between the two groups down the pub.

I was just polishing off my pint when I heard my phone ping with a new text message. "It's your round, lad!" was the instruction from Colin, the chief reporter of the Dorset area. He had been at the paper for five years, the longest of all the reporters with the exception of Katie who had been climbing the ladder since she'd arrived as a teenager. Colin was a friendly bloke from Bolton with a stammer, who despite being the best reporter at The Sentinel, kept failing his 'senior reporter' exam, which had been funded by the paper.

"I'll go and get them now," I texted back and went to get a round.

After I'd dished them out, Colin beckoned me over to sit next to him, so for once I found myself sitting in the middle of the Dorset lads.

"I liked that news in brief story you wrote about the terrorists targeting Appleton, you know the one?" he said.

"Yes, that's the county councillor. He keeps saying Al Qaeda is not going to target 'heavily protected London', when they can plant a bomb so easily in south Somerset."

"That's the type of story I would be writing about, rather than a smashed shop front," he said. I was disappointed he didn't like my front page, but it made sense.

"The problem is he's the only one who gives me stories, so I don't want to burn him," I explained.

"That's the problem with your edition," he said. "It's just too quiet. I would love to have a go at them one day. Perhaps when you are on holiday?"

"Fine with me as long they are still speaking to me when I get back," I said.

He smiled slyly which left me wondering if they would be.

"So how are you getting your stories?" he added.

"Mainly from council meetings, and by ringing around. I got given a good contacts book when I arrived so I use that."

"The thing is to listen out for any scrap of information," he said. "Just keep doing the rounds, asking 'what's new, anything going on?' The best stories come from the weirdest places. I interviewed the local drunk and found out he was a Falklands war hero. Got a Military Medal for bravery – brilliant story."

We chatted for a couple of hours before I staggered back to the flat, stopping on the way for a kebab.

My flatmates, an unemployed chef and a pregnant waitress, had left the kitchen in a state again. There wasn't a single clean plate and several had half eaten portions of food still stuck to them. To be fair, the waitress had warned me they were 'not a very tidy lot' when I arrived, but the place now resembled a student flat.

There was nearly always a mountain of plates with half eaten beans on toast, pizza, or whatever had been consumed for dinner, or a sink full of plates soaking to remove the hard crusts that had formed. A colony of flies seemed to constantly circulate.

I picked up a plate, washed it and ate dinner in my bedroom, falling into a deep sleep shortly afterwards.

I woke at 2am dreaming about my grandfather working at the local paper where he'd been a printer for 60 years. He showed me around one day and I saw the metal presses banging out the paper page by page – the end product streamed out at the end of the line, ready for distribution by trucks to all the local newsagents. I remember he told me that his work was 'upside down and backwards' because he had to check the spellings that way on the metal presses. He would have been proud that I'd become a journalist, I thought as I lay there in bed. But what would he have thought of my dishonest front page? The word 'shame' forced its way into my head as I tried haplessly to get back to sleep.

Chapter 5: Carrie

To save some time the next morning, I decided to forego a proper breakfast and force down some dry cereal straight from the packet. I'd chosen sugar coated corn flakes from the cupboard, which were fine for the first few mouthfuls. But with no milk in the fridge, I was forced to wash it down with a glass of tap water, which wasn't pleasant.

Yeovil's town centre is dominated by a pedestrian zone which runs through its heart. A side street runs parallel to the pedestrian zone, and I decided to walk that route because the hills sit serenely in the background.

A pub on the first corner was my local, the Unicorn, which was where I watched international rugby by myself on Saturday afternoons unless I could drag Sheffield along. He was more of a football fan. Turning right past the pub, a little further down the road, was the Indian restaurant where Colin had taken me for an evening meal with his girlfriend during my first week. He had taken me under his wing, partly, he said, because he knew how hard it was to get up to speed as a reporter.

My car was parked in a free parking spot a few metres further down the road. As I walked past, I fretted that it only had three months left on the MOT. I was already searching the paper for second hand cars, because I was certain I would have to scrap it. Working at a paper has some advantages, which included being able to check the sales section the night before the paper is in the shops. So I was scouring it each week for something under £200.

As I turned the bend at the bottom of the block and walked towards The Sentinel offices, I spotted the woman who'd approached me for cash the previous morning. She was asking for money again and, sure enough, she hurried towards me.

"My boyfriend has left me in town without any money, can you spare 20 pence for a bus?" she said, tears running down her cheeks.

For a second, I was furious at being conned the day before, but then I saw her deep sunken eyes and wasted body.

"Sorry, nothing for you today," I said hoping to skip past.

"Oh, it's you," she said clocking me. "You are the guy from The Sentinel, right? Thanks for the money yesterday."

"No problem," I said. "Better luck catching that bus today."

"Are you a reporter then?" she asked, blocking my way past.

"Yes. Excuse me I am going to be late," I said and tried to walk round her.

She grabbed my arm, her lips tight, eyes bulging and stretched forward to whisper something in my ear.

"I have a story for you if you want to hear about it?" she said in a loud whisper.

My first thought was to escape, but then I remembered Colin's advice the previous evening. Perhaps she was the type of unlikely source he had been referring to?

"Okay, I finish at 5pm so I can see you here after work, if you can make it?" I said not thinking things through.

"Suits me, but you'll have to buy me a drink," she said smiling.

I began to regret making the offer straight away, but I'd done it now and would have to go.

"I can meet you for a drink, but can't stay very long," I explained.

"Okay. My name is Carrie by the way, what's yours?"

"I'm Simon, I'll see you later," I said and she let go of my arm.

I tried not to fret about it as I sat down at my desk but I couldn't help wondering if I'd bitten off more than I could chew.

I flicked on my computer and scanned the room. Sheffield hadn't arrived yet and I could see that Katie was clock watching. He was the only reporter not in, so I assumed she was waiting to catch him arriving late. He walked in a few moments later, dead on 9am. I watched her take a quick look at the clock as he barged through the door and then quietly carry on with her work.

"Morning boss," he said sitting down with a heavy thump. He was stocky, but still in good shape.

"You were lucky - Katie was ready to pounce if you'd been late," I said.

"I know. Bloody hell, she had me in the editor's office after I was two minutes late last week. She said lateness would not be tolerated and that this was my only warning. It was way over the top."

The newsdesk had a zero tolerance policy to lateness, convinced that if they allowed any of us to be late, we all would be.

"They are paranoid," I said.

"Yes, but I am not going to push it," said Sheffield.

I couldn't help but think he already was.

The news room was about 15 metres long by five metres wide. The reporters sat around the perimeter facing inwards to where Katie and Sofia were seated.

Sheffield was the only reporter who sat on my left. His patch covered the towns of Somerton and Langport. Don Bradley who sat on my immediate right, was covering Crewkerne. Both were decent, busy patches compared to Appleton.

Further to the right were Tim and Jason, who covered Yeovil. With sales of 18,000 papers each week, it was by far the most important edition. My patch sold a little under 2,000 copies for instance.

To Jason's right was Jack Walton, a Geordie who covered the town of Chard. There had been a story about him in the paper a few months earlier. He'd had a skin full of drinks and wandered around town in nothing but his underpants. The paper had a policy of never shying away from stories about its staff to avoid accusations of hypocrisy, so Jack had to face the council sniggers the following weeks. He told us he was too drunk to remember details but he had decided to go for a walk after returning home inebriated, and had locked himself out. When he rang the police for help, they arrested him for being drunk and disorderly.

The seating in the newsroom turned ninety degrees left after Jack, and was populated by reporters from the north Dorset editions. Colin, the chief north Dorset reporter, covered Blandford. Next to him was Duncan who ran the Sherborne edition which is where I'd stayed in bed and breakfast accommodation when I first arrived. To his right were Bob, Don and Bert who ran Gillingham, Shaftsbury and

Templecombe. Don and Bert were great mates, always watching each other's backs, just like Sheffield and me.

The subeditors sat on a row of tables opposite the Somerset reporters. They occasionally walked across to query facts or the spelling of place names, but they never came for a drink after work. Subs were mostly ex-reporters, and a few years older. They had made the first step into management, although the pay was still pretty awful. It felt like the industry was dying because sales were falling steadily each year, although production costs were also coming down and the suspicion was, the paper was making a large profit on the back of low wages.

Sofia, the chief reporter, was an attractive thirty something with an athletic build and long flowing brown hair. She had a flair for writing but Tim said she wasn't keen on doing much leg work, so would pounce on the best stories as they came into the newsroom, writing them up with the minimum of effort. Her main role, though, was to rewrite and correct the news stories filed by reporters, particularly trainees, so I had spent a lot of time with her over the past few months. She was slowly training me up, but it was a painful process which included many public bollockings to make sure lessons were not forgotten.

News editor Katie Edwards was a classically attractive redhead. She was tough, always demanding better quotes and forcing reporters to re-interview people, which could be humiliating if it meant knocking on their door again. She was the daughter of a grammar school headmaster, and particularly detested poor spelling. Boyfriends had been dumped for making grammatical errors in emails, but fortunately the current one was an English teacher so we were keeping our fingers crossed for him. Unlike Sofia, though, Katie wasn't much of a writer. She had the reputation of a fearless but limited reporter, and both attributes were reflected in her editorial style. My copy was often 'hardened up' with tougher language. Mildly annoyed residents became 'angry' after she had edited the copy and were in the habit of 'slamming or blasting' the council, which lost me most of my contacts.

Sheffield and I were checking our inboxes for stories when Katie got up from her desk and came over. It was an involuntary action, but my eyes darted momentarily towards her legs; she was wearing tight white skirt which hung just above a delicate knee. Despite her good looks, she had been deemed as 'unattractive' by my fellow reporters because of her harsh attitude. I wasn't so sure.

"Okay you can bring up the papers," she said unfazed by my glance.

Collecting the papers was a Thursday morning ritual. We reporters would all march down to the basement, where unwanted copies of each edition were piled up. Before modern technology had made it redundant, the basement had been home to the paper's 'hot metal' printing press. I imagined the clatter of machines as the papers were pumped out each week. My grandfather would have recognised the dank smell from the basement where he had worked for so many years. You could still see scrape marks from the machinery. During my job interview I asked which one of the sub editors would have been a compositor. "That's my job," said the chief sub editor proudly. So my grandfather was on a par with Katie.

The height of your pile gave a good indication of how popular your edition had been that week; the higher the pile, the fewer papers demanded by shopkeepers. But many of these extra copies did not go to waste, instead they were used as giveaways at supermarkets to bulk out circulation figures.

My first few weeks had been embarrassing because the piles kept getting bigger reflecting a gradual loss of interest amongst my readership. In the end, the pile was too big to be brought up in one go, so I had the humiliation of having to make multiple trips while the other reporters watched. Colin's pile was never more than a handful.

That Thursday my pile was down a little, which enabled me to carry the bundle upstairs in one go even if I couldn't see over the top it as I walked.

"Better than last week, boss," Sheffield said as he split his pile up ready for two visits. We had been competing for last place for months and this week it was his turn.

"Looks like my front page went down quite well, even if it upsets the chairman," I said.

It meant that my sales might break through the 2,000 sales-barrier for the first time, although I wouldn't know until the following week when the sales team totted up the numbers.

We hiked upstairs and put our bundles on a long table which ran the length of the newsroom's side wall. Sales staff would occasionally pop down from their office one floor above us and grab a few copies for promotions. To me, the size of the pile was a constant reminder of how well or badly things had gone, especially as it was right in my line of vision.

We had a couple of quiet hours to plan our editions before we needed to start digging for stories. Some reporters, like Colin and Tim, were always ahead of the game and would head straight onto their patches confident they would dig up a good story. Sheffield and I were less experienced and couldn't take the risk of drawing a blank. So we would ring our contacts instead.

No stories were filed on Thursdays, but all the leg work has to be done for pages eleven and nine, which had to be sent through to the newsdesk the next day along with enough 'news in brief' articles to fill the pages. The deadline for page eleven was 12:30pm on Friday, while page nine had to be filed by 4:30pm the same day. Photos had to be arranged for each lead story, or a separate photo story would need to be found and organised through the picturedesk. Thursday afternoon was a good day to stand up the dullest articles gathered at council meetings earlier in the week. Sofia called these the 'bread and butter' of the paper. But she said that good journalists got 'off diary' articles by digging for them on patch. So it was a vicious circle; if you weren't good enough to go on patch, you wouldn't get the best stories.

Every edition of The Sentinel was 58 pages, so much of the paper was made up of stories from the other patches. A features department upstairs contributed to the midsection of the paper and three sports writers covered the back pages. They sat separately from us and we rarely spoke. They were not considered to be 'real' reporters because the 'couldn't write news,' and were generally keen sportsmen who'd turned their passion into a job. We only mixed with them at Christmas parties and during Teeline shorthand lessons.

Like all the other news reporters, each week I had to fill pages 11, 9, 7,5,3,2 and 1 of my edition. Each lead article had to be between 12 and 15 paragraphs while the news-in-brief stories, called nibs, were generally around 50 – 100 words. We organised photos through the picturedesk, which had two full time 'snappers,' or by taking our own photos using the office cameras. Unless you booked out one of the two digital cameras, precious time would be lost developing photos at the local photo shop.

It was 9:15am, so I still had time on my side. To my right was the depressing sight of Don, tall athletic and blond, rifling eagerly through his note pad and typing up stories at 100 words a minute. Despite starting his trainee position at the paper just before me, he was already a polished reporter, drilled in the art of journalism during a year-long journalism course. He had worked on the student newspaper at Oxford University, so not only was he extremely bright but he had also developed a great news sense, and had shorthand skills far superior to mine. Like the most experienced reporters in the office, he already had most of his lead stories lined up for the week.

Sheffield was more like me, so I decided to strike up a conversation.

"Are you going on patch later?" I asked.

"I want to get page 11 sorted out first. Have you got any story ideas?" he said.

"Nope, but I might do a ring around in a minute."

We were both on six-month probation, which was not great because the paper had fired people when they had failed to come up to scratch.

A few weeks' earlier, I had been struggling to find a front page story so had spent Tuesday evening, the day before the paper went to press, desperately searching for a splash in Appleton. I returned empty handed. So in desperation I filed a weak story about a county councillor calling on farmers to trim their hedges along the country lanes. It was a nib really, but I had spun it out into a 15 paragraph splash, hoping the newsdesk wouldn't notice. Sofia was furious.

"The readers will laugh at us," she'd shouted in front of everyone. "And you haven't got a page two story, have you?

A bit more experience would have saved me a lot of heart ache because I did have a splash, but my news sense had been too poor to recognise it. I had come across what I thought was no better than a page two story while searching for my front page the night before. A shopkeeper was calling for more regular police patrols after a burglary went unnoticed for several hours. Looking back it seems obvious it was a good story, but at the time I thought it was too old for a splash because the burglary had taken place more than a week earlier. I thought that front page stories had to be new.

"I do have something for page two," I said hesitantly.

"What's that?" she said surprised, looking up from her desk.

"A shopkeeper was burgled last week and wants more police patrols because no one spotted the break-in until the next day," I said.

"That sounds like a splash," she said exasperated. "Have you got a photo?"

"Yes I took one of the owner last night at the shop. But the burglary was ten days ago."

"That's fine, put through all the quotes straight away," she said. "Just say it took place recently."

Peter even congratulated me for digging it out because, as he said, "the police aren't giving us much anymore." It was one of five consecutive weeks, including my latest splash, where I found myself without a front page as I walked into the office on Wednesday morning. The stress was taking its toll. I constantly thought of resigning but decided to keep trying. My grandfather lasted six decades in the business after all, so the least I could do was to see the year out and then maybe move back to London.

But with a new week came new hope and I was in good spirits.

Sheffield lifted his paper above the partition between our desks, showing me a picture on his front page.

"Look at that photo I took," he said shaking his head in admiration. "It has everything; people, the shop, genius."

He hadn't been coached yet by the paper's chief photographer, Len, and I didn't have the heart to tell him it broke all the rules of a decent newspaper picture. During a ten minute lesson he gave to all new recruits, Len taught me to snap people at an angle so they were bunched in the frame. There should never be gaps between people, and the closer you were to the subject the better. By contrast, Sheffield's picture looked more like a holiday snap with everyone standing square on, a few paces apart from each other and looking like stick men in the distance.

"Have you asked Len for a lesson yet? He gave me some great tips," I said.

"With genius like this I don't think I need one," he grinned.

"It's not quite how Len told me to take them, the people are too far in the distance."

He looked at the photo again. "But it has everything in it – the sky, the fields, people...."

"It's not bad I suppose," I said, not having the heart to continue

"What were you talking about with that beggar this morning?" he asked.

"Oh that," I said. "Nothing really, she's just a potential source. She says she's got some big story for me so I have agreed to go for a drink after work."

"A drink with the town beggar?" he mocked.

"All the best stories come from unusual sources, according to Colin," I explained. "So I thought I would give it a go."

"Oh right," he said. "When are you seeing her?"

"After work tonight."

"Well let me know if you fancy a drink after that," he said.

He was probably right about the girl but I figured it was worth it. As the day dragged on, it became clear I wasn't getting much from my ring around despite hitting the phones for several hours.

Sheffield and Don headed off to their patches after lunch but I stuck to the phones for the rest of the day. All I got was a lot of voicemail messages, and a few nibs about church events. I wasn't too concerned and left on the dot at 5pm.

Carrie was waiting for me outside.

"You still want to hear about this story then?" she said clasping her hands tightly together.

"Of course," I said "Let's go to the pub to discuss it."

Being the cheapest pub in town, Wetherspoons attracted an eclectic mix of afternoon customers, including drunks, drug addicts and prostitutes.

Carrie led me inside and said "hello" to a large group of drinkers who were sitting silently consuming their beer.

"How are you doll?" a man in the group said.

"Fine, just having a quick drink," she replied.

He stared at me disapprovingly.

"Who's the fella?" he asked.

"A friend," she said fiercely. "And mind your own business."

He looked away. She was tougher than I thought.

We settled at the bar and I ordered some drinks.

"So I guess you are wondering what the story is?" she said taking a slurp out of her pint. Her cheeks were redder now, less sallow. Her face was animated, bright and friendly. "I don't fancy you, if you are thinking that?" she laughed. "But you were nice to me the other day and I know a story that you might be interested in."

She had smartened up and was wearing a clean white shirt. Her nails were painted pink, and she had put on some makeup. I detected a bit of mascara.

"I'd be interested to hear what it is but can't promise it will make the paper," I said trying to limit expectations.

"That's up to you," she said. "I don't care one way or the other. But I get to hear the odd thing or two on the street, as you can imagine."

"Yes I can," I said. "So what have you heard?"

"There's a girl I know. She's a stuck up cow who's in with all the posh people," she said lowering her voice to a whisper. "The rumour is, she arranges sex parties for them. I'll give you her name but you'll have to take it from there. But you didn't get her name from me, okay?"

"Of course. I would never reveal a source," I said.

"Most of Fleet Street will be down here if you get this story, I can promise you that," she said adamantly.

"So what's her name?" I asked.

"It's Selina Goodson - she's the daughter of the mayor of Yeovil. She does all their pimping."

Naturally, I was a little sceptical at first. I knew it could be a good story, but I reckoned it was just an urban myth at that stage, and it wasn't even on my patch.

"There's a whorehouse between Appleton and Longley called The Lodge," she added, causing my ears to prick up. "She hires the girls who work there – that's all I know."

Chapter 6: Back Pages

An approaching deadline concentrates the mind of a reporter, and I had two pages to worry about when I arrived at work on Friday.

I booted up my computer and looked eagerly at my inbox, hoping something had dropped in since 5pm the previous day. And for once I was in luck because Sofia had sent through court copy about a cold case. It had been sent to the newsdesk by a freelancer who covered Bristol Crown Court.

It brought a big smile to my face because court copy was the easiest of all page leads. Court reporters write a dozen stories a day, emailing the copy to whichever local papers can use it. In my case, the reporter discovered that the perpetrator was born in Appleton but left after just a few months, which seemed quite tenuous, but had obviously satisfied Sofia.

A quick review confirmed, as is usual with court copy, it needed a bit of tinkering. That is not a criticism of the reporter, who was understandably not interested in writing a prize winning introduction. They had to bash out so many stories to make a decent living that the copy was simplistic at best, and often confused. All they really needed to be successful was great short hand and a sound knowledge of sub judice, which ruled me out on both counts.

I read the copy:

Appleton man convicted of rape

A rapist has been sentenced 15 years after he committed the crime.

Thomas Snide, 43, who was born in Appleton, must have thought he had got away with the brutal rape of a student in Bristol more than a decade ago.

But the father of three had to give DNA to police after he stepped into a fracas his son, 18, was involved in.

The court heard he dragged the 18 year old down an alleyway in Bristol where he raped her.

Judge Jeffrey said: "This was a brutal attack on a young woman as she walked home. You dragged her into an alleyway and committed a violent attack. You must have thought you had got away with it but justice caught up with you today."

Mr Snide who was sentence to 9 years in jail denied being in Bristol at the time, claiming he was 'fitted up' by the police.....

I had to read it three times to be sure what the '15 years' referred to in the opening paragraph. But all the facts were there, so I didn't need to track down the freelancer which could take days, and potentially blow my page 11. Once I was sure of the facts, I rejigged things a little:

Rapist caged after escaping justice for more than a decade

It is fifteen years since a south Somerset man brutally raped a student after dragging her into a dimly lit alleyway in Bristol.

But the long arm of the law finally court up with the Thomas Snide, 43, this week.

The married father of three, who was born in Appleton, was arrested after he got into a fight involving his 18 year old son.

His DNA was later matched with the brutal rape of an 18 year old student.

Sentencing Snide to a minimum of nine years, Judge Jeffrey said: "This was a brutal attack on a young woman as she walked home. You dragged her into an alleyway and committed a violent attack. You must have thought you had got away with it but justice caught up with you today."

Mr Snide had claimed he was not in Bristol at the time of the crime and had been 'fitted up' by the police....

With page 11 filed, I had most of the day to find a page nine story. And my lucky streak continued when Sofia came over with a story.

"This fella who's been convicted of pot smoking wants to put his side of the things," she said. "Arrange a face to face interview. Take the digital camera. The story should do for your page nine."

Sofia handed over a note with his details scribbled on. "Don't stuff it up," she added.

Carl Cook lived in Bishopswood, which was good because I hadn't written many articles for that area despite it being a relatively large village in my patch. I gave him a call and we arranged to meet at his house - a pebble dashed three bedroom semi on a council estate.

He was friendly enough until I drew my reporter's pad from my jacket pocket, which had the effect of a gunslinger in the old West – his face instantly froze and turned ashen when I pulled out a pen.

It took me an age to warm him up after that but bit by bit, the information started to flow. He revealed that aged 48 and had been given a £100 fine and a conditional discharge a month earlier for 'producing and possessing' cannabis. At first he didn't give away much more than that, but then we struck a rapport and he explained that he'd grown the weed to ease his arthritis.

"I've suffered a lot less from arthritis over the last thirty years because I have regularly used the drug," he said smiling sadly while perched on the end of the living room sofa. I was sitting opposite in a leather armchair, trying to jot down the quotes with my amateurish 50 words a minute shorthand.

"The one thing that has always upset me though, is that there is so much smuggling and terrorism related to drugs," he continued. "So if I were to buy cannabis, I know there would be a good chance some of the money would go to the mob or terrorists. So I started growing my own a few years ago, for personal use only mind you, knowing that no gangster was going to get involved. So no money would go into the wrong hands you see. When you think of all time and money the police spent, well it's a farce really - they had four police vans and about 15 police officers staking my house out. Then there are the court costs and the forensics; all for a £100 fine."

I was nodding my head in an effort to chivvy him along, but I was also in agreement.

"It seems a bit ridiculous to me too," I said. "But what do you think should be done about it?"

His face froze again, and deep lines spread across his face as felt the strain.

"Well I don't know if I should say much more," he said shaking his head slowly. "Can you go on what I've told you?"

I pictured Sofia yelling at me from behind her desk, and Katie instructing me to 'go back for stronger quotes.'

"Not really," I said fighting the urge to plead with him. "The story would be a lot better if you said what you think should be done about

38

it all. If you call for a change in the law for example, that would be good. As it is, we've only got you complaining about the police."

"Well I don't know," he said scratching his head. "I'll might get some negative comments from people who are anti-drugs. They'll be saying I've got a big mouth."

"It's up to you," I said desperately trying to think of another reason. "But I reckon that most of our readers would agree with you - a good proportion at least. The younger ones anyway, and you wouldn't be the first to stick your neck out. There was that politician who said something similar recently."

"Oh yes, what was her name?" he said.

"Clare Short," I said.

"She did take a stance, didn't she?"

"That's right," I said.

He was on the verge of going for it, but I resisted the temptation to put pressure on.

"Okay then," he said finally. "You can quote me saying this: no wonder the police have so little money. The Government has forced police to spend huge amount of money on a battle they can never win. All drugs should be decriminalised and taxed for the treatment of drug addicts."

"Even hard drugs?" I asked.

"Everything - you could give hard drugs to known addicts at special centres where they could take them without harming themselves or anyone else. Crime would plummet, the dealers would go out of business. The gangsters must cheer every time the Government makes another drug illegal."

It was like a great weight had been lifted from his chest, which was puffed out a few inches. It was impossible to stop him now.

"I sometimes wonder who the police are working for," he said slapping the sofa. "It seems to me that the only people who benefitted from busting me were the dealers. Really what are they thinking?"

I had an uneasy feeling that the story was about to turn into a conspiracy theory, so as quickly as I could, I wrapped it up.

"Thanks. I think I have everything I need," I said. "Although I still need a picture of you to go with it."

His face froze for the third time.

"Oh no, I'm not sure about that, people might recognise me," he said.

"I need a picture to make it into a page lead. Otherwise the newsdesk might make it into a short story which wouldn't do it justice," I said.

It was only a half-truth: the newsdesk would prefer a photo of him, but it would still be a page lead. I would have to find another picture story by 4:30pm if he refused though. The newsdesk would probably give me a bollocking too.

"Okay I guess I can have a picture taken if you think it is really needed?" he said.

"It really is. And I think you should be proud of it," I said sounding like a second hand car salesman.

Before he could change his mind, I snapped a couple of photos of him standing in his living room. It wasn't the best photo but under the circumstances I thought it was a belter. We shook hands and I thanked him for the story.

"Hopefully you will like it," I said, although I was never brave enough to ring people after an article was printed. Sofia said that some people adored seeing their name in print even when they were being panned, while others would take offence at a seemingly harmless nib.

We shook hands again at the door, and I drove to Bishopswood town hall to check the information board for some nibs on the way back. I scribbled down one about a charity which was arranging an arts and craft sale, and another on a school jumble. Standard stuff.

It was just after midday when I got back to the office. The story took 90 minutes to bash out because my short hand was almost unreadable and I needed an age to decipher:

Pot smoker calls for drug decriminalisation after police raid

A Pot smoker convicted of a Class-B drug offence has called for a change in the law to free up police to target hardened criminals.

Carl Cook, 48, of Newtown Road, Bishopswood, was fined £100 and given a 12 month conditional discharge last week for growing his own cannabis.

Mr Cook, who smokes the drug to ease arthritis, said: "It's a farce. They had four police vans and about 15 police officers staking my house out. Then there are the court costs and the forensics; all for a £100 fine.

"No wonder the police have so little money. The Government has forced police to spend huge amount of money on a battle they can never win. All drugs should be decriminalised and taxed for the treatment of drug addicts…

The newsdesk was quiet so I should have been happy with a successful day but I kept thinking about what Carrie had told me about the council. Any story would pale into insignificance compared to that.

Chapter 7: Mayor's Daughter

"I need a volunteer to attend a charity dinner this evening," Katie demanded from her seat an hour after I had filed page nine.

Since Sheffield and I were ahead of schedule for once, we had been horsing about trying to think of scenarios under which we could call Tim, Timmy. But as soon as the call for volunteers went out, we fell silent like naughty school boys.

Unsurprisingly, there was a frosty silence as none of the other reporters was willing to volunteer away their Friday evenings either.

"You two," Katie said looking at Sheffield and me. "You haven't written any county pages since you've been here."

I saw the colour drain out of Sheffield's cheeks, and felt a knot in my stomach too.

"What hideous plan has she got for us this evening?" I whispered to Sheffield out of the corner of my mouth.

She beckoned us over with a curled index finger and we walked slowly to her desk accepting our fate like condemned me, heads hanging a little in misery.

Tim reclined in his chair, a smile breaking out across his face.

"About time too," he said barely able to repress laughter.

"Thanks Timmy," I said without thinking. His lips tautened in anger. I regretted the jibe knowing there would be payback.

County pages were the ones not covered by the reporter editions: pages 4, 6, 8, 10 and 12. It was true that we hadn't filed any, but that was because we were struggling to fill our own pages.

"We shouldn't have filed our page nines until closer to deadline," I whispered to Sheffield as we approached Katie.

"What was that?" she snapped.

"Oh, just said we've filed our page nines at least."

"I know," Katie said tartly. "And so has everyone else in the office. You really must get used to knocking out the back pages more quickly. Three a day at the very least."

That was ridiculous because even Colin didn't write that many.

She handed over a print out of an internet advert about the charity do.

"This should be good enough for page four," she said. Page four was the most important of the county pages because it was the first published across all editions. So it attracted the attention of the editor and managing director.

"Sheffield, you can be hypnotised," Katie said without explanation. "Simon, you can write up the story on Monday."

Sheffield had drawn the short straw. His face was a picture of misery. My evening would be wasted but his humiliation would last far longer, depending on how he performed.

"I *can't* be hypnotised," he said quickly.

"What do you mean you can't be hypnotised?" Katie sneered. "Everyone can be hypnotised."

"I tried in once on holiday in Spain," he said. "Some people can't, that's all."

"You'll have to go on stage and try," she snapped.

Poor Sheffield. I hated the thought of going on stage. He looked so miserable. In a split second I did something that surprised me.

"I'll do it," I said. "Sheffield can write it up - easier for me that way."

Katie looked at me quizzically, and for a moment she was weighing up whether to let Sheffield off the hook.

"Okay, but don't mess it up," she said. "It's the mayor's charity do, and you will be representing the paper so make sure you dress appropriately."

She left us alone after that, so for the first Friday in weeks there was no walk of shame about spelling mistakes or grammatical errors. It might have been that we'd been word perfect, but I suspected she thought we had paid our dues for the time being at least.

Sheffield thanked me for taking the fall for him. We were pretty subdued but eventually I asked him if he really had tried it in Spain.

"To be honest, it happened to a friend," he said. "It's my worst nightmare, I'd prefer to pack in the job."

We grabbed a bite to eat at the pub near his place after work and discussed our plans for the evening.

"How are you going to play it?" he said biting into a burger, grease oozing over his fingers.

"My plan is to remain fully compos mentis during the whole thing – do just enough to give you a story," I said. "You may have to embellish it a bit."

"What if you fall under, against your will?"

"Can't really see that happening," I said. "The way I see it, you can't be hypnotised if you don't want to be."

After the meal, we went back to his place and sprayed on some of his aftershave to ward off any smells that may have built up after a day in the office.

Top buttons were done up, and ties pulled up to the neck. He didn't have a mirror so we relied on each other's judgement.

Sheffield didn't have his own car, so we had to take mine.

It was a Seventies Vauxhall Viva, coloured brown tan, which I parked between a Jag and a brand new Mercedes. It was the only rust bucket in the car park. Sheffield got out and I noticed his brown shoes looked out of whack with his black trousers.

"How do I look," I asked.

"You've got a stain on your tie," he said pointing to a curry mark. "Hold on, things are looking up," he added looking at an exquisitely dressed twenty something woman greeting people at reception.

She was wearing a silky black evening dress and high heels. Her long brown hair had been straightened and fell behind delicate toned shoulders. She greeted us with a warm smile which made me feel human for once.

"I'm Selina, your hostess for tonight's dinner party." she said warmly.

"I am Simon, and this is my friend Sheffield. We're from The Sentinel," I said.

"The car rather gave you guys away," she grinned, looking out onto the car park.

"Unfortunately I have to be hypnotised for a newspaper article we've been sent to do," I said.

"What's your friend here for, moral support?" she asked.

"No he's writing up the story."

"I'd say he got the best deal," she said.

Sheffield and I nodded in agreement.

"I'll have a word with the hypnotist so he knows to get you on stage," she added before ushering us to our seats.

We joined a circular table set for eight people, which had a couple of spaces left.

"This is my father, John, he's the mayor of Yeovil," she said introducing us to a huge fat man with a bald head. "Perhaps you'll get a story out of him too?"

I must have been mesmerised by her looks, because it wasn't until that moment that I realised they were the father and daughter in Carrie's story. I found it was hard to believe there was any truth to it, as I watched Selina saunter back to the reception looking the height of propriety.

"Trust The Sentinel to be late," the mayor joked as we sat down. A brassy blonde woman next to him laughed loudly at our expense.

Sheffield glanced at his watch. The invite said the event started at 8:30pm so we were only 10 minutes late.

"No good looking at your watch young man, you are still late," the mayor added.

Once again the lady with him roared with laughter.

The lights dimmed to indicate the evening's entertainment was about to begin. Sheffield leaned over to me "It wasn't that funny," he whispered into my ear.

Even though she was half his age, I assumed the brassy blonde sitting next to the Mayor was his partner. Her hand caressed the sleeve of his suit lovingly.

Clockwise to her right were a couple in their fifties who laughed like drones every time the mayor cracked a joke. Next to them was a fat lady, with a corkscrew perm, who was accompanied by an elderly man. He barely said a word all evening.

Selina walked back to our table. "I've spoken to the hypnotist and he's happy to put you under. I've pointed out your table, so all you have to do is raise a hand when he asks for volunteers. There probably won't be that many," she said and placed a reassuring hand on my shoulder.

"Good luck then, I will be watching," she added before leaving for another table, flashing me a smile as she went.

The mayor was swilling back a large Gin and Tonic, his face reddened by years of heavy drinking. It was hard to imagine they were father and daughter.

"Hope he doesn't make you take your clothes off," the mayor joked to a cacophony of laughter. "I do love it when the reporter becomes the story."

"You have to be able to take what we dish out," the brassy blonde said to him.

"We try to be good sports, especially as we are supposed to be the eyes and ears of the people," I said.

"Ears and eyes of the people," he spewed, his voice raising a couple of octaves. "I agree with the mayor of London, you behave like concentration camp guards 'just following orders.'"

"We need a free press to stop political corruption though," I said cheekily.

"What!" the mayor shouted loud enough for guests at another table to swivel their heads round. "Total tosh!"

"Yes, total rubbish," the fifty something gentleman said. "A bloody nuisance is what the press is."

The master of ceremonies wandered on stage and introduced the hypnotist. "Ladies and Gentlemen, this act is not for the faint hearted or those of a nervous disposition," he said melodramatically.

"I give you the master persuader himself; all the way from Rome, Italy, the Great Mesmorisimooooo!"

A wave of applause greeted the final sentence and the Great Mesmerisimo walked onto the stage.

He was wearing a stereotypical long black cloak with red trim. His hair was long, swept back into a ponytail and dyed jet black. I guessed he was in his late forties but he could have been a lot older.

"Think of a shape," he said holding out his hand and forming a semicircle with his thumb and index finger. "Any geometric shape."

I thought of a dodecahedron.

"Now think of a vegetable," he added holding his palms open to the audience.

He was walking back and forth across the stage, staring wide eyed at the audience as he spoke.

"Now imagine those objects in your mind's eye," he said, putting his hands to either side of his temple as if to concentrate.

I was thinking of the least likely objects I could come up with - a sprig of broccoli inside the 12-sided dodecahedron.

He paused for a few seconds to give the audience time to think.

"Using the powers of the Great Mesmerisimo, I have implanted into the brains of the most telepathic of you a shape and a vegetable."

I looked across at Sheffield - his face was contorting in mental gymnastics.

There was another pause, this time for dramatic effect.

"You have the shape and vegetable in your mind's eye now," the Great Mesmerisimo whispered into the microphone. I felt my eye lids start to drop, made heavy by the soothing sounds of his voice.

"Now those of you who see a triangle put up your hands."

The audience murmured and about one half held their hands aloft.

"In addition to the triangle, those of you who see a carrot within the triangle, lift your hands," he said.

A gasp rang out as about one third, around 100 people, responded.

I shoved my hand in the air.

"Congratulations, you are receptive of telepathic messages," he said.

"All those who have received this message are suitable for being hypnotised by the Great Mesmerisimo," he continued. "But I only need six volunteers to come on stage."

He scanned the room and pointed to a woman near the front. "You," he said. She got up and started making her way to six seats set up on stage.

His gaze zeroed onto our part of the room. "The young man there," he said pointing at me.

My stomach in knots, I stood up and walked over to a ripple of applause.

"Another there," the Great Mesmerisimo said pointing to another table.

One by one, the volunteers made their way over to the stage and sat down.

The stage lights lit up, blackening the audience from view. Occasional laughter rang out from the darkness.

"The Great Mesmerisimo will now hypnotise these volunteers," he said to the audience and turned towards us.

He began by walking up and down the line of chairs, speaking to us each in turn in a slow comforting voice.

"Imagine you are outside in a wonderful place – the most comfortable, warm place you have ever visited," he said staring into my eyes from a foot away. My eyelids started to droop, like I could fall asleep. He moved to the person next to me.

"Now a warm wind is starting to blow softly against your skin, the sea is lapping at your feet," he said.

I felt warm water lapping at my feet, the sun gently caressing my skin.

The Great Mesmerisimo placed his hand lightly on my shoulder. "Deeper now, you are feeling calm, relaxed, close your eyes." I went into a trance, I couldn't move.

"You are falling deeper, deeper into relaxation. Think of the perfect place you like to relax. You are there."

Perhaps I could have broken out of the spell, but I didn't want to. I was back on White Sands beach in Koh Samui where I'd visited after university.

"Now my friends; imagine you are at the Grand National, sitting on your horse Red Rum, which is favourite to win the race. Give him a slap on the side for encouragement."

I slapped the side of my chair, it was easy to imagine I was riding the great horse. Laughter spewed out from the audience.

"Now, get ready to start the race. The umpire is out, he is steadying the horses. Hold the reigns."

My hands lifted up to grab them.

"They are set, under starter's orders – and GO!" he said.

I started to bounce up and down on the chair as if the horse was beneath me, barely noticing waves of horrified laughter coming from the audience. In my mind, I was in the middle of the pack, steering a careful line amongst the other six riders.

"You are reaching the final furlong now, double your speed," he implored us.

I started bouncing double time on the chair. It felt like a performance but it was easy, too easy perhaps. I had lost all inhibitions.

"And you have crossed the line in first place, well done you have won the race," he said.

I gave the pretend horse a slap and then a hug as I pulled back on the reigns.

I heard the footsteps of The Great Mesmerisimo approach me. He tapped me on the shoulder.

"Now I want you to imagine you are the Mick Jagger, the greatest rock star the world has ever seen. Imagine you are at a concert, on the stage and about to perform. The audience is going wild," he said. "Slowly open your eyes now and stand up to hear your fans."

A huge round of applause rose up from the back of the hall as I stood.

Music started to pump out from loud speakers behind the stage.

"I can't get no… satisfaction," I sang, and started to prance about the stage with a pretend microphone.

"And I try, and I try, and I try, and I try! I can't get no… satisfaction!"

The audience were in hysterics as I sang along to the karaoke for the rest of the track.

Finally, the music came to an end and the Great Mesmerisimo told me to sit down.

"Close your eyes," he said. "You are no longer Mick Jagger."

"You are back in you warm place, where you are resting, relaxed." he added.

He took every one through a different act; a ballerina, a boxer, a tight rope walker, a tap dancer and Madonna.

Then when we were all done, he brought us out of the fog.

"You are slowly coming out of your special place," he said.

"You are less sleepy now, feeling awake, open your eyes. You are no longer hypnotised," he said and tapped me on the shoulder. He pointed towards the tables and I walked calmly back to my seat still convinced I had been playing along, not hypnotised at all.

The Mayor's face was a picture of joy.

"I shall buy The Sentinel this week," he said.

Sheffield waved his notepad and camera at me, "got all your quotes and a few photos while you were up there," he said.

"Great, how was I?"

"Brilliant boss, it will make a good story."

After about twenty minutes, I'd had enough of being quizzed and spotting Selina at the bar, escaped to buy a drink.

"Quite a performance," she said. "I'd say you've missed your calling as a rock star."

She was smiling broadly, sympathetically. "So what's it like to be hypnotised?"

"I didn't think I was hypnotised while I was up there," I said. "But the thing is I would never sing that song unless I was. Your father and the others certainly enjoyed it."

She held my gaze for a few seconds, as though she was thinking about saying something.

"I could tell you a few stories about them," she said.

"Please do. I'm always looking for new sources."

"Some things that happen in this town would make the front page of The Sun," she said. "But can I trust you, Simon?"

"Of course, I would keep your name out of everything, if that's what you want?"

"I can't tell you any more just now, but would you think less of me if I told you I am involved?"

"Of course not," I said.

"Well I'm tired of the whole thing, but in too deep to get out."

Chapter 8: Blogger

"If you want to learn about the way things work around here, then find out what happened to the council's tractor," county councillor James Dunne told me after I phoned him for a story on Monday morning. Once again, I was desperately in need of a lead story. Dunne was pretty used to my begging calls, and at first I got the feeling he was fobbing me off.

"Why what has happened to it?" I asked pushing for more to go on.

"It's gone missing," he said flatly. "It's your job to find out where but I reckon there's a story in it if you dig hard enough."

Word had got round the office about my performance at the charity do, so I was quite happy to do a ring around that morning. Tim had collared me before I sat down, singing a rendition of Satisfaction in front of everyone. He'd bumped into Sheffield and Jason at the pub on Saturday night, and they'd spilled the beans. For once I'd stayed in to save some money so had missed my chance of getting the ribbing out of the way before work.

Councillor Dunne was the seventh person I had called that morning, and the first to give me a sniff of story. The town councillors treated him with reverence because the county council wielded far more power than the parish council. They only controlled small budgets, called precepts, which focused on leisure facilities, the town's car parks and hedges. County councils were big employers which ran major services such as education, social services, highways, libraries and waste disposal. Appleton's budget was £60,000 a year while the county council had a budget of tens of millions.

"What council tractor?" I said still slightly bemused. "I haven't heard anything about a tractor in council meetings."

"Maybe not, but plenty of people are talking about it. If you lived in Appleton you would know."

It was a dig at The Sentinel because in years gone by, all reporters lived on patch, chatted to locals and would hear every rumour. But at The Sentinel at least, that requirement had ended many years earlier. We could only afford the cheapest digs in Yeovil these days, and were lucky if we visited our patches once or twice a week. Instead we relied on periodically telephoning key contacts, and gathering stories at council meetings.

"What are they saying about it?" I pressed.

"To be fair, it's before your time," he said relenting a little. "A couple of years ago Appleton council blew its entire budget buying a new tractor to clear walkways, tidy up verges etcetera. But no one has seen hide nor hair of it since they bought it. You should find out what happened to it."

"Do you know what happened to it?" I asked. "There is no point me asking people at random if you can tell me."

"Well, the rumour is that the council are using it for personal purposes. But you didn't hear that from me," he said.

"Is that illegal?"

"No but it's a disgrace if the councillors are the beneficiaries rather than the town. But don't quote me on that. I can trust you I hope? A blogger has written about it so you can find out more from that. It's called the Three Wise Monkeys. The whole town is talking about it."

I was too embarrassed to admit that I hadn't even heard of the blog. But it only took a few seconds to find on the internet. I clicked on the latest link 'Mystery behind Appleton's missing tractor'.

Next to a picture of a gleaming red tractor, the blogger had written:

"When asked where the vehicle was, the town clerk was unable to supply an answer. I rang the council chair who also failed to respond. Surely even the most incompetent of councils will know where the £49,000 tractor, bought with residents' money, is stored?"

It looked like a good story, but I would need to 'stand it up' by proving that councillors were using it to landscape their gardens or something similar. Like Selina's sex party story, it had the whiff of 'slow burner' about it. I'd have to find out where the tractor was kept for starters. If I didn't nail down the facts, the paper might be sued for libel. I'd never be allowed to print a word about it without strong evidence. In the British courts it is up to the newspaper to prove 'beyond reasonable doubt' that a story is true or face a hefty fine. And papers were so unpopular they nearly always lost.

One thing was for sure, I wouldn't have it done by 2pm, the deadline for page seven. I checked my watch - 10:10am. Then I thumbed down my contacts list: Tom Falding, the chairman of Bishopswood, was next.

I rang his home number which went to answerphone. "Hello, this is Simon from The Sentinel," I said, and asked if he had any issues to raise. "I'll try again later, or perhaps give me a call if you have time?" I added, trying not to sound too desperate.

Next, I rang a shop owner in Appleton, Pauline Jarvis, who picked up. "I'm ringing a few people this morning to see if they have heard of

any stories, or know any issues that might be of interest to the paper."
I droned.

"Sorry, nothing this week," she said and the receiver clicked. This job
really was like being a salesman, I thought.

I sat back in my chair and let out a huge breath. Sheffield was busily
typing something but I decided to interrupt him.

"You need to be a good salesman to do this job," I said, sticking my
head over the partition. "You have to get people on side before they
give you a hint of a story."

He stopped typing and grinned. Sheffield always had time for a chat.

"Are you stuck for page seven then?" he said.

"Yes - and that's my problem, I'm always chasing the next story. How
are you getting on?"

"Sofia sent some court copy through, so I'm working on that."

I let him get on with it and thumbed further down the contacts list.
But I'd gone beyond the point where I recognised any of the names.
The list had been put together by Camilla, a reporter who ran the
Appleton and Longley patch before landing a job at a daily. She was a
local girl so had great contacts but I was a new face and finding it hard
to get hold of them.

"You have the quietest patch by far," Sheffield said. "When you went
on holiday they struggled to get the edition out. You need some better
contacts."

"I need to make some of my own," I said thinking out loud. "And I
might just have one."

The blogger's name and contact number were on his website. The blog described itself as 'a tale of life in deepest darkest Somerset' and it was a relief when Roy Easter, the self-styled citizen reporter, answered his phone.

"Now there's a coincidence," he said after I'd introduced myself. "I had been meaning to get in contact with you about your front page story."

I was always on tenterhooks when someone said they were calling me about a story because it was usually followed by a complaint of some sort. But there was a friendly tone to his voice, which made me relax.

"Why's that?" I asked. "Have you spotted something?"

"Yes I have!" he said. "It's an absolute disgrace that the chairman blamed the town's youngsters for his shop fire when he doesn't have a jot of evidence to back it up."

"You are absolutely right," I said. "I hadn't thought of that. If you don't mind being quoted, I can write a story about it?"

"That fine with me," he said. "I'm already a thorn in the council's side."

"What makes you think it wasn't youngsters?" I said trying to chivvy him along a little.

"The point is it could have been anyone. But this council, and the chairman in particular are always keen to blame 'young yobs' for every misdemeanour, even when there isn't a jot of evidence to back it up. It could be a pensioner for all he knows. But he wouldn't dare blame anyone older because he'd lose votes at the next elections."

He was starting to rant which was testing my short hand skills.

"Blaming young people is just dandy for him. I tell you, I wouldn't want to be a young person in this town - the council does nothing for them. The skate park has been kicked into touch so many times I doubt it will ever happen. They blame the youngsters for all social ills – vandalism, graffiti and now arson it seems. Far more likely it was someone with a grudge against the chairman, or is it just a coincidence that the only shop ever to be fire bombed in Appleton belonged to him?"

"Probably not," I said, delighted he'd given me enough for my page seven. "Are you around this afternoon for a photo?"

"Well I suppose so, if it's really needed?" he said, and I booked it with Len on the photo desk.

It was my first 'running story', which are old stories refreshed with a new angle. So I only needed to change the intro of last week's splash, add some fresh quotes and the job was done.

A more experienced journalist would have pursued the story rather than leaving it to luck. But I was chuffed to file it anyway:

Blogger slams council for blaming youngsters over shop fire

A south Somerset blogger has blasted Appleton Council for blaming 'young yobs' for an arson attack on a shop.

Roy Easter, 52, of Southview Road, Appleton, says the attack against the chairman's barometer shop was much more likely to be an adult with a grievance.

The shop was set alight last week causing thousands of pounds of damage to antiques.

Mr Easter said: "It could have been anyone. But this council, and the chairman in particular, is always keen to blame 'young yobs' for every misdemeanour, even when there isn't a jot of evidence to back it up. It could be a pensioner for all he knows. But he wouldn't dare blame anyone older, because he'd lose votes at the next elections."

Mr Easter said youngsters were being ignored by the council.

He said: "I wouldn't want to be a young person in this town - the council does nothing for them. The skate park has been kicked into touch so many times I doubt it will ever happen. They blame the youngsters for all social ills — vandalism, graffiti and now arson it seems. [It is] far more likely it was someone with a grudge against the chairman, or is it just a coincidence that the only shop ever to be fire bombed in Appleton belonged to him?"

Chairman Ripley last week denied that he had been targeted because of a grudge.

He said: "No one in this town with a grudge against me. I'd say it was mindless yobbos getting teenage kicks by smashing up other people's property."

He has offed a £10,000 reward for information that leads to the arrest of those responsible.

Chapter 9: On patch

With page seven filed, I'd won myself some breathing space. Appleton council was meeting that evening, so I figured I'd get a couple of leads out of that. With luck I would be able to use those to fill pages five and three at work the next day, which meant Tuesday was sorted. That would leave me just needing a splash and page two by Wednesday morning. So with that in mind, I decided to drive to my patch and try to dig something out.

Appleton was the largest and richest town in my patch, with beautifully maintained houses built with locally quarried limestone. But like many affluent neighbourhoods, it wasn't the most welcoming of places. People spoke about house prices a lot, and there was a hint of snobbery in the air. By contrast, Longley's streets were slightly more dishevelled with the occasional buildings appearing as blots on the landscape. But the town made up for it as a place to live, by being more friendly and embracing of outsiders. There was a greater sense of community too, which even reached out to me. If shopkeepers had a story, they were more likely to share it. I felt at home in Longley.

Unfortunately, things hadn't started out so well with Longley council, though, after I had reported on what was supposed to be a discreet conversation at the end of a meeting. People had relaxed as it was drawing to a close, and the deputy chairman made a remark about the recent revamp of the town centre being 'a disaster' because it had taken so long to complete, driving visitors to other towns. "I could lob a grenade down the high street and not hit anyone," he said. It wasn't off the record, and the chairman hadn't officially ended the meeting. The truth is I needed a front page, so my ears pricked up and I jotted down the conversation. Unfortunately the councillor for development, John Marshall, had agreed with the deputy, saying "It will take decade for the town to recover." This was somewhat indiscreet because it was his project, and he had spent the past two years denying there was a problem.

Deputy chairman Alan Johnson later told me that the council had considered shunning me after the story came out, but dropped the idea after he said I had reported the conversation accurately.

"I asked them, 'what exactly would we be banning him for - writing an accurate report?'" he recollected over a pint with me at the Dancing Bear one evening. "It was Marshall's fault for saying such a daft thing," he added.

Even Marshall remained friendly, although I lost contact with him after he was voted out at the next parish council election.

So I drove straight through Appleton's picture postcard setting of stone houses and medieval churches, to Longley in search of a friendly chat. The Dancing Bear, which was situated near the town's entrance, was a good place to start looking for a story especially as I hadn't had lunch and fancied one of their homemade pies. So I parked up and went inside.

The landlord, Sam, was always happy to pass on stories he'd overheard from customers in the hope that I would write a few paragraphs about his pub in the paper. Sam had moved to Longley five years earlier and had made a lot of friends chatting to locals over the bar. He stood well over six feet tall, was ruddy faced from years of drinking and had a friendly smile, although one or two teeth were missing. His wife, Jane, cooked while Sam worked 'front of shop'. She kept the books, while he chatted to the punters, which suited them both perfectly.

"Have you got anything for me this week Sam?" I asked after ordering a bite to eat.

He pursed his lips and rubbed his chin. "No, there's nothing going on at the moment," he said. "So what stories are you working on now then? I saw the front page about the shop, terrible thing that is; local hooligans no doubt?"

"Maybe, Sam, but I'm working on a story about the council's missing tractor. Have you heard anything?"

"Oh yes, lots of people have been talking about that," he said. "It's the talk of the town."

"Who's been talking about it Sam?" I asked.

"We had some of his guys in here the other day, the ones that work at the industrial estate for that council fellow."

"Tom Ripley?"

"Yes, that's him. Well his men were in here yesterday saying they have been using the tractor for two years moving stuff around the yard. They thought it was his before they saw a picture of it."

"In the Three Wise Monkeys blog?" I said.

"Yes that's it. Now how about a story about the pub?"

"What story though Sam?"

"The story is, it's a bloody good pub," he said.

After lunch, I drove past Ripley's industrial yard. It consisted of a large metal barn situated inside a storage yard. A variety of trucks and mowers were parked outside, but no tractor. It could have been hidden in the barn, but I'd have to jump the fence and peer through the window to get a look.

I turned my car around further up the road and pulled up opposite the main gate. The place was deserted, so I climbed over the metal gate, grabbed hold of a window ledge and heaved myself up so my eyes were at window height. To my delight, I could make out a gleaming red tractor standing in the middle of the building. Before I could be spotted, I lowered myself down and jumped back over the fence and quickly drove off. I couldn't take a photo because it would have to be snapped on private land, which breached privacy laws So I figured I would need to catch his men red handed using the tractor, although that was less likely now that the blog had printed the story. It was frustrating, but the story wasn't stood up just yet.

My phone rang so I pulled over in a layby. It was Sheffield.

"Do you want to share a story?" he said enthusiastically.

"Of course," I said, "What is it?"

"Katie says there's been some sort of riot in a village between our patches. She said you can do it if you want?"

"Yes of course. Where is it?"

"It's in a place called Otherby, do you know it?"

"I've seen it on the map but never visited. What's the story?"

"It's about a bunch of kids wrecking the place."

He gave me the name and a number of the pub landlord, Tom Shelling, who'd phoned the story in. I telephoned him from my car and we arranged to meet straight away at his boozer, the Old Heavy Gate Inn.

I got there about twenty minutes later. The village consisted of two rows of houses running either side of a quiet country lane, with a pub in the centre. There was a village green, where the blacksmith might once have plied his trade and a Norman church with a defunct drinking water pump next to it. On the outskirts of the village were several art deco semi-detached homes, while at the centre were about a dozen thatched cottages.

I parked up and took a moment to admire the lush green rolling hills. A kestrel was hovering over a hay field.

Mr Shelling guessed who I was as I walked through the door. He was around six feet four inches, with a slight stoop from decades of serving customers. A receding hairline betrayed an otherwise youthful appearance. His blond hair was complimented by a deep mahogany tan.

"As you can see, we're a bit isolated here," he said, "the nearest town being ten miles away. The Police ignore us, so we hope this story will get us on their radar a bit more. It took them an hour to get here after we called them."

He told me it had all started after a kids party had got out of hand.

"About fifty people came out of one of the houses on the high street at 9pm. They ripped down the pub's sign, smashed up a Portaloo and set fire to one of the scarecrows. We went outside and saw a lorry slam on the brakes and slide into a scarecrow they had left in the middle of the road. I saw him get out and check; he must have thought he had killed someone."

While he was talking, a young man, perhaps in his mid-twenties, sidled up to the bar and sat down next to me.

"Tony," Mr Shelling said, nodding towards him. "You saw the kids play a game on the road?"

"The kids call it dead man's bluff," Tony said. "They took it in turns to lie down in the road and wait for cars to come along. The idea was the one who jumped out of the way at the last point is the winner, unless he is run over of course. I was watching from my bedroom window, they were all drunk and swearing. It's the first time we've had this sort of thing in the village."

They took me outside to show me the damage. They pub sign had been uprooted, revealing a clot of cement at its foundations. I got them to pose next to it, and snapped off a couple of photos. I was chuffed - all I needed was a quote from the police and the story was ready for page five the next day.

I rang Avon and Somerset police press office for a comment before heading back to the office. Their quote was on my voicemail when I arrived.

It was late afternoon by the time I sat down at my desk, but I had enough time to bash out the story ready for filing the next day:

Mob rule as cops take an hour to arrive at riot

Residents in a remote community have slammed police after rampaging youngsters were allowed to go unchallenged for almost an hour.

Villagers in Otherby called emergency services after a house party turned into a riot.

Around 50 youths, who emerged from a house party of the high street, were seen vandalising property, ripping up a pub sign and playing a game of 'dead man's bluff'.

Proprietor of the Old Heavy Gate Inn, Tom Shelling, 56, of the High Street, said: "About fifty people came out of one of the houses on the high street at 9pm. They ripped down the pub's sign, smashed up a Portaloo and set fire to one of the scarecrows. We went outside and saw a lorry slam on the brakes and slide into a scarecrow they had left on the middle of the road. I saw the driver get out and check; he must have thought he had killed someone."

Tony Hill, 27, also of High Street, watched from his bedroom window as the party turned into a riot.

Mr Hill said: "I saw the kids dare each other play a game on the road. They call it dead man's bluff. They took it in turns to lie down in the road and wait for cars to come along. The idea was the one who jumped out of the way at the latest point was the winner, unless he is run over of course. They were drunk and swearing. It's the first time we've had this sort of thing in the village."

A spokesman for Avon and Somerset police confirmed that it took officers almost an hour to attend. He said: "Officers spoke to a group of youths who were not thought to have committed any criminal offence..."

Chapter 10: Appleton meeting

"Order, Order," barked Ripley, signifying the start of the meeting.

He was sitting in the middle of a row of three desks facing the public, which the council were perched on. Some ten or so residents had turned up to watch the monthly debate and were lined up in chairs facing the Appleton members. The clock had just ticked past 7:30pm, the official starting time. Ripley's timing was second perfect.

I was sitting at a table to the right of the councillors, facing them rather than the residents. My desk had Press written on a place name holder, so I knew exactly where to sit.

"Point one of the agenda," Ripley said, but the audience carried on chatting. "Order!" he shouted and, grabbing hold of what looked like a judge's gravel, he thumped the table.

The room fell silent.

"Good," he said looking to the floor. He glanced slyly at me briefly, then back at the public.

"Item one: Apologies," he said and read out a list of people who could not attend.

"Item two: Media Coverage." I hadn't seen the agenda until I sat at the press table, and I felt a knot in my stomach as soon as I read it.

"This is a matter which I wish to bring to the attention of the council following recent media coverage in the local paper," he said, glancing at me again to check I was listening. His deputy Pat Cummings who was sitting next to him, was nodding in zombie-like in agreement

"I'm sorry to say that again The Sentinel has printed an irresponsible article, full of inaccuracies," Ripley said. "This time it was about the break in on the high street, which they erroneously claimed was a vendetta despite me explaining that this was absolutely not the case."

Again he glanced at me, sneering. "I need hardly tell you how damaging this type of reporting is to this council and the wider community," he continued. "It is an example of the worst kind of tabloid journalism, which unfortunately is the style of this particular newspaper."

He paused for effect, looking round at the other councillors who were murmuring in support.

"I'm hacked off about it," he said tersely, banging his fist on the table. "And I don't intend to put up with it any longer."

He was speaking more to the members of the council than the public at that point.

Sofia had warned that reporters could become the focus of council meetings. The secret to dealing with such occasions, she said, was to remain calm, yawn and put your pen down. She might have been cool enough to do that, but my heart was in my throat. My fingers were so greasy they could barely grip the pen.

"He wouldn't be allowed in the room with us if it were up to me," said Cummings, speaking as if I wasn't in the room. Again there was a murmur of agreement amongst the council.

"We are all hacked off with this particular reporter," said Ripley. "So to prevent any more inaccuracies, I motion that no town councillor shall speak to The Sentinel except through the official channel of the town Clerk. Naturally, the county councillor will make his own mind up whether to communicate."

"Seconded," said Cummings immediately.

"Those for?" said Ripley. All but Cllr Dunne held up their hands. "Those against?" he added, and no hands showed. "Abstained?" he said. James Dunne lifted a finger wearily.

"The motion is carried," Ripley said, flashing me a triumphant smile. "Let it be minuted that none of the town councillors will speak to The Sentinel. All media enquiries should be through Sean, the town clerk."

He looked at me for a few seconds, waiting for a response. I tried to yawn, but my jaw was locked.

"Item two: Members' Attire," he said looking towards the public.

In the commotion, I hadn't noticed it on the agenda. It looked like a quirky story perhaps good enough for page three.

My pen dropped to the floor breaking the silence. I reached down and picked it up. Ripley was staring angrily at me but continued.

"I believe the deputy chair has something to say about this agenda item," he said.

"Thank you chairman," Cummings said. I was aware enough to jot down each of the members attire as they spoke. Cummings was wearing a double breasted blazer with brightly polished brass buttons, a cream shirt and pink tie.

"I have been contacted by several residents who are very concerned by the attire of some of the members," he said solemnly. "They say that we are the elected representatives of Appleton, a beautiful town.

and should be dressed accordingly. I agreed to raise the point at tonight's meeting."

Councillor Tim Lyon, wearing shorts and a tee shirt, raised a finger to signify he wanted to butt in. He and Cllr Dave Johns who'd been elected a few months earlier, were the fresh blood on the council and twenty years younger than the others.

"I saw this item in the agenda and I knew it was about me and Dave because we wear shorts," said Tim. "I always wear shorts even in the winter. I just don't feel comfortable in trousers."

Dave Johns then took his chance to speak. "I wear shorts most of the year because I work outside and find them the most suitable type of clothing," he said. "But the shorts I wear to council meetings are as smart as trousers, they are just cut at the leg."

Ripley looked slowly around the table for others to speak.

"I agree with the residents," said Councillor Roy Phelan, wearing a tweed jacket, tie with grey slacks. "In my experience in life 'if you think champagne, you drink champagne," he added.

Next was Councillor Pauline Smith, wearing a smart green blouse and skirt. "I don't think it is the style of clothing that matters, but the smartness of the clothing. We can all make an effort to represent the town."

Ripley, wearing a checked jacket and open necked shirt, had the final word. "Well I think that we should dress formally for meetings. After all, this is a council not a barbeque. I don't propose to have a vote on this matter, but the clerk will note the comments in the minutes," he said before moving to item number three.

The rest of the meeting was a disappointment as far as lead stories were concerned, but at least I had something for pages three and two. There were plenty of nibs too, because they had spoken about their usual hobby horses; the skate park, the car park, grants to sports clubs and the state of the town's walk ways.

Finally Ripley called for 'questions from the audience' and when no one spoke, closed the meeting. I packed up and followed the residents out of the building thinking about the gaps I still had in the paper – everything was covered apart from the splash.

The public melted away to their homes, leaving the high street empty apart from a line of people queuing at the fish and chips shop. I walked to the car park, which was dimly illuminated by public lighting from the road opposite.

As I approached my car, I heard the rapid scuffle of footsteps making their way towards me. I turned just in time to see a clenched fist fly towards my face. Jolting my head backwards instinctively, I managed to parry the blow, his knuckles grazing the top of my forehead. A second blow rained down on me, this time connecting with my shoulder, deadening my left arm. I jumped backwards to avoid a third punch, and shuffled to my right to gain some space.

Lit by the street lighting, I could see he was wearing a balaclava, his eyes burning brightly with adrenaline. Having missed his best chance, I could see he was sizing me up. I was a couple of inches taller, but he was a bit broader. Within moments, he'd swung a lazy karate kick towards my head, but it was so telegraphed that I easily managed to pull back, and his boot flew harmlessly past my head missing me by more than a foot. Of balance, I took my chance to throw a punch, and felt it crunch as a tooth shattered.

He screamed, but the blow only seemed to energise him and again he rained down blows. The first missed by a whisker, the second smashing into my cheek. I felt the side of my face go numb, then turn warm but there was no pain.

He threw another punch, which landed flush on my jaw. I staggered to one knee and a kick came in hard against my ribcage, knocking the wind out of my lungs.

"Fuck off back to London," he yelled while I was at his mercy.

It gave me just enough time to stand up, and stagger backwards to my car. He bolted in the direction he had come from, jumped the perimeter wall and disappeared into the darkness.

Chapter 11: Members in shorts

"What the hell happened to you?" Sheffield asked as I sat down at my desk, his eyes wide open with shock. I had spent more than two hours icing my cheek the night before in a vain attempt to hide the bruising, but it was still pretty puffed, red and sore.

"Someone jumped me after the council meeting," I said quietly, not wanting to attract the attention of the newsdesk.

"Jesus, what the hell is going on?" he said. "It can't be something to do with your front page, can it?"

"I guess it could have been anyone." I said. I was certain Ripley was behind it but wasn't going to let anyone know my thoughts, even Sheffield. I'd decided to play it down.

"Are you going to tell the newsdesk? It could be your splash," he said. "At least if you want it to be?"

The newsdesk would probably have accepted it as a splash, but that would have given Ripley the satisfaction of seeing my bruised face all over the front page. I wasn't going to give him the pleasure.

"I want to deal this another way," I said. "Don't let on to the others. Just say I fell over jogging or something, okay?"

"Okay boss," Sheffield said. "It's your call."

I already had a plan, of course. It had been festering in my mind from the moment my assailant had told me to get back to London. All I needed was some cutters, a can of spray paint and a large sheet of cardboard.

"Do you know where I can get some bolt cutters?" I asked Sheffield.

"There's a hardware store in town, but what do you want those for?" he said looking surprised.

"Oh just for a padlock I've lost the key for. Nothing to worry about."

My plan was going to have to wait until after work that day, and I still needed to get page three sorted out. It was a good story, showing up the council as a bunch of buffoons, and would probably be good enough for the splash under different circumstances. But I needed a couple of pictures of the councillors.

Tim Lyon answered his mobile straight away.

"Morning," he said in a heavy West Country accent.

I explained why I needed his picture for the dress code story. "It's not much of a story without a photo of you in those shorts," I said.

"Well I'm not sure I should even be talking to you. But the way they treated us last night, I'm thinking screw them - you can call me any time. I'm not sure about a photo though - it will only make me look even more stupid."

Without a photo of at least one of them, there was a chance newsdesk wouldn't accept it as a page three lead. I'd be doing the walk of shame again.

"I don't think you will be humiliated," I said. "It is going to be a light hearted piece and it's the council who will look small-minded. Let's show them up for what they are."

"I don't know," he said pondering. "But I'll do it if Dave does."

"Okay, I'll give him a call," I said.

Fortunately Dave had also decided to ignore the gagging clause "I was going to call you to be honest," he said. "I can't see the point of not speaking to the press. The chairman will just have to lump it."

"That's great, Tim just told me the same thing," I said. "That's why I'm calling you. He said he'll have his photo taken if you do?"

"Well if Dave is game then so am I," he said.

Tim kept his promise, so I booked Len to take the photos at 10am and 10:30am. And with that all arranged, I filed the page five blogger story along with half a dozen short nibs from the meeting.

That gave me the rest of the day to bash out page three. But the newsdesk had spotted by bruised face and Katie came over looking angry. She'd assumed I'd got involved in a fight.

"How did you get those bruises?" she demanded to know.

"Out running," I said.

"What do you mean running?" she asked, her face contorted with rage.

"I fell over while jogging, and bashed my head on a tree root." I explained.

She stared at me blankly for a moment, then burst out laughing.

"You do know the paper has banned reporters from playing football in case they get injured don't you?" she said barely able to get the words out. "Well, perhaps they should add jogging to the list of dangerous sports!"

It must have really tickled the newsdesk, because outbreaks of laughter continued for the rest of the day. Sofia's occasionally joined in, her laugh sounding like a machine gun against Katie's high pitched screech.

But I thought it was better than having my face all over the front page. So I knuckled down to write up the dress code story, which required a big mental effort from me since it needed lots of puns. After about 20 minutes, I only managed to think of one for the intro:

Two councillors were given a public dressing down this week over the smartness of their clothing....

But that was about the extent of it with me and puns. I decided to leave the rest to Sofia who no doubt would write something brilliant. She cooed with delight when she saw the story drop in. "This is excellent Simon," she shouted from her desk.

When she had finished polishing it, she came over.

"What you put through was okay," she said, which was code for pretty average. "It's fine; everything was there, all the facts. You had the introduction right, but you needed more puns."

"I drew a blank after the first one," I explained.

"That's fine but take a look at what I did later. Are you sure you don't want to use this for your splash though?" she said. "It's easily good enough – really quirky. The type of thing the Daily Mail might go for if you call them on Thursday."

"I'm working on something else for the splash," I said.

"Okay, well I'll put it through as page three then," she said. "If you are sure you have a splash?"

I nodded.

I looked at the story she'd put through to the subeditors before I left for the day. It was good but I decided I didn't really like puns in articles. They might show how clever the journalist was, but they also trivialised the story in my eyes:

Dressing Down for Councillors in shorts

Two councillors were given a public dressing down this week after residents complained about the smartness of their clothes.

Appleton councillors Tim Lyon, 35, and Dave Johns, 33, were told the secret to 'thinking smart' was 'dressing smart' after the pair's casual attire of shorts and checked shirts failed to impress the public at a recent council meeting.

But despite soaring temperatures the two refused to get too hot under the collar, and gave short shrift to the fashion critics, saying they could do just as good a job as those in cravats and blazers.

Deputy chair Paddy Cummings, wearing double breasted blazer and cravat said. "I have been contacted by several residents who are concerned by the attire of some of the members. They say that we are the elected representatives of the town, and should be dressed accordingly."

Councillor Roy Phelan, wearing a jacket and tie with grey slacks, agreed. "In my experience, if you think champagne, you drink champagne. So if you want us to be smart then require us to dress smart."

The dress code debate was stylishly handled at Monday night's meeting, when the pair were asked to air their views and iron out any problems.

Tim Lyon, a keen gardener, arrived at the meeting in shorts and a checked shirt.

He said: "I saw this item in the agenda and I knew it was about me and Dave because we wear shorts. I always wear shorts, even in the winter; I just don't feel comfortable in trousers."

Dave Johns, a farmer, added: "I wear shorts most of the year because I work outside and find it the most suitable type of clothing. But the shorts I wear to council meetings are smart."

Chairman Tom Ripley, wearing a checked jacket and open necked shirt, said the item was raised after complaints from members of the public. "This is a council not a barbeque," he said....

Chapter 12: Missing tractor

'Cutters, Cardboard, Spray paint' – the shopping list was short but I had to make sure I wouldn't be traced after buying it. So believing that purchasing the stuff locally would give the game away, I drove to a hardware store near Taunton.

The advertising on the bolt cutters boasted they could slice through 8mm of steel, which I was confident would do the trick. It only took a few minutes to find a can of red metal oxide spray paint, which I imagined with glee that Ripley would have to scrub for hours to remove from the barn. But finding the cardboard proved to be trickier than expected until I spotted a discarded box made of the material in a skip at the back of the store. I had some string and a small torch at home, which were the only other items I thought were needed.

Everything was in place, but that didn't stop me spending the night tossing and turning with worry about the plan.

I aimed to turn up at 5am when I was certain that Ripley's yard would be deserted. So it was still pitched black as I crept out of the flat with a rucksack full of paraphernalia. It never occurred to me that I might have looked suspicious as I walked to the car.

To minimise the risk of being spotted at the scene, I parked in a layby and walked the rest of the way to the front gate.

It was a dark, cold and lonely walk in the rain to the entrance. I leapt over the gate, which lurched forward, creaking loudly. Pausing for a moment, I wiped the dew from my hands onto my jeans, and reached into a rucksack for the cutters. My target was a brass padlock which fastened the barn's giant sliding doors. I'd spotted it the day before.

Gripping the arms of the cutters tightly in each hand, I squeezed hard and they snipped through the bolt like plasticine. "What a con," I said to myself, thinking how easy it had been to break in. It was my first time after all. I picked up the broken pieces of the lock and placed them safely away in the rucksack.

The giant French metal doors slid open with an ear splitting scream. I yanked them far enough apart to drive the tractor through, and grabbed my torch to illuminate the inside of the barn.

The tractor sat gleaming in the moonlight which flooded in through the open doors. I clambered into the tractor's cabin and quickly found the keys on a hook next to the ignition - exactly where we'd kept them when I worked for a motorway maintenance company during a summer job a decade earlier. The lads had taught me how to hotwire a car while I was there, so I had a Plan B. Thankfully it wasn't needed.

I climbed down from the cabin and grabbed the rucksack and pulled out the cardboard which I'd curled into a tube. It unfurled to reveal the writing I had sprayed on earlier:

MYSTERY SOLVED: COUNCIL TRACTOR

FOUND IN CHAIRMAN RIPLEY'S YARD

It seems a bit daft now, but I had tied a long piece of string between two holes either end of the cardboard, so I could hang it somewhere. I looped the string over a bar at the front of the tractor so it sat flush against the front grill, and clambered back up into the cabin to fire up the machine.

It coughed into life, puffing great black clouds of smoke into the back of the barn. I jammed the machine into first gear and it lurched forward, and chugged through the sliding doors into the front yard. I slammed on the brakes and it slid to a halt. Then I switched off the engine, locked the cabin door and put the keys in my pocket. Finally, I pulled out the can of red paint and sprayed over the front of the barn:

"MYSTERY SOLVED: COUNCIL TRACTOR FOUND HERE"

Droplets of red paint ran down the front of the stainless steel panels as it dried, giving the graffiti a ghoulish expression.

Confident I hadn't been spotted, I jogged back to my car and drove home sedately, content that everything had gone to plan.

I'd calculated the first commuters would see the tractor around 6am, so after getting a 'tip off' I could safely arrive any time after 6:30am without raising suspicion. I started my way back at 6:10am and drove past the gates.

The place was empty, but I was prepared for that - I drove a circular route along some back roads to eat up some time.

As I repeated the 15 minute loops, the roads started to fill with cars and by 7:30am a steady stream of vehicles were driving past the gates, illuminating the tractor with their headlights as they rounded the bend.

I parked up outside to take a photo.

Several other people were milling outside the building. Two were standing at the gate, their figures silhouetted against the barn. I took a couple of photos and drove off home satisfied the job was done.

Katie called me excitedly at 8:30am. "We've just had a call about a commotion at Ripley Light Industries," she yelled. "You know the place?"

"Yes, I'm working on a story about it."

"Better get down there then and check it out."

For the third time in as many hours, I drove to the yard, this time parking in front of the gates. I could see Ripley's Jag parked round the back, although he was nowhere to be seen. The cardboard plaque had been removed, of course, and someone had tried to scrub the red paint from the building, without success – the red lines only slightly blurred by the scouring.

The tractor hadn't moved, although a locksmith was working on the cabin door. I took a couple of photos of him, nicely framed next to the graffiti.

I was about to leave, when Ripley walked out of front doors. But seeing me, he immediately doubled back inside.

It was my best chance to get a decent comment, so I jumped over the fence and followed him. He was chatting to a group of workmen, and one of them tapped his shoulder and pointed at me.

"This is private property," he yelled. "Get out or you will be thrown out."

"Have you a comment about the council tractor Chairman?" I shouted across the shop floor.

He didn't say another word but two of his men started walking over to me menacingly.

I turned and walked briskly out of the building, hurdling the gate to escape capture as they closed in. They patrolled the perimeter after that, so I snapped a couple of photos of them from a safe distance and left.

Sofia walked over to me as soon as I got in.

"You're on deadline for page two!" she yelled. "Ten minutes!"

"Okay, I'll type it up," I said calmly.

This time I was prepared because I had been thinking about the story overnight and knew exactly how I was going to write it. And I'd got all the quotes I needed the day before.

"Ten minutes!" she yelled again, disappointed not to get a reaction the first time.

"No problem, I'll do that now," I said. She looked at me blankly for a moment, then trotted back to her desk.

It was the 'chairman gags council' story which was a backup to my splash. I tapped it out and filed it with moments to spare:

Residents' anger as Chairman gags Council

Residents have slammed a chairman's decision to gag councillors from speaking to the press.

Appleton chairman Tom Ripley imposed the ban because he is furious at recent Sentinel reports about an arson attack on his property.

He claims an article which suggested the firebombing of the barometer shop was motivated by a vendetta against him was 'full of inaccuracies'.

But police confirmed that the vendetta angle is being investigated.

Appleton shopkeeper Mary Dodds, who runs Organic Foods, said most townsfolk thought the arson was motivated by a grudge against the chairman.

Ms Dodds added: "I don't understand this decision; if a council isn't about speaking to the media, then what is it for?"

Under the new regime, council official Sean Alderman will answer press enquiries rather than elected members of the community.

Chairman Ripley said: "I'm sorry to say that again The Sentinel has printed an irresponsible article, full of inaccuracies. This time it was about the break in on the high street, which it erroneously claimed to be a vendetta attack despite me explaining there was absolutely no foundation in this accusation.

"I'm hacked off about it and I don't intend we put up with it any longer..."

Sofia came over an hour or so later to check on my splash. "Was your being late something to do with the splash you've been working one?" she asked.

"Yes. A blogger has been writing about a missing tractor. It turned up in the chairman's yard this morning with graffiti accusing him of taking it."

"Lucky that happened or it wouldn't really have been a splash," she said quizzically. "But I guess all's well that ends well - you can put it through."

It needed a couple of quotes from Roy Easter and Cllr Dunne. Once I'd done that, I rang Sean Alderman who had already prepared something from the council:

Chairman slammed after missing tractor found in yard

Residents have accused the council chairman of using a top of the range tractor bought with taxpayers' money for personal benefit after it was found in his property.

Town blogger Roy Easter said it was an 'absolute disgrace' that the Mercedes tractor, pictured below, showed up at Ripley's and Associates yard. The town council had repeatedly refused to tell Mr Easter of its whereabouts despite numerous queries to the town clerk Sean Alderman.

The tractor appeared outside the front gates of the yard on Wednesday morning, next to graffiti 'Mystery solved: council tractor found here.'

Mr Easter said: "It appears that this was some kind of whistle blower action showing the missing tractor was being used by the chairman. It's an absolute disgrace if that's the case. He needs to come clean if it was used for his business and step down from the council if that is the case."

Mr Easter wrote a blog last week asking what had happened to the tractor, which was bought two years ago with council funds, but has not been seen since. It was bought to maintain the town's hedges and cut fields but the council has admitted that it has not yet been used for that purpose - instead contractors have used their own equipment.

County Councillor James Dunne said: "No one should be making money out of council property."

In a statement, Appleton council said: "The tractor was originally stored at Ripley Associates' yard as a temporary measure but has remained there because no other suitable storage facility has yet been found."...

Chapter 13: Morning meetings

My edition was starting to sell well, so my pile of papers in the basement was only a few inches high on Thursday morning. Sheffield's leftover copies were stacked in two huge piles. Feeling guilty, I grabbed some of his, added them to mine and we walked up the stairs.

We dumped them on the bench opposite our desks and each took a copy of our editions to read, swapping them over the partition once we'd finished.

"That's a great front page!" Sheffield said. "No wonder your paper is selling so well."

For a moment I thought I detected sarcasm in his voice and thought he was on to me. I felt like confessing all.

"I was gifted a lot of stories this week," I said. "How are you finding your patch?"

I knew the answer – he was struggling to find enough good stories, and finding it difficult to stand up the ones he did.

"Katie and Sofia had me in Peter's office again this week," he said despondently. "They were picking through each of the stories, telling me how to improve. You're flavour of the month – Sofia keeps saying that 'Simon had to start from scratch and he's got it'. Can you imagine that?"

The newsdesk's view was that there is always someone queuing to take your place if you're not up to scratch. They did a simple calculation – would it be easier to train up a new guy who might be better, or stick with someone who might never 'get it'? They were sticking with Sheffield for now but there was every chance they'd drop him after the six months' probation.

"We could try to do another boundary story this week, if you fancy it?" I said. "It worked well last week."

"Okay boss, I'll keep an eye out for something."

We didn't have many contacts in the wilderness, so I wondered how he would find something. It would probably mean driving out to the villages and knocking on a lot of doors.

I leafed through my note pad for some inspiration for pages 11 and nine - an update to an old story would do. While I was wracking my brain, the phone rang. I picked up eagerly.

"Well done lad," said Councillor Dunne enthusiastically.

"You mean the splash?" I asked.

"Yes lad," he said. "Well done for getting it into the paper. You'll be pretty unpopular, although you weren't flavour of the month anyway, were you?"

He chuckled down the line. "Since you did so well with that story, I thought you might like another?

"Of course," I said thinking he was becoming a top source.

"There is a brothel between Appleton and Longley called The Lodge, you know it?"

"No," I said, but thinking it must be the one Carrie had mentioned.

"Well some important people in the town have an unhealthy interest in it. If you get what I am saying?"

"Customers?"

"No, no," he said.

"What then?"

There was a pause. "A financial interest," he explained.

Ripley?" I said instinctively.

"You'll have to work that out for yourself," he said. "I've had some complaints from residents, so I've put it on the agenda for Monday's meeting at Longley. Make sure you're there to cover it."

The trouble was I wouldn't be able to file the story until Tuesday at the earliest. So I decided to give the phones a rest for once, and take a calculated risk by driving into Appleton to flush something out.

According to my old lecturer at journalism school, information boards were the key to local stories. But I was beginning to wonder what paper he worked on because all I could find were nibs. I jotted down some adverts about a 'dog walking service' and 'paper rounds offered'. It was real cat-up-a-tree stuff.

Fortunately, I spotted a group of archers practicing on the common. I snapped them sideways on as they lined up to fire their bows. I figured it was worth spending half an hour chatting to them just in case I could turn it into a lead.

"Are you training for the Olympics?" I said hoping for something.

"No, just practicing. We practice once a month here at the common," Mark Metcalfe, the captain, said guardedly. I suspected that he didn't like the press.

"But are you entering any competitions? Any stars in the making?" I pressed.

"I'm afraid not, we don't enter competitions at the moment. But our membership has doubled in the last year."

That was just about all I got out of him.

The trouble was the endeavour had cost me the afternoon, so anxiety levels were starting to rise the next morning as I arrived at work. Then Katie called an editorial meeting, which cost me more time.

We all trudged into a small, dingy, meeting room next to the editor's office, waiting for Katie and Sofia to arrive. Sheffield and I sat down in our usual spot around one corner of the large rectangular meeting table. Next to us was Len and his assistant Zoe, who we rarely saw because of her busy schedule. We'd complained to him about the quality of her pictures which were completely uninspired. He'd explained she didn't have time to get out of her car on most jobs. To meet deadline, she'd wind down the window, snap the shot, and drive onto the next destination.

Sitting next to Zoe was Luke, the 21 year old editor's assistant. Despite having a couple of years in the job, his copy wasn't great and the newsdesk was conspiring to get rid of him. He was nearly deaf and when he asked if he could install some special software to help, they suggested he might want to leave instead. His mother was friends with the owner, though, so they couldn't sack him.

It was in these editorial meetings that we reporters were asked to reveal our story ideas for the week ahead, only to have them picked apart by the newsdesk. It was a game of cat and mouse – the newsdesk would try to prise out the best stories and the reporters would endeavour to keep quiet, knowing they might pinch them for county pages.

For me there was the added humiliation of having to reveal my non-existent story list. Tim would snigger at my incompetence; only Sheffield would get the same treatment.

The din of chattering reporters was growing to a crescendo as we waited for the Katie and Sofia, the occasional bout of laughter ringing out. The door swung open and they strode in, the room immediately falling into obedient silence. They sat poker faced at the opposite end of the table.

Katie started by explaining she had just come from a meeting with the editor and 'he wasn't pleased' with the standard of this week's editions. This was usual, but what happened next wasn't.

"Sales were down by nearly 3,500 copies – that's in just one week," she added. "We're below 41,000 sales for the first time so Peter wants us to pull out the stops. The stories were flat with no colour at all! There are too many council stories, not enough off-diary pieces. You need to get out on patch and hunt down better leads."

Nobody dared say what I was thinking - that we didn't have time to go on patch because of the huge number of stories we had to write.

"What articles? Which editions?" Tim demanded to know. "We've busting a gut to get the paper out all month."

"Peter didn't pick out any particular edition," Katie said. "It was just that he felt the stories are too grey. He wants people to get out and speak to real people rather than boring councillors."

The paper was selling more than 46,000 copies a week when I started. I knew it was vital sales were kept high because advertising revenue was linked to circulation

I lifted a hand, and she nodded in my direction.

"All the stories are published on the website right?"

"Yes, everything goes online the day we go to press," she said.

"Well perhaps those 3,500 people are using the web rather than buying the paper?" I asked.

Katie was furious: "The website is the future Simon," she said slowly and in staccato. "But we do not make any money out of it at the moment, which is why we have to work harder to find better stories."

It seemed like the website had become another stick to beat us with, although no one was going to say that in the meeting. We'd have a chat at the pub later and draw our own conclusions, which usually blamed the paper.

"We've had a tip off that the organiser of the Griffin Music festival has got cancer," Katie continued looking at Tim since the festival was in his patch. "Ask him when you see him."

"That's crazy," Len said. "He's not going to give us any more free tickets if we run that story. It is the one good thing about working for this paper."

"Then we must try to broach the subject discretely," Katie said. "Use your contacts to confirm what type of cancer it is, Tim. Say that you would like to do a piece thanking the hospital or raising funds for cancer research. Make it something he'll want to be involved in."

She read a list of events taking place in Yeovil over the next week, trying to prompt some more ideas. So it looked like the Yeovil edition was the main problem. Tim and Jason were under the cosh.

Sofia then took over to discuss our story ideas.

"What have you got planned for today's pages?" she said finally getting to me.

"There's an item about a brothel at the Longley meeting, so that's my splash," I said.

"The Lodge?" she said.

"Yes, that's right."

"Wonderful," she said. "Some of your predecessors wanted to run that story, but could never stand it up. But if it's in the public meeting you can report it."

Journalists had 'qualified privilege' to report just about anything in public meetings without being sued, as long as there was no malice.

"Anything else?" she asked.

"I have a feature on the archery club."

"Okay fine," she said. "Anything for page nine?"

"Not yet, I'll do a ring around after the meeting."

As usual, Sheffield's list was better than mine but she had a go at him for failing to stand up his stories. "It's all about facts, facts, facts Sheffield," she said.

We trudged back to our desks and I rang the archery captain for some more quotes. His phone went to voicemail so I left a message to call me back.

With time running out, I started to write it out as best I could:

Accountants swap quill for bow and arrow

They are accountants, shops workers and businessmen, but once a week this army of office workers swap the quill for Robin Hood style sharp shooting.

An Appleton archery club has doubled in size in recent years after setting up residence on the local common.

The Appleton Archers was established three years ago in response to a booming demand from highly strung enthusiasts.

It now attracts dozens of bowmen and women from across south Somerset who hone their skills regularly on Appleton Common.

Club captain Mark Metcalfe, 38, an accountant, said: "Our membership has doubled in the last year. We practice once a month here at the common."

But the sharp shooters are not planning to get too competitive, and admitted they are not even considering entering for the Olympics.

He said: "I'm afraid not, we don't enter any competitions at the moment. We just do it for fun."

But they are now calling for new members to start separate men and women's teams. Mr Metcalfe said: "Ideally we need another couple of dozen people to join the club so we can set up men and women's teams this year."

I counted up the eight paragraphs - four short of the minimum. So I searched the internet for something to bulk it out and found a few paragraphs in the GB Archery Club's official website. I attributed the final two paragraphs to a spokesman, which is strictly against the rules:

The archers are reviving an age old Somerset tradition, according to official GB Archery Club. The oldest bow ever found on these shores, dated to around 2700BC, was discovered in Somerset. But it was only when William the Conqueror defeated English King Harold at Hastings in 1066 that the longbow was developed into a weapon of war - and archery became widely practiced.

Kings went to great efforts to ensure that enough men had the proper archery skills. They banned games such as football, bowls, golf and cricket because not enough men were practicing archery.

A spokesman for the GB Archery club said: "The gradual introduction of firearms from the 15th century cut down the need for archers but never quite quelled a national following for archery as a recreation.

"As early as the 16th century, societies dedicated to the bow and arrow sprang up to satisfy the demand for competition, with modern target archery beginning in the 18th century."

With page eleven, pic and nibs filed, I turned my thoughts to page nine. But before I had a chance to pick up the phone to anyone, Sofia beckoned me over with an outstretched index finger.

"Walk of shame," Sheffield said meanly as I lumbered past.

"This is a picture story," Sofia snapped. "You'll need to get them to talk about what inspired them into taking the sport up, why it's become a popular pastime again, or it's a nib. What else have you got?"

"Just The Lodge story," I said, my cheeks turning red as I realised that the whole office was listening in.

"Go and make some calls," she said. "See if you can turn this into a page lead or come back with your note book. Ten minutes – you're behind deadline already!"

Sheffield wanted to chat but I was too stressed. I telephoned the captain again, but his phone went straight to answerphone. Thing were getting desperate.

I rifled hopelessly through my notes to see if I'd missed anything from the Appleton meeting. Nothing!

"What did you put through?" Sheffield asked.

"A story about an archery club asking for more members," I said still paging through the reporter's pad.

"That's a nib," he said. "What are you going to do?"

"Go back with my notebook if I can't find anything in the next five minutes," I said.

I considered writing the story about terrorists targeting leafy Somerset. But that would burn my best contact. So I trudged over to Sofia with my notebook, and no ideas.

"What else have you got?" she snapped.

"There was a discussion about the council donating £40 to the air ambulance," I said.

"Err?" she sneered.

"And there is one about putting fencing up around the footpath on the common."

"Why are they doing that?" she said immediately.

I read my notes slowly out loud. "Some people are scared of walking over the common because of the cows so they want to fence it off. But others want to keep things as they are."

"That's a good story," she said clapping her hands together. "Put the quotes through straight away. Have you got a pic?"

"No."

"Okay I'll use the archery one. Have you got anything for page nine?"

"No."

"Then you better start ringing people once you've put the quotes through. You really need to get more organised."

It was tricky to decipher the mixture of scribbled full English, and tee-line short hand I'd written the council meeting in. I was shaking like a leaf by the time she'd called for the quotes for the fourth time. Finally, sweat pouring down my brow, I filed it:

Chairman Tom Ripley said: "Last year most people wanted to go ahead with the scheme. People want the path to be fenced off because they think the cattle will sit on the hard core that has been put on the path. They are frightened of being attacked. It's mainly newcomers who are in favour but there are plenty of old townspeople who are afraid as well….."

Councillor Hill said: "Cows have been allowed to graze on the common for hundreds of years and to my knowledge there has never been an attack. If they come over to you, all you have to do is say 'boo' and they will run off. We don't have the money for this and in my opinion it would be foolish to do it …."

She left me alone after that so I chatted to Sheffield for a bit who was trying to make the most out of my misfortune. I took a sneaky look at the story though, once she's sent it to the subs:

Walkers fear attack from grazing cattle

Sightings of big cats may have inspired tales of the Beast of South Somerset but a less fearsome creature is terrifying a nearby community.

Marauding cows are in the middle of a fierce debate in Longley pitting newcomers against old townsfolk.

Recent arrivals want a popular walkway through a moor behind the town hall gardens to be fenced off because they fear being attacked by grazing cows.

But old town's folk, who have lived in harmony with the cows for decades, are fighting to keep the path free from fencing.

Council chairman Tom Ripley said: …

At least there hadn't been a blank page, I thought breathing a sigh of relief.

In all the commotion, I hadn't seen that my voicemail flashing – it was a missed a call from Roy Easter. I rang him straight away hoping for a lucky break.

"You made me look like a bloody fool this week, didn't you?" he said curtly.

"How do you mean?" I said, hoping he was joking.

"You've got me saying the chairman's an idiot for blaming kids for vandalising the town on one page, then turn over and you've written a huge article about youngsters rioting. It makes me look like a bloody fool."

"I don't think it does," I protested. "The point you were making was separate from the riot issue."

"Makes me sound like an idiot, there is no getting round it," he said adamantly.

He wasn't going to give me a lead after that and I was left wondering what else could go wrong. I spent the next hour ringing all my main contacts, without a sniff of a story. It was as if all the shopkeepers, businessmen and town busybodies had been told not to speak to me.

Then I was struck by a flash of inspiration, and called Longley chairman Ben Webster.

"Are there any stories from tomorrow's agenda which I can cover today?" I asked thinking it was a great idea. Surely there was no reason why a story couldn't be brought forward a day or two.

"Well I suppose you could write up our plans for the pet cemetery," he said. "We're putting forward proposals to use the town's cemetery for the burial of pets. The idea was backed by most councillors earlier this year but has been delayed because the councillor who suggested it retired from the council. We'll be rubber stamping the plans on Monday evening."

Delighted, I organised a photo with Len, got some reaction from a Crufts dog breeder I knew and filed the story:

Animals may go six paws under

Plans to develop a pet cemetery at a town's graveyard have been given the green light.

Longley Town Council has approved the proposal to use an unused section of the community's graveyard for the burial of pets.

The idea was backed by a majority of councillors when it was raised by Tom Kite earlier this year, but was shelved when he retired from the council.

Chairman Ben Webster said the council wanted to gauge public opinion before moving forward....

Chapter 14: Sham stories

Sheffield and I sat down in the pub's window seat next to Colin, Bert and Bob. They briefly said 'hello' to acknowledge us, and carried on with their conversation about a reporter called Paddy. It was Friday night and as usual, all the reporters had trooped down to the local drinking hole near the office.

"Who's Paddy?" I asked while they took a breather to drink their pints.

"He was an Irish lad who worked on one of the north Dorset editions a couple of years ago," said Bob downing the last few inches of stout, and licking a creamy residue off his lips. "He worked with Colin then left without a word's notice."

We turned our gaze on Colin, who had been listening to the others but contributing very little.

"He was always late with his stories," he said ruefully. "I'd be saying, 'what have you got lined up for the front page?' and he'd have nothing, zilch. His news list was virtually non-existent. And then, right at the last moment, he put through these amazing articles."

Colin, was struggling to get his words out because of his stammer. "He worked for around six months," he said with great effort, "then just disappeared without saying a word. I was suspicious about all those great stories, of course."

"So what type of stories were they?" I asked.

"There was a lot of court copy, some burglaries and death knocks," he said. "Never any pictures though – 'they didn't want to have their faces in the paper', he'd say. So when he left, I checked out some of them. It turned out he made them up – the people, road names, everything. That was his trick you see – he made it all up, so no one would recognise a road name or place. They would just assume it was somewhere in the town "

"So why did he leave?" Sheffield asked.

"Ah well, that was a different matter," Colin said. "You have to have a driving licence to do the job, and he'd told Peter that he had one. But he didn't have a car, and so the newsdesk needed to see his licence to insure him for the pool car. He drove it around patch for six months, stringing them along saying he's lost it and had applied for a replacement – 'It will be coming through any time now' etcetera. And it got to the point that they said if he didn't find it, he would be sacked. A couple of days later he disappeared."

"But how do you know that he didn't have a licence?" I asked.

"Paddy's mother rang the paper a few weeks' after he left to apologise for him failing to work out his notice, and to tell Peter that Paddy was fine. She says that 'Paddy just wasn't cut out to be a journalist.' Then Peter asked her if Paddy had 'found his driving licence' yet - typical journalist, still trying to get the full story. His mum laughs and says: 'Is that what he told you? - he's such a liar, he's never had a driving licence.'"

I was trying to laugh along but it was a bit close to home for me to see the funny side. Everyone apart from me was grinning madly though.

"Have you ever thought about making up a quote?" Bob asked me.

"No never crossed my mind," I said truthfully.

"Come on it must have crossed your mind," he said. "It crosses everyone's mind. Are you telling me that when Katie and Sofia are jumping up and down demanding another quote, it doesn't enter your head momentarily to make something up - just by attributing a sentence to a made up name and busy road on your patch?"

I was feeling uncomfortable with the line of questioning, but it was true – I really had never considered making up a quote, even for a moment.

"I've always written the truth," I said adamantly.

"The truth!" Bob barked. "Don't ever think that what you write is the truth. What we do is write stories based loosely on a few facts, that's all. Never confuse that with the truth."

Everyone was staring at me, waiting for me to argue the point. My cheeks flushed red with embarrassment.

"I've never done anything dishonest though," I said defensively.

Sheffield broke out of his slumber, almost falling off his seat.

"Are you telling me you've never done anything dishonest?" he demanded, making me think he might be on to me at last.

"Nothing that wasn't in the public interest," I said and was relieved when he let the subject drop.

Chapter 15: Road Trip

It was the first time that any of us had escaped to the coast since arriving at the paper. Bert picked up Sheffield and me from my place after breakfast. Bob was sitting in the front seat, holding a football in his lap, so it was pretty obvious what the plan was once we got to Lulworth Cove. Sheffield and I sat in the back of the car, and we all chatted about the paper while we drove to the sea.

"When have you got your six month review?" Bob asked Sheffield as we motored out of Yeovil and onto the country roads.

"It's still a couple of months away," he said.

"They'll probably wait till both your probationary periods are up and bring you both in the same day," Bob said. "The most important thing is not to complain about anything. They will ask you if you are enjoying working at the paper, and if you say no, then they'll have a real go at you for not fitting in. Not being cut out for journalism. You must say that you are loving it, even if it's a complete lie."

Bob and Bert had been at the paper a year longer than us, and had several run-ins with Katie and Sofia.

"Have they ever sacked anyone?" asked Sheffield.

"A couple of years ago they sacked this 18 year old guy. He went into the review and then came out, packed up his things and left. It only took them a day to replace him – they keep a long list of people who they've interviewed."

"That's what happened to me," I said. "They said I hadn't got the job but was next in line."

"We knew you'd be hired as soon as you walked in the newsroom," Bert said. "Katie and Sofia were full of smiles. Ever wondered why the reporters they've hired are all guys?"

"Perhaps they prefer managing them?" I asked.

"Something like that - whatever it is, we could tell they liked you straight away. You should have heard the reaction from the rest of us after you'd left."

It hadn't even occurred to me that they might like me. I'd honestly thought I must have had the strongest CV. "You two lads are like me and Bert," Bob said. "I reckon you look out for each other like we do. You need someone watching your back at this paper."

It was the first time I'd heard them let rip at the newsdesk in this way; obviously there was some pent up frustration.

"So how are you two finding the paper?" I asked.

"Like everyone else, it's terrible," Bob said. "I'll give you an example - they sent Katie on a management training course a few months ago, and she came back saying 'they were going on about how to motivate your staff, but you don't need to do that with reporters. By definition, journalists are self-motivating'. That about sums it up."

The paper viewed itself as a training paper, and expected reporters would move on once they'd learned the ropes. In the meantime they could treat us how they liked, I thought.

"Have they said anything about training yet?" Bert asked Sheffield. We were perched on the edge of the back seats like two children listening to our parents.

"We've had shorthand lessons, but nothing about our seniorship exams." I said.

Bert smiled at Bob. "We've been at the paper nearly a year and a half, and they still haven't signed us up on the seniorship course. They keep saying it is fully booked, but we checked and it's not. Bob knows one of the trainers, so we know for sure they have places."

"Why are they doing that then?" I said.

"It takes 18 months to complete the seniorship," Bert said, "and once people have passed, they tend to leave straight away for a better paper. The longer they leave it till you start training, the longer they have you for at The Sentinel."

It was a depressing thought but I wasn't even sure if I was eligible for the seniorship exams because I hadn't done the recognised junior reporter exams.

"So what are you two going to do?" I asked.

"We're going to leave in the next few months – to try somewhere else." Bert said.

We were winding our way through the lush green hills of south Dorset, which helped take our mind off the paper and improve our mood. We parked at the visitors' car park above the cove and took in the view.

It is an idyllic spot – the cove is a near complete circle cut into the Jurassic coastline. The sea, having sliced its way through a clay bed thousands of years ago, had at first created a limestone arch, which allowed tides to gradually eat into the Weldon Clay to form the circular cove. A shingle beach packed with millions of tiny fossils makes up the shoreline.

We walked into the visitor's centre, which was displaying a dozen or so fossils from the coast. Sheffield picked an ammonite, its spirals fanning out to the size of a dinner plate.

"We should set up a business digging these things out if we don't make it through the review," he said.

"I'd be up for that," I said dreaming a little.

Apart from the visitor centre and car park, the cove was unspoiled. We walked around the beach for half an hour, trying unsuccessfully to find a fossil and then walked back to a flat field near the car.

"You know the reason why Sandra banned staff from playing football after work?" Bob asked kicking the ball to Bert and positioning two jackets as goal posts.

"Because of time off work?" I asked.

"We had a game a year ago and three of us ended up in hospital with sprained ankles. She was furious and sent everyone an email which said she was disbanding the paper's football team. She doesn't know that we still play unofficially, so don't ever let on. We'd all get the sack."

We played a game of 'head volley'. With Bert in goal, Sheffield and I had to score eight volleys to win. Bob needed four intercepting headers.

I stabbed at the ball ambitiously with the toe of my boot after Sheffield sent over a cross. The ball dribbled feebly along the ground and stopped just short of the keeper.

"That was the weakest shot I have ever seen," Sheffield grinned.

They were all football fanatics, while I was more of a cricket fan - not that I was going to admit it that day. I'd played a bit at school after all.

"What position do you play?" Bob asked me.

"I was a striker," I said. I'd played one game in that position at university because the rest of the team were so slow.

"I see you as more of a full back," he said. Adding, "With the silky skills of an Alan Hansen," after seeing my disappointment at being relegated to the backs.

Once we'd finished the kick about, we bought ice creams from a vendor and ate them on a grass bank overlooking the cove, chatting about what we wanted to do after leaving the paper.

"Local journalism will do me from now on," Sheffield said.

"Really," I said. "Don't you want to work at a national one day?

"No, it's not for me," he said, "I'd be happy to go up north and work at a local paper there for the rest of my life."

We admired the sentiment, but it wasn't what I had in mind - I wanted to work at a national broadsheet.

Bert told us that he'd studied English at Cambridge and Bob revealed he'd done the same at Oxford, which made me appreciate getting a foot in the door at The Sentinel.

We headed home at dusk, a perfect day by the coast never to be repeated. Bert dropped me off first, and I was about to slam the door when Sheffield noticed something had dropped out of my bag.

"I think you've forgotten this," he said handing me the broken padlock I'd taken from Ripley's yard. I took it without saying a word, and walked to the front door silently berating myself for being so careless. It wouldn't take much more to be rumbled.

Chapter 16: Satisfaction

Editorial staff were summoned into the managing director's office on Monday morning to discuss the results of a staff survey the paper had been forced to carry out by head office in London. All the group's papers had been asked to survey staff to assess job satisfaction, pay, management as well as training and facilities. We were one of the most successful papers in the group, well regarded in newspaper circles and had won many local journalism awards. The results would make interesting reading to the bosses in London who we heard were keen to hear what lay behind our award winning journalistic performance.

The managing director, Sandra Lavis, was standing next to the projector looking distinctly unhappy as we walked in, which didn't come as a complete surprise as the post mortem into the survey at the pub had revealed we'd all slated the paper. Tim had even predicted job losses when Sandra saw the results. "We're probably all get the sack for telling the truth," he'd said. The survey's timing wasn't great because the paper been slashing overtime and mileage claims, which was costing people a lot of money.

We sat in two rows of seats facing her, with the projector screen over her left shoulder as she faced us and waited in silence.

Each section of the survey posed a question, for example about 'pay and conditions' and then asked us to rank the paper's performance from 'excellent' to 'very poor'. I had only been at the paper for a month when the survey was foisted on us, so was at my keenest. Even so, I ranked nothing above average, and pay as 'very poor'.

The results were presented in a series of bar charts. Sandra, who was calm at first, gradually let her emotions take over as the results lit up the screen.

"Editorial staff has given the worst of feedback of all departments," she said kicking things off, "Far worse than Advertising. And I just don't understand this response about pay."

The bar chart for 'pay and conditions' showed all but two of the editorial staff felt them to be 'very poor'. And presumably the exceptions were Sofia and Katie.

"I make no apologies for saying Advertising is better paid because it earns three times as much revenue for the paper as Editorial," she said. Until that point, I had no idea there was a gripe between the two departments about pay so she was completing my education. Sandra explained that the money brought in from paper sales, which was considered as Editorial's contribution to the balance sheet, was less than a third of that from advertising revenue. The logic didn't work for me - after all there wouldn't have been much advertising revenue if no one bought the paper. But Sandra's doctrine was law, and nobody questioned it. There was just a stony silence.

"I have made a huge improvement to the pay and conditions of reporters in recent years," she continued, "wages have doubled in the last five years."

This was true but I quickly calculated that was only because the minimum wage had come into force during that time. Before that people often had to take second jobs while working at the paper.

"Salaries cannot increase further at this time because paper sales are down. I hope people can understand that?" she said before moving to the next histogram. I was dying to ask whether production costs were dropping as fast as sales, because it was rumoured that the paper had a 50 per cent profit margin. But it wasn't that type of meeting, particularly if you were on probation.

"There were comments about profits," she added, unable to hide her anger. "Anyone who wants to know what our profits are can come to my office and ask!" She was referring to criticisms made in the feedback section. It looked as though people's suspicions had been put down in black and white. Bosses had been cutting costs for years but still taking big bonuses. We reporters thought it was a 'race to the bottom', with ever poorer quality and declining sales.

The next histogram was about 'training and development.' Again all the bar charts were heavily built up towards the 'poor' or 'very poor' end. Two said 'very good' – presumably Katie and Sofia – and the one said 'average', which must have been me.

"I really don't understand this because the training opportunities offered to editorial staff are excellent," she barked. "We are fastidious in ensuring that you are all trained to the highest standards in shorthand, and send people on a very highly regarded seniorship course, so this makes no sense what so ever."

Without pausing, she moved to 'management and motivation.'

Again the histogram showed the same pattern.

"Management is always ready to help with any issues you have," she said, "So I really can't comprehend why the results are like this! As reporters, I would expect you all to be self-starters. If you are not, then perhaps you are in the right profession."

She moved swiftly on to 'facilities and equipment' and again staff were critical, mainly because of our antiquated computers.

"We were considering moving headquarters to an industrial estate, but decided against that because of the view of staff, so I would have thought that might have registered here," she said. "Sadly it appears not!"

It was clear she'd made her mind up that editorial were the 'awkward squad.'

Without summing up, she switched off the projector and said, "My office is always open if you have any further questions."

It was one of the shortest presentations I'd been to, lasting less than 15 minutes. We gathered afterwards that she had been required to do it by head office.

We trooped quietly out to our desks, with no one daring to say a word about it in the newsroom in case we were overheard.

Thankfully my phone rang, so I could get on with some work.

"I would like to speak to the reporter Simon Turner please," a woman said in a posh voice.

I admitted he was me, wondering if I was about to receive another complaint or a story. It turned out to be both

"I'm ringing about the rape story you published last week. I am the wife of the man who was convicted," she said referring to the cold case conviction of a rapist who'd been jailed after raping a student in Taunton many years earlier.

"My parents still live in the area – can you imagine what it was like for them to read the story?" she said.

"I can only imagine," I said uncomfortably. "It was court copy though, so we tend to publish whatever the court reporter puts through."

"The conviction was unsound," she snapped, prompting me to start scribbling down her quotes. "It was based on DNA evidence alone. There was no corroborating evidence whatsoever, which means he was convicted entirely on the DNA found more than a decade ago. In America you have to have corroborating evidence to convict someone of a serious crime, otherwise the conviction is dropped."

"So you are saying he is innocent?" I asked to get the quotes I needed.

"Yes of course I am!" she said. "The police made it clear when they arrested him that they didn't like him. They said that if they ever saw him again, they'd make sure he was sent to jail for a long time. Then they pinned this on him. Do you think I would stay with him if I thought for one moment he could have done that? He is a gentle giant not a monster."

She demanded I print her side of the story, and said I would ask the newsdesk. Sofia was delighted to run the piece so I filed it for my page seven:

Rapist's wife claims conviction was unsound

The wife of a south Somerset man jailed for the brutal rape of a student claims the conviction is unsafe.

Thomas Snide, who was born in Appleton, was last week convicted of the rape more than a decade after the offence took place following a cold case police investigation.

The married father of three had his DNA taken earlier this year after getting into a fight with a man who was involved in an altercation with his 18 year old son.

He was sentenced to nine years behind bars for raping the student after dragging her into an alleyway in Taunton.

His wife Julie Snide, 52, said: "The conviction was unsound - It was based on DNA evidence alone. There was no corroborating evidence what so ever, which means he was convicted entirely on the DNA found. In America you have to have corroborating evidence to convict someone of a serious crime, otherwise the conviction would be dropped."

She claims the police investigation was malicious.

Ms Snide said: "The police made it clear when they arrested him that they didn't like him. They said that if they ever saw him again, they'd make sure he was sent to jail for a long time. Then they pinned this on him. Do you think I would stay with him if I thought for one moment he could have done that? He is a gentle giant not a monster…"

Chapter 17: Longley meeting

The atmosphere at Longley's council chambers was far more convivial than its Appleton equivalent the week before.

Chairman Webster lounged back in his chair, welcoming me with a warm smile as I rushed in a few minutes late. He was a conciliatory figure amongst the bombastic folk who become councillors. Red faced and cheerful whenever I saw him, he gave the impression of a man who'd had a couple of gin and tonics at home before arriving at the chambers. The other councillors were huddled around him, sharing a private joke or two. Several of them acknowledged me with a smile or a raise of the hand as I sat down in the press chair. I mouthed 'hello' in response and picked up the agenda waiting on my desk. Just as Councillor Dunne had promised, item number two was marked as The Lodge.

I noted that two seats had been put out for journalists, which seemed ambitious since The Sentinel was the only paper to attend while I'd been covering the patch, although Peter had warned that our rivals, the Western, might make an attack on my patch at any time. I made a note to ask if they were expecting any one else to attend.

"Can we start the meeting?" Chairman Webster said laconically. He looked up at the public momentarily and content he had their attention, started proceedings.

"Item number one – Footpaths," he said, "Councillor Townin have you an update?"

Freda Townin was tall and thick set, with unusually broad shoulders. She was in her late sixties and gave the false impression of smiling when she spoke, when she was in fact grimacing. This could lead to some unfortunate miscommunications, particularly with people who didn't know her.

"Funding is the main problem in the short term," she said with a hint of smile, which I was unable to determine the nature of. "So we have been concentrating on the most used pathways. It's upsetting, but the others will have to remain untended until we can find the funds."

Webster tapped his pencil on the table, deep in thought for a few seconds. "Could we have a list of paths the council wishes to adopt in time for the next meeting? So we can concentrate our efforts on those which are most important." he said, having decided the course of action. He led the meeting from the chair, but was happy to be challenged by colleagues or the public.

"Of course," Townin said. "But may I suggest that we put some signs up asking people if they want the other paths to be maintained. If we don't get a response, we know they aren't being used."

Webster nodded and we moved onto the next item.

"Point Two," said Webster, "The Lodge - I believe the County Councillor has something to say about this?

"I do," Cllr Dunne said turning his head towards the public, which consisted of about 20 people - a very large turnout for a Longley meeting. I noticed two elderly women and a middle aged man with a greying beard sitting together alone in the front row, watching proceedings intently.

"I have been contacted by several parents who are concerned about the goings on at The Lodge, which as many of you here today will know, is a property of dubious reputation on the main road between Appleton and Longley."

"It's a whore house!" one of the elderly ladies in the front row shouted, leading to a burst of laughter from the people sitting further back.

"Quiet please, ladies and gentleman," Webster said calmly and the noise slowly died down.

"It does have that reputation," Dunne continued. "But it's not primarily that activity which I am concerned about today because there is no law against prostitution so the police are powerless to take action unless they can prove a particular establishment is a brothel, which isn't easy. But selling drugs is a different matter, and now we have evidence that that is happening, so I suggest we ask the police to take action to shut the place down."

Gentle applause rang out and several people raised hands into in the air, including the ladies in the front row.

"The public will have a chance to speak in a moment," Webster said and the hands dropped down. "First though, I would like to hear from the member for community cohesion."

Vice chairman Peter Dean was dressed from head to foot in tweed, which suited his style – that of the English gent. Whether he was or not was still to be established. He wore a handlebar moustache which was twisted at the ends, and he tugged on it as he spoke. "It is wrong to accuse people of a crime without hard evidence," he said. "If people have evidence then they should take it to the police, that's my view. It is not for the council to be judge, jury and executioner."

"I disagree," Townin responded. "It's the council's business to remind police of their duties. Lord alone knows why they haven't done anything yet."

She pointed a shaky finger at me: "Let's use the paper for our benefit for once. The least we should do is to write an official letter to the police demanding they investigate."

"I second that motion," said Councillor Dunne.

"Those in favour?" said Webster, and all the members apart from Dean lifted their hands in support. "Those against," he added. Dean slowly lifted his arm.

"The motion is passed," Webster recorded. "The council will write a letter outlining our concerns about The Lodge to the police and ask them to investigate. I will draft the letter with Councillor Dunne."

"Point three," Webster said. But before he could continue, he was interrupted by the woman in the front row.

"You said the public would have its chance to speak!" she demanded.

"You are quite correct," Webster said apologetically. "And your name please?"

"I'm Lady Fothergill, as you know Ben. I've lived in Longley all my life after all," she said. Laughter rang out behind her once again.

"Yes, Lady Fothergill, what is it you wish to say?" Webster said.

"I want to say that I'm not sure what good a letter to the police is going to do!" she said looking towards the other residents. "They have known about this for months and done nothing. The place is attracting the wrong type of people to the town and it needs to be shut down now. Let's take some direct action and picket the place."

Webster pointed to the man next to her who'd raised his arm after she'd finished.

"I am Sam Smith, the coach for the Longley football club," he said. "Several of our younger members have spoken to me about The Lodge. They tell me there is a large scale commercial drug dealing operation taking place there. Lady Fothergill is right about the need for action. The youngsters say that the kids are literally queuing up the street to buy Ecstasy some nights. The police seem unwilling to take action."

There were shouts of support from behind him, prompting Webster to ask for quiet again.

"Your remarks are noted, along with Lady Fothergill's, and will be included in our letter to the police," he conceded. "This council does not recommend direct action, but there is nothing we can do if you wish to pursue it. However I would urge you to remain within the law in your protests."

"May I move to item number three?" he said scanning the room. There was no protest. "Good, then let us move to The Pet Cemetery. Many of you will remember this item from earlier this year but it was put on hold after the councillor in charge retired. The idea is to put aside a certain part of the cemetery for the burial of pets. The deputy chair has been revisiting these plans, so I would like to ask him to speak."

"I've been speaking to the clergy about this earlier this week," he said. "Unfortunately there is a snag. The area we thought we could use was designated for paupers, meaning it has unmarked graves. So we can't move forward until another part of the cemetery is found. I've asked the vicar to look into this and he has promised to let me know by the next meeting."

"Then we will hope to hear from you about this next month," Webster said looking anxiously in my direction. "Until then our plans will have to remain on hold."

I felt the pit of my stomach churn with anxiety. I'd either have to tell Sofia my page lead was wrong, or risk her finding out after the story came out.

I was too busy worrying about the pet cemetery story to take much notice of rest of the meeting, but jotted down some quotes about 'signage at accident spot'.

After that, the chairman ploughed through a dozen or so planning applications, which I wrote down half-heartedly, then he called the meeting to a close. But as the public began to drift home, I was with it enough to make a beeline for Lady Fothergill.

"Could we have a chat about The Lodge story for The Sentinel?" I said putting my worries about the cemetery to the back of my mind.

"Tell me a bit about yourself first?" she said smiling. "Where are you from?"

"Marlow which is a town twenty or so miles west of London," I said.

"You'll be heading back to London soon enough, no doubt," she said warmly. "Once you've got the experience you need from our little community."

We walked past the local Chinese takeaway and through the town square, chatting all the way.

"I can see you are right on the money," she said. "I've seen how you've been taking on Appleton Council. You'll find that there are quite a few people don't like the ways things are done. But there are not many who will speak to a newcomer – that's the way it is in this part of the world."

We stopped at a row of beautifully maintained limestone terraces. "Would you like to continue this conversation over a cup of tea?" she said. "I live here."

She's stopped at the door of her cottage. "It is made from limestone quarried from Bishopswood," she said. "It's such a shame that new residents living there want to close the quarry down."

"Do they?" I asked unaware.

"It's mainly the newcomers in Bishopswood these days," she said. "And because those people don't work in the quarry anymore, they don't like their houses being coated in lime dust. Bishopswood was built for the quarry workers, so no one complained in days gone by. But less than half are quarry workers now."

She opened her front door and led me into the front room.

"Would you like a cup of tea or perhaps a glass of wine?" she said.

I asked for tea because I was driving.

"As I say - right on the money!" she said.

The interior walls of her house were decorated with gold patterned wall paper and Chinese rugs covered its oak floors. There was a selection of watercolours on the walls next to photos of Lady Fothergill's family on a side table. A bronze figurine stood next to them.

"They are my granddaughters," she said. "That bronze is me when I was young."

"Beautiful," I said, hoping it was the right thing to say.

"Are you married Simon?"

"No," I said.

"Oh you are still very young. No doubt you will meet someone in London when you are working for one of the big papers."

We sat down on a leather settee and sipped our tea. I must admit I was wondering quite what to say.

"I'm glad I've had a chance to talk to you because my friends and I wanted to warn you to be careful. Ripley won't stop until he's got you out of his hair. You've upset him too much already. He went to great lengths to remove one of your predecessors after he started asking difficult questions too."

"What was his name?" I said startled.

"It was Ted. I'm afraid I don't remember the details very well."

I'd heard about Ted in passing. He'd covered my patch before landing a job as a producer on national television.

"That must have been three or four years ago?" I asked.

"That sounds about right. He was probing the Council's plans to build a community hall," she said. "That rattled them. Normally Ripley would send a couple of his thugs to put the frighteners on. But they couldn't do that with Ted."

"Why not?"

"Because they were terrified of him - he was six feet six inches tall and a black belt in karate. He sat at council meeting staring at them. They wouldn't say boo to him."

"So what happened?" I asked.

"They set a different kind of trap. I believe you call it a honey trap? But one thing you need to know about Ripley is he's not that bright. They tried to get him in an uncompromising position with two girls. But it all failed miserably."

"Why?" I asked.

"As I said, Ripley is not that bright at times. Determined, dogged, ruthless, yes - but not that intelligent. The plot failed because Ted was gay." She placed a friendly hand on my arm. "You had better watch you back though, Simon. I am sure he will be plotting to get rid of you too."

"Tell me about the community hall Ben was investigating," I said trying to change the subject.

"Ripley owns property called Alma Court which the council wanted to turn into a community hall. Someone is making a lot of money out of the deal, I promise you that. Ted was looking into the title deeds before he left."

"I'll do some digging then - try to find a paper trail."

"As I said, you're on the money," she said smiling.

Chapter 18: Midweek manoeuvres

The knot in my stomach tightened as I arrived at my desk the next day. I'd resolved while fretting in bed the night before, that the first thing I'd do would be to tell Sofia about my mistake and have done with it. At least that would bring things to a head, and hopefully get the article corrected.

She was writing an answer into The Times crossword as I arrived at her desk and, seeing me, quickly closed the paper to hide what she was doing. I thought it best to pretend I hadn't noticed.

"I've realised I made a mistake with my page nine," I said.

"What story was that?" she said rolling her eyes melodramatically.

"It was the pet cemetery story," I said. "The chairman said they would be rubber stamping the plans at last night's meeting, so I filed it yesterday as if they had approved it."

"And what happened?" she asked repressing a yawn.

"Unfortunately they found out that the site has already been used," I said.

"So let me get this straight," she said curtly. "You filed a story about a council decision for a pet cemetery before the council had actually made the decision! And now they've decided not to go ahead?"

"Yes that's right," I admitted. "But it's more accurate to say they have put it on pause until they find a new spot."

"This is going to make us look like idiots," she snapped. "People will laugh at us."

"Can't we correct it?" I asked. "After all the paper hasn't been published yet."

"The page will have been sent to the printers by now, so it'll be set up."

She walked over to the subs' desk and spoke to the chief subeditor. I stood where I was, looking like an idiot, waiting for her to come back.

"It's too late, the page has been set by the printer," she confirmed. "Never file a story saying a decision has been made until it has. You could have said that plans for a pet cemetery are being revived, rather than they have been approved. That would have given you room for manoeuvre."

She waved me away in disgust, and I trooped back to my desk. It wasn't so much the view of the newsdesk that bothered me as the reaction I'd get from the people of Longley.

It was a great fat mistake, and there would be no hiding from it.

"What was that all about?" Sheffield asked sticking his head over the partition.

"A story I messed up," I said. "I said the council had agreed something but then they didn't."

"Sounds like a tense thing?" he said.

"No I it was a fact thing."

"What I mean is, if you said 'the council were planning to give the green light' about something, that way you can get away with it when they don't. I do that all the time."

"Lesson learned," I said crossly.

I needed to get on with pages five and three or face another bollocking. At this rate, I was getting more than the rest of the office combined.

I had the 'accident waiting to happen' story from the Longley meeting but needed a photo of Chairman Webster and others at the junction.

He agreed to a photo at 1pm, as long as he could invite other councillors. 'Otherwise some might feel excluded,' he explained.

Len had to phone a university student who doubled up as a freelancer outside classes, because everyone else was tied up. Still reeling from my latest cockup, I typed up the story:

Council urges improvement at death trap junction

A junction branded as 'an accident waiting to happen' is putting lives at risk in a South Somerset town.

Longley Council is demanding a reduced speed limit and better signage at the junction between Dark Lane and Appleton Road.

Longley Chairman Robert Webster said: "There have been several accidents at the junction because people can't see traffic approaching from Appleton as they pull out. There have been no serious injuries so far but it really is just a matter of time before someone is killed. We need a reduced speed limit and warning signs.

The Highways Authority, which uses accident statistics to determine where to make safety improvements, says the road is fine, according to the Chairman Webster.

Chairman Webster said: "Their system is flawed because it means there has to have been a serious accident before they will make changes. That is like shutting the gate after the horse has bolted...."

It was a bit weak but I watched Sofia take it from her inbox and send it through to the subs without complaining.

It was nearly lunchtime which gave me several hours to file a story for page three, so I decided to make a round of teas before Tim complained too loudly.

I plonked a cup on his desk.

"You do make a nice cup of tea, I'll give you that," he said. "You do it so quickly too." He said it so effeminately I wondered if he was chatting me up.

"It's all about pouring the water directly onto the bag," he continued. "A lot of research goes into getting the bags just so."

Jason was on patch so Colin was next down the line. I placed the cup carefully in front of him as he was finishing a call.

"Thanks, lad," he said.

"How's your week going?" I asked.

"Fine lad," he said. "How's your patch coming along?"

"You might have overheard I made a mistake on page seven," I said.

"Oh don't worry about that lad," he said. "Reporters worry about mistakes to start with but after a few years it's like water off a ducks back. I laugh when they point at mine."

"Oh right, I'll do that then," I said pleased at the thought.

With tea done, I sat at my desk trying to think up a story idea. I leafed through my notepad for inspiration but there was nothing other than nibs. Then I remembered the quarry story tip from Lady Fothergill, so I Googled the company name, Bishopswood Limestone, and telephoned its managing director.

His personal assistant, Josie, told me he was 'unavailable' so I explained the story I wanted to write about old towns folk versus newcomers and left my telephone number for him to call.

Then I recalled a journalist website thesplash.org posted story ideas for student journalists. It was a long shot because they usually couldn't be 'localised' but it was worth a look:

Quiet day in the office? In need of some inspiration to fill the features page? See our story ideas here:

Helping people enjoy a 'wheelie' good night

There's nothing more unpleasant than seeing a row of drunk men (and sometimes women) urinating on a shop doorways during a night out on the town. But police and Eastleigh Borough Council, in Hampshire, are considering leaving out a wheelie bin for people to wee in…

Aggressive children and stressed out teachers

The behaviour of primary school children is becoming more aggressive while a quarter of teachers are suffering mental health problems as a result. These and other startling findings are the result of research conducted by the Association of Teachers…

The second idea gave me the inspiration I needed. Thumbing through the contacts book that my predecessor had left me, I came across telephone number for *Newcross School (for special children) Headteacher, William Newman.*

"You've got a damn cheek calling me after the last story your paper ran about my school," he said indignantly after I'd said hello. "I've a good mind not to speak to your paper because of the inaccuracies – riddled with them it was "

I'd learned that people who don't want to speak to you rarely left you in any doubt, so I was encouraged.

"That is awful," I said. "But it must have been someone else because I'm new at the paper. I'll will make sure we're accurate this time I promise you."

"Well you say that. But then you have a clever way of twisting all the words. How do I know you will keep your word? I really don't know if I want to go through it all again."

I explained that I wanted to write a story about the stress levels teachers are under. "Why so many leave after a couple of years in the job."

"It is true," he said taking the bait. "We are under tremendous stress - more than ever because of all the new government initiatives."

I picked up my pen and started to scribble down the quotes, confident I had him hooked.

"Which initiatives are causing the most anxiety?" I asked.

"The testing regime is onerous. But it's the inspections that cause the most stress. We had to go through one recently and there is a tremendous amount of work that goes in. The push at the moment is about child protection, so if you haven't got all the appropriate plans in place then you will be marked inadequate, regardless of the academic qualities of the school. You could be teaching the children brilliantly and still be labelled as failing."

"So would you say schools are being asked to pick up the pieces for a broken society?" I asked picturing an easy headline.

"I wouldn't go so far," he said. "But the onus is on schools to do far more than we did a generation ago, and that creates stress. I expect half my new teachers to leave in the first two years, and it is particularly difficult to replace staff in a school for children with special needs. Morale is low because so many children are being moved into general schooling, which has left us with just 16 children and 11 staff."

My antennae immediately shot up at the mention of the staff pupil ratio, "So how many children are there in each class?" I asked.

"I must stress it's a temporary measure, because the school is being wound down," he explained. "We will be closing next year. But until then, the handful of staff I have will continue to teach the children in classes or four or three."

I'd made him a promise but it was still hard to suppress my journalistic instinct to pursue more quotes for a knocking story about the staff to pupil ratio. I wondered if my predecessor had encountered a similar indiscretion when they spoke to him. He was certainly a rich source of quotes and had given me enough for three separate articles in two minutes. No wonder he was wary of the press.

After the interview, I pondered which line to take. But I made the right choice, plumbing for original line about stress:

'One in two' teachers leave school due to stress

A south Somerset school for children with special needs is losing half of its new teachers every two years through stress, a Sentinel investigation has revealed.

Peter Newman, head teacher of Newcross School in Bishopswood, blames ever increasing paperwork to meet Government targets.

Mr Newman said: "The onus is on schools to do far more than we did a generation ago, and that creates stress. I expect half my new teachers to leave in the first two years, and it is particularly difficult to replace staff in a school for children with special needs."

"The push at the moment is about child protection, so if you haven't got all the appropriate plans in place then you will be marked inadequate, regardless of the academic qualities of the school. You could be teaching the children brilliantly and still be labelled as failing."

He said that while the testing regime is onerous, inspections cause the most stress.

Mr Newman said: "We recently went through one and there is a tremendous amount of work that goes in. Morale is low because so many children are being moved into general schooling, which has left us with just 16 children and 11 staff. We will be closing next year. But until then, the handful of staff I have will continue to teach the children in classes or four or three."

I filed the report by mid-afternoon, which won me several hours of freedom.

While I had been chatting away, Katie and Sofia had whisked Sheffield off for a meeting. He sat down looking dejected as I filed the story.

"They said I'm on my last chance," he said.

"They've said that before though, right?" I asked. "What do they actually mean?"

"If I don't come up to scratch in the next few weeks, they're going to boot me out," he said. "Me - a kid aged 21, and they won't give me a break."

"Have you got your pages covered today?" I asked, not knowing what to say.

"Yep."

"Your sales are going up aren't they?" I said.

"Over the last couple of weeks."

"So tell Peter things are improving. You might still be learning but sales are going up. Your copy is improving slowly and you're confident that you can pull through." He nodded and I got back to work.

My splash about The Lodge was pretty much stood up. So I arranged to visit County Councillor James Dunne at his home with the aim of getting the low down on another story.

Chapter 19: Dunne deal

County Councillor James Dunne was one of that very rare breed of politician you instinctively trust. He had no real airs or graces, instead connecting with people through his convivial nature and genuine commitment to the public. He had been repeatedly elected to the county council, easily seeing off determined rivals such as Ripley and Cummings who regarded him as a nuisance and an obstacle to their plans for power. And, what is more, the very act of being elected meant Dunne was revered by many on the Appleton town council, most of whom had been co-opted into office - a process by which existing councillors, such as Ripley and Cummings, hand pick new councillors when too few votes were cast at the ballot box to legitimately elect them. This strange quirk of democracy was instigated under electoral law because it was felt that it is more democratic to let a cabal of elected councillors choose their fellow civic leaders, than allow a few dozen voters elect them. So after bullying staff and business associates into voting for them at the town council elections, Ripley and Cummings were able to select the rest of the council until the recent bi-election, which saw Tim Lyons and Dave Johns returned to office.

Dunne's front door swung open to reveal him in a blaze of primary colours - his jacket was mustard yellow, his shirt a vibrant green. "Come on inside," he said jovially, looking ruddy faced after vigorously shaking my hand on the door step.

He took me through to the kitchen in his two up two down Victorian terrace, and then offered me tea and chocolate biscuits. Dunne lived in the hamlet of Hendon, which was made up of a smattering of identical terrace houses along one side of a country lane, facing farmland on the other side.

"Will you be running The Lodge story this week?" he asked enthusiastically while handing me a partially melted chocolate biscuit on a saucer.

"I'm planning on it being my splash," I said equally enthusiastically. "I should be able to run another story about it next week too, if Lady Fothergill arranges the sit in she's promised."

"Tiny Tom will be incandescent," he said with a roar of laughter. "You didn't hear it from me, but The Lodge is a cash cow for him, although nobody would dare say that in public of course. On that note, how will you be mentioning me in relation to the story?"

He looked a little anxious at being named as the instigator, and I was keen to put his mind at rest. After all he was my best source of stories and I wanted that to continue. "The article will focus on the comments made by Lady Fothergill and the football coach, with perhaps a few words from you towards the end." I said.

"That's probably the best way. And it allows me to continue to feed you stories without any repercussions from you know who."

He was pleased, and reclined in his chair contentedly. "That suits me perfectly too," I said. "But if you know that Ripley is taking money from The Lodge, then perhaps I should be pinning the story on him? For instance, I could check who owns the building?"

"You'll never get him that way," Dunne said emphatically. "He is a kind of Don Juan in these parts of Somerset and that means he knows how to launder money without getting his hands dirty. It is widely assumed he prospers from The Lodge, otherwise it would have been shut down years ago. But I have never seen any proof and he'd never be so stupid as to have his name on the deeds of the place. You'd probably find it was owned by a company based overseas – it's all about smoke and mirrors, you see?"

He was right but I made a mental note to check its ownership with the Land Registry at some stage anyway, just in case Ripley had got sloppy.

"Has Lady Fothergill been in touch about the sit in?" I asked.

"I wouldn't hold my breath about that particular idea either," he said. "Lady Fothergill often says things for effect - with the press in mind. Not that I don't admire her for doing so. The idea of some direct action will add to the story no doubt. It might even motivate the police into doing something for once."

"Oh I see," I said, disappointed that a potential follow up story was unlikely to amount to anything. "I have enough to write up The Lodge article for this week's edition in any case. But I actually came to see you today about an entirely different matter."

"I'd be delighted to help in any way I can, providing we keep to our agreement about using my name discreetly?" he said with a friendly smile.

"I give you my word," I said. "Lady Fothergill told me the council is involved in some, let's say, questionable deals over a community centre. Is that something you have heard about?"

"She's referring to the purchase of plots of land by the Ripley cabal," he said leaning forward. His face getting uncomfortably close to mine. "It is very murky stuff - she's right about that. I'll tell you what I know, but it's quite complex and I don't have all the facts. What I can say with confidence is that Ripley is using smoke and mirrors again to hide what's going on."

139

He reclined again, allowing me more personal space. "So what's the deal about?" I asked.

"I have no hard evidence," he said. "But I'd bet my mortgage that the purchases are cover for property development deals between Ripley and Cummings. Ripley buys or sells the plots to the council and then Cummings fixes them up, making a tidy little profit on the way."

"I thought there are rules against councillors getting involved if they have an interest?" I asked.

"There's no rule against them bidding for a contract," he said. "They only have to announce their interest and then leave the room when something is being voted on."

"And rely on the rest of the council to vote it through?"

"Precisely - don't forget most of them are co-opted, so they either owe him a favour or are in business with him. It's just a case of having a little word here and there about what the council wants, perhaps down the pub and word trickles down to the others. They are either too stupid to spot it, or they are part of the scam."

"What exactly is the scam though?"

Dunne paused for a moment, taking a sip of his tea while he recalled past events. "Over the past five or six years, the town council has been in negotiations over the development of the former police station site called Alma Court," he said. "They bought it from the county council at that time, saying it would be used for a community hall, which the town is lacking. Nothing happens for ages, then quite out of the blue three years ago, they decide to sell it. The council met behind closed doors to discuss the deal but we -that's me, Lady Fothergill and others – got wind of it, so we sent a former chairman to a council meeting to warn Ripley that we were onto him. Because of the secrecy, he could be liable if the deal falls flat you see. You can't go round making deals in secret like that. Anyway, Ripley went to the former chairman's house the next day and shouted through his letter box he'd sue him if he didn't shut up."

"But he is protected by free speech laws at public meetings so he can't be sued," I said trying to be helpful.

"We knew that, but who wants to be pursued through the courts? In any case, he claimed we were acting out of malice, which if proved true wouldn't be allowed. Whatever the rights and wrongs of it, we backed down."

He took another sip of tea, the cup rattled on the saucer as he raised his pursed lips.

"Do you do know Appleton has a star council?" he said.

"I have no idea," I said. "What's a star council?"

"It's an inner circle which makes all the decisions. Appleton has one. It consists of Ripley, Cummings and Alderman. I asked Alderman to release the minutes for the purchase of Alma Court but he blocked me, even though it's his duty as town clerk to hand over the files. You know town clerks are effectively the chief executives of the town council?

"I thought they were just administrators," I said.

"My dear fellow, they are far more powerful than that. Nothing can be done without the clerk's sign off, regardless of what the others want. So he effectively has a veto. He is also paid a handsome wage to run things. And in this particular case, he is also a close friend of Ripley and Cummings They got him the job."

He sat back in the chair and let out a long sigh and drained the last few dregs of tea from the cup. I could see a smattering of tea leaves stuck to his lower lip.

"I wrote to Alderman asking for the Alma Court minutes, and copied in the Member of Parliament and leader of the county council," he said. "After two months, I got a reply, which wasn't copied to the others, saying that the files had been misplaced and it would be too costly to search for them! So I paid him a surprise visit one afternoon, and told him the cost issue could be overcome if I searched for the documents myself. Not much he could do about that right? At first he tried to say that the files were confidential and could not be released without approval from the council, but I told him that was a lie and we had a blazing row. Eventually he allowed me to search the council archive."

"What did you find?" I said hoping to get to the crux of it.

"I searched high and low but found nothing. There were all the usual commercial documents about the sports club, the new BMX track but nothing about Alma Court. Not a jot. And the files were in complete disorder, either through incompetence, or a deliberate blocking tactic. Whatever is going on has at least three players in my book - Ripley who is the ring leader. As you know, he is a man with a finger in every pie. The second is Cummings - I'm sure he benefits from all the work the council contracts as well through his light furnishing company. And with the third is Alderman who benefits through a cosy job."

"Unfortunately, I can't write any of this without libelling someone," I said, "Though it might be a different matter if I could get hold of those documents."

"If you do find a smoking gun I'll back you when the time comes. But keep my name out of it until then."

"So what happened after you backed down," I asked.

"Everything went quiet again and then about a year ago, the council changed tack, saying they wanted to buy Breakers Gate which is right in the town centre, to develop the community centre - despite it having a doctor's surgery on the site with a 99 year lease. The council then sold a large proportion of the Alma Court site to a property developer called Compton House, which was part-owned by Ripley. Meetings were held behind closed doors, they said to avoid attracting outside interest in the purchase.

"As soon as the Alma Court deal is closed, the council buys Breakers Gate, again behind closed doors. They claimed it was another 'once in a life time opportunity' for the town. The whole thing was rushed through without by Ripley, Cummings and Alderman."

"How does The Ice House fit into the picture? Lady Fothergill mentioned something about it." I asked.

"I was getting to that," Dunne said. "Six months go by and then the council announces that it has dropped the plan to develop Breakers Gate, and instead will use The Ice House for the community centre. It is a derelict factory owned by Ripley. Then they sell Breakers Gate to Compton House. But as with Alma Court they make a small profit on the sale because property prices have risen, so no one complains."

"Did The Sentinel run any stories?" I asked, hoping there might be something in the paper's back catalogue.

"Just a basic story here and there - a couple of short stories perhaps. None of the reporters are around long enough to get to the bottom of this," he said. "What makes me suspicious is that six years after the plans for a community centre were announced, the council hadn't commissioned any architectural drawing for a community centre at

Alma Court site, Breakers Gate or The Ice House. But in truth, I can't make head or tail of it."

"The question is do you believe in cock up or conspiracy?" I asked.

"I'm a conspiracy man myself," he said.

Chapter 20: Drinks

The office was shut by the time I got back to Yeovil, so I texted Sheffield and arranged to meet him for a quick drink at Wetherspoon's. He was at the bar talking to Bob and Bert when I arrived, so I made a beeline for them.

"What are you drinking?" he asked immediately, so I ordered a lager and sat down with them. It was beginning to feel like we had formed a gang of four.

"I was telling Bert and Bob that I had yet another meeting with Katie and Sofia after you left. This time they've given me a month to improve or I'm out," he said.

It wasn't a huge surprise since they'd been ramping up the rhetoric for weeks and things hadn't really improved for him. But I thought he must have stuffed up another page for them to call another meeting so quickly.

"Did you mention that sales are going up?" I asked trying to remain positive.

"Yes, but I don't think they are bothered about that. They said they don't want to have to 'baby' me any longer. I've got to be 'more like you.'"

"I reckon they are bluffing," Bob said. "I overheard them saying they haven't got anyone decent lined up at the moment, so they would have to put themselves through all the hassle of interviewing people again."

Sheffield shook his head disconsolately. "They seemed pretty genuine to me," he said. "They kept banging on about how 'not everyone is cut out for newspaper journalism.'"

"It doesn't make sense," said Bert. "Why not wait until the six month review? It's only a couple of months away."

Unlike Bert I knew how much Sheffield was struggling. I had experienced the same problems finding stories myself until I'd started taking certain, shall we say, short cuts.

"What he needs is a few decent stories," I said injecting some optimism. "And some help writing them up. I'll keep an eye out for leads if you guys have a go at editing his stories?"

"Fine with me," said Bob downing the last few fingers of his stout. "Wing them through to me before deadline and I'll take a look."

Tim joined us at the bar for a few moments. He'd been drinking shots of whisky with Colin and was slightly the worse for wear, which was never a good sign.

"You are shit!" he said pointing to Sheffield and grinning. "And you are, well, okay," he said pointing to me. A nasty tight lipped smile having come over his face.

There was a long silence while we took it all in.

"We were all shit when we started," Bob said finally. "Even you, Tim."

"I was never that shit," he said pointing to Sheffield again, and walked off to join the others before we could think of a response.

"If being a journalist makes you like that," said Sheffield when he was out of earshot. "Then I'd be happy to get the sack."

"Did you hear what Sofia said to him the other day?" Bob said.

"No, we can't hear her from our desks, unless she is shouting at us," I said.

"She told him that they can't recommend him for a job at the daily paper unless he improves his personality."

Sheffield fell about laughing at the thought. "She's right about that but what can he do about it?" he said.

"By the way he just behaved, not much," Bob said. "After all it's not that easy to change who you are. You have to work on it. The thing for you to do, Sheffield, is to get some good stories and prove him wrong."

"I just need to find some inspiration." Sheffield said.

He was gazing at me again with an expression that made me feel like he was on to me. I knew very well how he could conjure up some stories – by smashing a few shop windows for instance, or writing graffiti on the town hall. But then he would be as unethical as me. It was better he kept his integrity, than go down the path I was on. That's what I told myself anyway. He'd probably be appalled if I told him the truth – so it was best to keep quiet.

"We'll help you find something," Bert said filling a pregnant pause which had emerged in the conversation. "What have you got for tomorrow's splash?"

"A story about a bloke who found an old wedding ring in his garden ten years after losing one!" Sheffield said excitedly.

It didn't sound too good to me, but it was hardly the time to criticise.

"What's yours about?" Sheffield asked me.

"It's about a drugs den called The Lodge," I said allowing myself to sound a little proud for once. It was a genuine story after all.

"That sounds legit," Sheffield said dryly.

"Of course it's legit," I said. "Why wouldn't it be legit?"

"I meant to tell you," he said ignoring the question and finishing off his pint, "Sofia came looking for you about half an hour after you left, but didn't say what about. I said she could get you on your mobile"

I checked my phone but there were no missed calls.

"I don't like the sound of that," I said. "Any contact from Sofia usually spells misery."

"It's probably nothing, I wouldn't worry about it," he said.

They were all waiting for me to finish my drink before we went home, so I forced down the last half and plonked the empty glass on the table. I couldn't help but wonder if Sheffield had twigged me as we left.

Chapter 21: The Lodge splash

It must have been threat of the sack that had jolted him into action, but Sheffield was in ridiculously early the next morning. Ridiculously early for him at least.

"Morning boss," he said cheerfully as I walked through the door.

"What's this - the new Sheffield?" I said looking at the office clock It was 8:35am!

"I decided I'd better make a go of it if I only have a month left." he said. "Have you got all your pages finished?"

"I'm still searching for something for page two," I said. "Fingers' crossed there is some court copy."

I was pinning my hopes on the paper's freelance court reporters filing some stories before the paper was put to bed. It happened most weeks, so the odds were quite good.

"I've sent you my splash to look at, if you get a chance," Sheffield said while I booted up my computer. "I thought I'd show it to you before Bob?"

"Okay mate, just let me get my pages sorted out first though."

My screen flickered into life but I was dismayed to see there was nothing in my inbox. I was just about to panic when the phone rang.

"It's John Perry from Bishopswood Limestone, returning your call," said the caller.

"Thanks for calling back," I responded, delighted he had bothered to ring. "I am hoping to run a story about the row over the quarry between newcomers and old towns folk? Lady Fothergill told me about it."

"Never mind about that now," he said bluntly. "I want you to report something else. I've been double crossed by Natural Britain. If you do this one fairly, then I'd be happy to do more stories. But your predecessors only took the campaigners' side, and you won't hear from me again if you take that approach."

"I have no axe to grind," I assured him. "What's the story?"

"We submitted an application to extend the plant four months ago and Natural Britain had every chance to comment at that stage, but didn't," he said. "Now after the application has gone in, the local branch has written a strong letter of objection. The upshot is we will have to spend a huge amount of money on an environmental report."

"Why did they do that?" I asked.

"They have taken a political position," he said angrily. "If they fight us there is a good chance we will have to drop the application."

"But what is the motivation?"

"Can I tell you something off the record?

"Yes of course," I said hoping I wouldn't regret it. I didn't like 'off-the-record' chats because if they gave you the information you needed to run the story, you'd be left with a tricky ethical dilemma – print the story and break your word, or keep the story secret and fail as a journalist.

"The real problem is that I'm not a member of a particular gentleman's club," he said.

"What club?" I asked wondering what on earth he could mean.

"You'll have to work that one out for yourself," he said. "But one thing I can assure is it's not the bloody golf club."

Regardless of what his obscure clue meant, I had enough for a page two lead. There was a headshot of him in our photo library, so all I had to do was put in calls to the district council and Natural Britain and wait for their response. There was a couple of hours before deadline, which was plenty, so if they didn't get back to me I was within my rights to say they were 'unavailable to comment at the time of going to press'.

I filed the story with 'more to come':

Quarry director accuses group of double cross

A quarry boss has accused an environmental group of 'double crossing' him after it objected to a planning application for a new lime manufacturing facility.

John Perry, managing director of Bishopswood Limestone, says Natural Britain did a U-turn over the planning application leaving him out of pocket.

Bishopswood Limestone submitted an application to South Somerset District Council to extend the town's lime manufacturing plant.

Mr Perry claims Natural Britain were given the opportunity to object but failed to do so. But a month after the planning application was submitted they wrote 'a strong letter of objection,' forcing him to commission an expensive environmental report.

He said: "They have taken a political position. If they fight us there is a good chance we will have to drop the application…."

It was only 9:30am, so I had more than two hours to finish The Lodge splash.

My notebook gave me a confusing myriad of different angles for the story. So I took a few minutes to jot them down. The first was 'Residents demanding police shut down drug's den…..'

Next was 'Residents poised to take direct action …'

Then I pondered 'Police slammed for failing to shut drugs den…..'

I settled on the first and typed it up:

Police action needed to shut drugs den

Residents are demanding that police close down a South Somerset premises which they claim is being used to sell drugs to youngsters.

At a packed Longley Council meeting on Monday, residents claimed The Lodge, on the Appleton Road, is also being used as a bordello.

Lady Fothergill, 82, said the council's plan to write a letter to police demanding action did not go far enough:

She said: "I'm not sure what good a letter to the police is going to do? They have known about this for months. The [Lodge] is attracting the wrong type of people to the town and it needs to be shut down now. Let's take some direct action and picket the place."

Sam Smith, coach of Longley football club, added: "Several of our younger members have spoken to me about The Lodge. They tell me there is a large scale commercial drug dealing operation taking place there. The youngsters say that the kids are literally queuing up the street to buy Ecstasy some nights. The police seem unwilling to take action…"

I filed the story confident it would win plaudits from the newsdesk and then took a look at Sheffield's splash. Unfortunately I could not make head or tail of it.

Resident finds gold ring 10 years after losing his own.

A man found a wedding ring after losing his 10 years earlier.

He found it in his garden using a metal detector…

"Was it his own ring he found? I asked politely.

"No," he said.

"So what's the story?"

"The story is that it is an amazing coincidence that he also lost his wedding ring," he said enthusiastically.

"They both lost rings in the same garden?" I asked wondering if I'd grasped it.

"I don't know where he lost his ring, but he found one in his garden."

"Where did he lose his then?"

"I haven't asked him."

"Better ask him then. If he says he lost it in the same place - then I think you might have a story about an 'amazing coincidence.' Otherwise I don't think it's a story."

His face dropped at my assessment.

"You're sounding just like Sofia and Katie," he said.

"Oh, sorry," I said trying to backtrack, "If that doesn't work, you could say he's calling for the owner of a wedding ring to come forward after finding it in his back garden. But you need to exaggerate the value of the ring, or its age or something."

"Okay boss I'll phone him," he said picking up the receiver.

Sofia called my name just as he started speaking.

"Simon!" she shouted from her desk.

I walked over to the newsdesk wondering what the hell I'd done wrong this time. My patience was wearing thin.

"Have you been round to The Lodge to give them the right to reply?" she asked.

It was another rooky mistake.

"No, I thought it would be okay without it because it was a public meeting?" I said.

"You must have to give them the chance to respond, or we can't run the story," she said rolling her eyes. "It a rule of the paper. Get down there straight away and ask the occupants if they are dealing drugs. Have you at least got the photo organised?"

The knot in my stomach tightened as the mistakes were totting up.

"I forgot," I admitted. "But I can take one while I'm down there."

"Ring Lady Fothergill and ask if she'll have her photo taken," she said. "And try to remember to take the camera!"

Sheffield was smiling as I sat down, but not at my discomfort. "I'm going with the line about him calling for the owner to come forward," he said. "It turned out the ring is worth thousands. It's got some big diamonds in it. What were you talking to Sofia about?

"I forgot to give to give the right to reply to the people at The Lodge," I said. "Glad you're having better luck though. Send it to Bob."

Luckily, Lady Fothergill picked up her phone when I rang. "Hello Simon, lovely to hear from you again – how can I help?" she said.

She agreed to meet me outside The Lodge half an hour later, which would give me just time enough to speak to the occupants beforehand.

I jogged up the hill to my car, trying to keep my nerves under control at the thought of confronting drug dealers for the first time. I imagined they'd probably be huge, and own a viscous dog.

At least the drive gave me a chance to think of a way of approaching them. As usual, I would need to be sneaky and make out I was on their side.

The Lodge was a dilapidated Victorian house of gothic architecture. It had beautiful red brick bay windows, filled with diamond shaped leaded glass. But the front garden was full of junk. Two cars were rusting in one corner, and the remnants of a huge bonfire was in another.

I walked up a pathway leading to a grand oak front door and knocked loudly.

I heard a door slam inside and footsteps pattered their way towards the door. It opened slowly to reveal a young blonde woman, perhaps in her twenties. Her hair was in a bob and she was wearing bright red lipstick.

"How may I help you?" she said sweetly.

"I've come to give you the opportunity to respond to something the council said at a public meeting yesterday," I said. She looked blankly at me. "They said that drugs were being dealt from this property," I added. "So I wanted to give you a chance to respond for an article I'm writing for The Sentinel."

She seemed stunned for a moment and then said "no comment" before closing the door in my face.

I was desperate to leave just in case that dog appeared out of nowhere - but turned to see Lady Fothergill walking up the path towards me.

"Bravo Simon, how exciting!" she said. "Do you want me to speak to them?"

"No, let's walk to my car and take the photo?" I said shepherding her back down the path.

"What did she say?" she asked as we walked to a suitable spot.

"She said 'no comment,'" I said.

"Oh that's a shame, do you want me to go back and make a scene?" said asked.

"Really no," I said. "I have all I need for the story. I just needed to give them a chance to respond and take a photo."

I snapped a few pictures of Lady Fothergill looking cross with The Lodge in the background, and then offered to drive her back to her car.

"No I'll walk," she said. "But it's been fun. Bravo Simon."

Chapter 22: Ice House

Sofia was content with the 'no comment' response, Natural Britain and the district council came through with lines for page two, and even Sheffield's splash got the green light from the newsdesk without too much quibbling. It showed how quickly fortunes can change in the newsroom, which is one of the things I like about it.

"It was a good splash this week in the end," Sofia conceded as I trudged off with the reporters for le petit weekend. I was lost for words for a few seconds before finally spluttering 'thanks'" as I walked out the door.

We headed to a more upmarket establishment for once – a wine bar a few metres further up the pedestrian zone. The change of atmosphere seemed to bring on a better mood and even Tim was being friendly. Six of us - Bob, Bert, Colin, Tim, Sheffield and me - sat on high chairs around a table chatting about the scrapes we'd been in that week.

"Why is it that no matter how hard I try, I never have enough stories in the bag?" I asked Tim in an attempt to stroke his ego. "I'm always desperately trying to conjure something in time for the next deadline."

"It took me a year before I had half an hour to myself," he said smiling empathetically. "I drove to the beach and lay down for half an hour, resting with my eyes closed. But the news monster always needs feeding."

It seemed like a breakthrough in our relationship but then, as if a switch clicked on in his head at the thought of being overly friendly, he reverted to type. "But no talking about work outside the office," he said and raised the palm of his hand up to my face. A thin mocking smile had replaced the warm one.

"Are you going to play for the football team this year," Bert asked Tim. "We are playing the Gazette next week."

"I don't play, you know that," Tim said emphatically.

"You are the only one that doesn't play," Bob said. "It doesn't matter what standard you are - you could even play in goal if you wanted?"

"It has nothing to do with my playing standard," he said tersely. "I am just as good at kicking a ball around a field as the rest of you. It's just that I choose not to play that's all. I don't have to give a reason."

With Tim back to his usual self, I decided to head off and try to find a story to feed the news monster. I had resolved to spend some of my spare time investigating the community hall story, so I took the opportunity of paying Sean Alderman a surprise visit at the council's offices in Appleton. I wasn't really expecting to find any more than Dunne had, but it was a good place to start, and they say that good journalism is about finding things out first hand rather than relying on the words of others.

I parked in the town centre car park early afternoon and walked briskly to the council offices, arriving at 1:45pm. The building had been a court house during the 18th Century and the roots of the 'hanging tree' were rumoured to be still visible in the back yard. I got the feeling that some people's attitudes hadn't changed much since those days, and many on the council would have liked to seen that old hanging tree replanted.

The front door of the offices was locked, which was a surprise since it was still opening hours. I knocked loudly just in case Alderman was taking a convenience break, but no one came. So I sat down on the steps and waited, and waited. After 30 minutes I grew impatient and walked around the back of the building and peered through a window just to check no one was in. The place looked empty, and I was about to head back to the car when I noticed a door to the kitchen had been left ajar. I pushed it open and stuck my head inside. A light was shining through a panelled window of a door inside which lead to an adjacent room. I circled further round the back of the building till I got to the lighted room, and peered inside through a window.

Alderman was sitting at a desk, sifting through a large bundle of documents. He pulled one out and filed it in a cabinet next to the desk. I watched him repeat the process for a few minutes before heading back to the front door.

I tried knocking again, this time as loud as I could. Again there was no response. I thought about knocking on the back window, but I didn't want to reveal that I'd seen him. So I walked back to my car and sat inside considering my options. Finally, I decided to try ringing the council on my mobile phone. The phone rang and rang, and finally he answered.

"Good afternoon Appleton Council," he said.

"Good afternoon," I said politely and asked if I could visit the office to take a look though the council's files.

"Which files?" he said curtly.

"The ones relating to the sale of the community centre. I want to take a look at the documents for Alma Court, Breakers Gate and The Ice House."

If you can feel a frosty atmosphere down the phone, then this was it. There was a long drawn out pause which I had to stop myself from filling.

"I'm not sure you will find those here," he said coolly. "Councillor Dunne tried but was unsuccessful. You can take a look but I would not hold out any great hope of locating them."

Reluctantly he agreed to meet me at the office 20 minutes later. I waited in my car for a few minutes and then trudged over.

"I'm afraid the paperwork isn't in any particular order," he said as he opened the door. "All the council papers are filed in these cabinets but they are not kept in any particular order." He pointed to two grey metal cabinets in reception, and handed me the keys.

"I close at 3pm but you are free to look until then," he said.

He sat at a desk in the same room and watched as I systematically grabbed bundles of files then scanned through them as quickly as I could. Just as Dunne had described, there was no order to any of the papers and I couldn't find anything of relevance.

At 3pm, I thanked him and walked back to my car and waited. I wanted to give him plenty of time to lock up and leave, so I sat patiently in the car park for an hour before walking back.

As expected, the front door was locked so I was confident he had left. I circled round the building again and this time crept through the open kitchen door, closing it as quietly behind me.

Alderman had locked the cabinet in the room where he had been secretly working but I found the keys easily enough in the desk drawer and opened it. The files meticulously indexed by date and subject so it didn't take long to find the documents:

Community hall

Contract for the Council purchase of Alma Court.

Scanning down the document, I saw the heading *Covenants*.

There was a clauses about "section 106 agreements", which I recognised from stories I'd written as standard clauses which require future developers to provide some money for good causes, such as libraries or children's playgrounds.

I noticed another clause which I hadn't seen before, a '316 agreement' which seemed to relate to the number of houses that a developer could build at the site.

No more than 6 residential properties may be built at the Alma Court site under the restrictions of the 316 agreement with Appleton Council.

Paper clipped underneath were the sale documents to Ripley's company, Compton House.

The section 106 agreement was repeated, but I noticed there was no Section 316 clause.

The Council's contract for purchase of Breakers Gate had a similar 316 agreement this time for 12 properties but again the clause was missing from the sale to Compton House.

I jotted down the details as quickly as I could and hurried back to my car elated at the find.

Councillor Dunne was not expecting my call. He was in the process of striking a four foot putt on the 18th green, which he had carefully lined up for several minutes, when the mobile phone vibrated in his pocked, causing him to yip the ball to the left of the hole.

"Dammit," he said in frustration down the line. "Sorry, I mean, what is it?"

I had some sympathy since he had recently undergone a course of hypnotherapy to cure the yips - a condition which causes a golfer to inadvertently twitch the putter head as it strikes the call.

 "Can you tell me how 316 agreements work?" I asked, not put off by his bluster.

"316? Why, what have you heard about them?" his said as his anger gave way to intrigue.

"Let's just say I've had a tip off about them regarding the community hall, but I don't understand how they work."

"You might be onto something," he said. "Section 316 prevents a developer building more than a certain number of homes on a plot of land, over a certain period of time. Typically a section 316 lasts two years, and it's up to the council to renew it. If they don't the restriction is lifted and the developer can apply to build many more homes and the land is worth a lot more money."

"So what's the purpose of it?" I asked.

"It's to protect the character of the area. To stop over development," he said. "Is that what they've been doing – failing to renew the 316 and selling to Ripley? All he'd need to do is wait for a couple of years for the heat to die down before submitting new housing plans. It could explain all those closed door sessions."

Chapter 23: Encounter

Selina was waiting at my doorstep as I arrived home. Beautiful, bright and humorous, my delight at seeing her was only slightly tempered by bemusement over why on earth she would track me down.

"Don't worry I'm not stalking you," she joked and greeted me with a firm hug.

"How did you know where I lived?" I asked. It seemed a fair question, even if I was too dazzled by her looks to really care.

"I rang your office and got your address of your friend Sheffield," she said. "I swore him to secrecy though, because I wanted to surprise you. I thought we might go out?"

I was flattered of course, but couldn't help but think it was too good to be true. Stunning women like Selina don't track down penniless reporters and take them out, do they?

"Of course I would," I said nonchalantly, trying to sound cool. "But what's the catch?"

"Catch? You do know how to make a girl feel special," she said melodramatically.

"Sorry, I just meant the offer seems too good to be true." I was digging myself a hole and knew it. I felt my face redden with embarrassment.

"I was joking Simon," she said. "I had no idea you were such an easy wind up!"

"Oh, okay, well I'm glad we cleared that up," I said.

She had cropped her long locks into a bob, which made her high cheek bones look even more prominent. I thought about telling her how it complimented her delicate features, but thought better of it.

"I have to be honest with you though Simon," she said. "I am guilty of mixing business with please because I want to chat about the issue I mentioned the other night."

I was part relieved, part disappointed that my instincts had been right - she wasn't after me at all. But at least it showed my antenna was working.

"You mean the stuff about how 'certain goings on' might attract tabloid headlines?" I asked.

"Yes that's right. I've made a decision - I want to give you the whole story. And I want you to publish it in The Sentinel."

I smiled and thanked her, thinking it would need ultra-careful handling given who her father was. I suggested we go to the nearest café for a chat, to get to the bottom of it.

The sight of crowds of people jostling for lattes and bagels seemed to make her nervous, and I assumed she was on edge about being spotted with a journalist.

"I want to nail the whole lot of them," she said quietly after we'd sat down. "All the dodgy councillors and businessmen, and that includes my father, Simon."

It wasn't my place to judge but I wondered if she might back out when it came to the crunch. I wasn't going to get too carried away with the story.

"I know you must think I'm dreadful wanting to do this to my own flesh and blood?" she asked. Her face had moved closer to mine, and I could see anguish in her eyes. "You don't know the history, Simon," she said. "He deserves everything he gets and more for involving me in his disgusting life."

"I'm not here to judge," I said. But I was judging. Judging her father that is. And thinking that perhaps Carrie had been right. Perhaps there was some kind of sick sex ring involving him and Ripley.

"Think of me as a journalist objectively looking at a potential story," I said. "Tell me what you know and I'll see if it's something I can run."

"I might need a little more from you than that Simon," she said. "I need to know you are on my side - that I can trust you?"

"I promise you can," I said. "I won't run the story unless you give the green light, if that helps?"

"It's is a start," she said. "The other night I hinted that the council is corrupt, but it goes much deeper than that. And the truth is my father is at the heart of it. They are all gangsters really – handing out contracts to their friends. Pretending they are doing the community a favour. It's all bullshit."

"It sounds like a story I am already working on," I said half-jokingly.

She fixed me with a hard stare. "You have no idea, Simon," she said. "They organise sex parties for the councillors, business leaders and the police."

My appetite was wetted of course, but the bigger the claim the more a story needs standing up. So I was still sceptical about whether I'd be able to run it, even if it were true.

"Exactly who are 'they'?" I asked.

"One of them leads a council in your patch," she said.

"Tom Ripley?"

"That's right," she said. "That's why I came to you, Simon. It's fate that we met."

I was never a believer in fate, and even less so since I'd been creating my own through do-it-yourself journalism. But there was no harm in going along with it.

"Tell me how you are involved?" I asked.

"My father introduced me to Ripley a few years ago. There is no easy way to say this Simon – I set up the parties for them. My own father asked me to do it."

"But why would you want to do that?"

"The money of course. He's bought me."

She'd been entrapped by her own father. I could see why she wanted revenge.

"So how are we going to nail them?" I asked.

"By setting up a sting at one of the parties," she said. "I'll be arranging one soon, so all you need to do is turn up and report it. I imagine it will be a big scoop?"

"It will as long as we have enough evidence to print the story," I said. "Otherwise my bosses wouldn't run it because we'd get sued. Something as big as this could bankrupt us."

"But surely you being an eye witness would be enough?" she said, a hint of desperation in her voice.

"I'm afraid not, we'll need something much better than that. But don't worry I think I know of a way to make this work."

"Okay, well I suppose I'll leave you to work on that then?" she said. "Just be honest with me Simon, that's all I ask."

"I give you my word," I said.

It was a moment of no turning back for both of us. We'd both made a commitment to pursue it. We got in my car and she directed me to a country home where the parties took place. It was set on a piece of raised ground in the Somerset levels which I imagined must form an island during heavy flooding.

"As you can see, it's far away from prying eyes," she said as we pulled into a driveway big enough to turn a car in. Shingle sprayed from the tyres as we skidded to a halt.

"I am planning to move out of the area once this is all done and dusted to start a new life," she explained. "I have some savings so no matter what happens I'll be okay financially."

I kept quiet, but wondered why she was telling me everything. We were still virtually strangers after all.

The party house was built in the Thirties, had a painted grey render exterior and a grand oak front door. Selina took me in through the side entrance on the east of the building, which opened into a double aspect pine kitchen. A fine Welsh dresser stood proudly in one corner.

There were seven circular bells above the kitchen door. I pushed a buzzer on the side entrance and one of the bells chimed out.

"Each of the five bedrooms has a buzzer," she explained. "A sixth bedroom, about half the size of the others, was built for servants. If the guests stay the night, they can ring for the girls if they wish. It's my job to make sure they get everything they want."

We walked through the kitchen to an adjoining breakfast room which in turn led into the dining room. A mahogany dining table sat proudly in the middle with seating for eight people. Sliding French doors led out to the long thin garden which stretched into the distance like a short golf hole. A door led from the dining room to a drawing room which had two dusty leather sofas facing a grand bay window.

"I close this room when we have parties in the dining room," she explained.

"Do you have the keys for the door?" I asked immediately.

"Yes I do, but what for?"

"I might need to hide somewhere during the party," I said. "This would be perfect, providing they can't get in?"

"The room is usually locked up so they can't see what a mess the rest of the house is in. I could give you the key."

She pulled a key from a bunch she was holding and passed it to me.

"It's the only one I know of, so you should be safe enough."

We sat at the dining room table and looked out on the lawn which was set on three levels, each one higher than the last.

"It must have been a stunning family home," I said.

"I imagine so. We cut the grass twice a year, but it is still beautiful in the summer."

"How often does he hold the parties?" I asked, getting down to business. "How many have there been?"

She totted up the numbers on her fingers.

"I'd say eight or nine over the last year," she said "They took place more often during the summer when they were in recess. Idle hands really do make the devil's work, Simon."

"And how many people attend?"

"It can be anything from four to ten. We are only limited by the size of the table," she joked.

"Tell me exactly what happens?" I said. I could see from her face that she was finding it hard to speak about the details.

"It usually starts with a formal meal, they discuss their little business schemes. Then it's down to pleasure."

"You mean girls? Where do you get them from?"

"The Lodge and one or two other places. There are drugs as well, and it's all done very openly."

"Who attends? I need names really."

"My father for one." she said. "And there is Ripley and some other business people. A police officer sometimes comes along too, although I can't remember his name. They have a common interest – making money."

She suddenly got up to leave, so I followed her out of the building. Leaves crunched underfoot as we trudged over to the back lawn to a doorway on western side of the house.

"You can get into the drawing room through this entrance," she said handing me another key.

"Ripley trusts you to look after the place?" I asked.

"That's one of the things he pays me for. I do everything from fixing leaks to organising parties. So you can see, I'm no angel either Simon.

"He trusts you completely because your father is involved?" I said.

"Yes and he knows I'll ensure they are thoroughly entertained with fine wine, food, women and the best quality drugs."

"What type?" I asked.

"Cocaine," she said. "You'd be surprised just how much they use."

I tried the lock which worked smoothly enough, and then we got into my car to drive back to Yeovil. But before I could start the car, she asked if I wanted to go for a drink. I accepted eagerly.

"Let's go somewhere near my flat," I suggested.

"I don't think we should go out in Yeovil again in case one of my father's spies spots us – it could blow the whole charade," she said. "But we could go to the Arthouse cinema in Taunton if you want?"

"I've never been but it sounds good," I said.

The Arthouse cinema was one of the town's hidden gems. Built within a former college premises, it was full of little nooks and crannies filled with paintings and sculptures from local artists. It was my first date since I'd finished journalism-college and I felt a little out of practice in the art of essential small talk.

"So have you any idea what they are showing?" I asked.

"No, but they have very comfortable sofa seating, I think they call them lovers' seats," she said flashing her gloriously white smile.

"I haven't tried those before," I said nervously.

A waitress came over and we ordered a couple of glasses of white wine.

"You know Ripley will get nasty when you run the story," she said taking a slurp. "It's only fair to warn you."

"Don't worry, I already know about his tactics," I said. "And it makes me even more determined."

"I guessed you would understand, but wanted to be sure," she said.

"You don't get much bigger than councillors setting up a drug fuelled sex orgy," I said. "I mean, the story has everything – drugs, prostitutes, politicians, corruptions and even a beautiful female victim - although I'm assuming you want your role kept out of this?"

"Thank you and yes definitely keep me out of the article," she said smiling "As I said, I want to be able to start a new life afterwards."

"That's fine but the bottom line is that the story will be hugely damaging for all the men involved, so we need cast iron evidence "

"How will we get that?"

"We will need to video it," I said. "They won't be able to contest that in court."

"Can you set that up Simon? I can't go through all this only for you to drop the story," she said.

"Don't worry, I know a place in London where I can get all the kit we need. You keep your side of the bargain and I'll keep mine – I give you my word."

"It's a deal then," she said and put out a hand to shake on it.

"Partners then," I said shaking vigorously. "Let's do the world a favour and put these guys out of business."

Selina gave me the choice of movie, which was tough because none of them were particularly to my taste. Two were in French so I immediately wrote them off as unwatchable, and the third was a love story about a casino worker called 'The Croupier."

"Let's go for the English one," I said plumping for it. "At least we won't have to read subtitles."

"Don't you speak French?" she asked as if expecting me to be fluent.

"Not since school," I explained, although the truth was I'd never been able to converse in it.

We were directed to a 'lovers' seat' in the row nearest to the screen. They were more like sofas that seats, and had spare cushions for extra comfort. We lay down sideways using the cushion as a pillow. My arm went dead after a few minutes but I decided to endure it rather than spend the entire movie wriggling about.

Selina seemed comfortable enough though, so I contented myself with occasionally alleviating my pins and needles by lifting my arm a few inches in the air, allowing the blood to flow.

At least the movie was better than I was expecting. It was about a dreamer who spent his life working in a sweat shop casino before predictably meeting the perfect girl. He was an aspiring writer, so I could imagine a parallel to my own life. I couldn't help but wonder if I had met my own perfect girl too.

"What did you think?" she said after the curtains went down.

"I thought it was pretty good. An optimistic tale," I said.

"Optimistic?" she said. "Why not realistic?"

"You think it was realistic then?" I said realising too late I was in a debate.

"You are the movie critic," she said. "I was just wondering why a happy ending has to be optimistic. I mean, life can be like that can't it?"

"Well I'm not much of a critic really," I said. "The newsdesk like us to either slam a movie or say it was amazing. Whereas I said the one I saw had a good start but an uninspired twist at the end. They didn't like the nuance."

"Well I'd prefer nuance if I were reading the paper."

It was a little thing to say, but it lifted me to know that someone - a real person - was on my wavelength.

We walked back to the car, and she looped her arm around my elbow as we went.

"I wanted to be an actress once, but my father said it was a waste of time," she said sadly.

"It's not too late," I said. "Perhaps you could take it up once this is all over?" All I could think about was kissing her, but I had no idea how to try.

As we approached the car, I thought about making a move, but courage failed me. I kidded myself that women always take the initiative, and there had been no signals.

"Perhaps you are right," she said. "Perhaps I'll sign up for a course, or join a theatre." Her face lit up with a smile and she squeezed my hand.

We stopped at the passenger side door. She smiled and gently pulled me a few millimetres towards her, and we kissed.

It's a strange thing, but public displays of affection are only socially unacceptable when you are watching them. All the rules go out of the window when you are actually one of the participants. Dozens of people walked past while we embraced. No words were said between us, no promises made.

The cinema car park was empty by the time we got into the car and I drove us back to Yeovil. She lived on the first floor of a converted Victorian terrace house and invited me in for a glass of wine after we pulled up outside. I eagerly accepted.

"Be quiet and don't forget to lock the gate," she said intently.

I closed it carefully behind me as she watched on. Then we walked up a flight of steps which led to a small hallway at the top.

To the left was the kitchen, straight ahead was a spare room and to the right was the living room, which had a brown cotton sofa and matching chair. A small television sat on a chest of drawers in one corner.

"The lady downstairs is mad, she'd rant at you if you left the gate open," she explained as we sat down.

"You mean she actually watches people go in and out?"

"All the time, I call her the troll; Kate Bush is terrified of her!" she said.

"Sorry, but what has Kate Bush got to do with it?" I asked.

"Kate Bush is my cat," she said "I didn't name her, the cats' home came up with it."

"Oh brilliant, I love cats. But where is she?"

"She's is probably under the bed upstairs - she's terrified of new people. Would you like to go upstairs and look for her?"

"Of course I would," I said, perhaps a little too quickly.

"Then let's go and take a look," she said squeezing my hand.

Chapter 24: Press Day

Kate Bush woke me with a loud purr in my ear, then licked my hand to show she wanted to be petted. I stroked her a couple of times while I came to my senses and reached for my mobile phone – it was 8:30am. I was late.

I jumped out of the bed, waking Selina.

"What's up?" she asked, stretching out her arms and yawning contentedly.

"I have to go – I am going to be late unless I get my skates on!"

It was less than half an hour to work, so I could make it if I left immediately. But it would mean avoiding a long goodbye.

"The newsdesk has a zero tolerance policy to lateness," I tried to explain as I pulled on my shirt and trousers, then sat on the bed pulling on my socks.

"You get two chances, and then you are sacked," I said before quickly kissing her farewell.

"You better get going then," she said flatly.

"Pray that my car starts," I said, but she wasn't listening.

I was panicking because I'd pictured the time Sheffield was late at work. Katie seemed to delight at reading him the riot act, and I didn't want to give her the opportunity of doing the same to me. Poor old Sheffield, the reporters had taken bets on the next time he'd be late. He'd shrugged it off, but I could see he wasn't happy about it. The days passed, and time and again he made it in the nick of time, sweating heavily as he burst through the door. Katie and Sofia would look up at the clock, and then back at their computers. On one occasion, he clattered the door open with just five seconds to spare, prompting money to change hands down the pub.

"Wallet, phone and keys," I said checking the essentials before slamming the front door.

It had rained overnight and my car refused to start. With each turn of the key, I became more desperate, bashing the steering wheel. I could smell petrol and realised I'd flooded the engine, so I waited a couple of agonising minutes before trying again.

With a twist of the key, it sparked into life and I chugged off into the line of traffic.

The traffic lights were against me all the way to the office, and I was cursing my luck as I parked at The Sentinel car park at 8:58am. I sprinted up the stairs, only slowing to compose myself over the final few strides, and walked in as calmly as I could.

Sheffield was watching the clock as I arrived. "Fifty seconds to spare," he said enjoying the spectacle.

"Were they watching the clock?" I asked avoiding eye contact with the newsdesk.

"Of course. You would have had a bollocking for sure."

I sat down at my desk and booted up my computer, then gazed over towards Katie and Sofia who were working away as if nothing had happened.

"What time did you get here?" I asked wiping sweat from my cheek.

"I've been here since 8:30am," he said.

With the emergency over, I was about to settle down to check my mail when Peter made a rare appearance in the office and made a beeline for me. He tapped me on the shoulder, and dangled a copy of the paper in front of my nose.

"William Newman is in my office with a complaint about your page five," he said. "Come to my office in ten minutes to discuss it with him. Make sure your short hand notes are accurate."

I assumed that was code for doctoring your notes, although he'd never say so. Short hand notes are admissible in court as an accurate depiction of a conversation. So no one would be able to 'prove' you were reporting an inaccurate account.

He dropped the paper onto my desk. "See you in my office in ten," he said walking over to see Sofia and Katie.

School with 16 children and 11 staff complains of high work load

A School which has eleven teachers for 16 pupils made a shock claim that staff are leaving due to the stress of work.

William Newman, head teacher of Newcross School, in Bishopswood, whose staff teach class sizes of "three or four children" blames the high turnover on low staff morale caused by mounting Government paperwork.

He said: "The testing regime is onerous, but it's the inspections that cause the most stress. We recently went through one and there is a tremendous amount of work that goes in.

"The push at the moment is about child protection, and if you haven't got all the appropriate plans in place then you will be marked inadequate, regardless of the academic qualities of the school."

The Government says inspections have helped to drive up standards in recent years. The number of children in failing schools has dropped by hundreds of thousands.

A spokesman said: "Child protection is rightly a high priority but it is not being put ahead of educational achievement..."

I read in horror the changes made by the newsdesk.

"That's not the story I put through to the Sofia," I protested to Sheffield.

"You mean they changed it without telling you?"

"Yes that's exactly what they've done," I said. "The angle is totally different. He must be furious."

I passed the paper over the partition so he could take a look. "That must have been what Sofia came to see you about the other day," he said sheepishly. "You remember; I told you about it the other day when you were on patch?

It was exactly the newsdesk's style, hardening up the intro and not caring a jot about the consequences.

"No wonder she didn't ring me," I said.

"What are you going to say?" Sheffield asked.

"I have no idea, what would you say?" I said. "I don't think there is anything I can say?"

"They've stitched you up this time," he said unable to stifle a grin. "You can't tell the truth or they'll make your life hell!"

Peter had asked Katie and Sofia to attend the meeting with me. They walked breezily past me, out of the newsroom and to his office. I was still desperately trying to think of a way out.

"You'd better go," Sheffield said. I had the kernel of an idea but had not time to think it through.

Mr Newman was sitting at the far side of the editor's desk, with Peter and Katie either side of him. Sofia was sitting facing them, and I sat in the spare seat next to her.

"Morning," I said nervously to Mr Newman. He looked furious but said nothing.

"Thank you for taking time out of your busy schedule to join us," Peter said politely to me. "Mr Newman has come to see us about the story about his school, which he feels was not properly reported."

A copy of the paper lay open on the desk at the offending page. Peter pushed it towards me as if showing it to me for the first time.

"Yes, I remember it," I said innocently.

I could see that Mr Newman was incandescent but Peter spoke before he could explode.

"He says you agreed to run the line about staff turnover, so he feels very let down by the focus of the story on staff ratios," Peter said as a matter of fact.

I could feel Mr Newman's eyes boring into my head. "You gave me your word!" he said. "You promised that you would not run another knocking piece. Perhaps I should have recorded you because I have no doubt you are going to deny it. But it's the truth! I am sorely tempted to write a letter to the Press Complaints Commission."

"I don't think that will be necessary," Peter said. "Simon, perhaps you explain what happened?"

I looked at Katie, and then to Sofia, hoping I would spot a hint of guilt on their faces but there was none.

"I'm afraid it's one of those awful miscommunications," I said to Peter. "I had absolutely no intention of breaking my word, and am as devastated by the article as you are."

This maddened Mr Newman even more. "What do you mean you are devastated!" he yelled. "You wrote the damn thing."

"Well there's the crux of it," I said looking at Katie and Sofia, hoping they might be just a little concerned I was about to blame them. They looked totally relaxed. "I was in such a rush to meet someone about another story that I just put through the quotes without a proper introductory paragraph," I said. "The newsdesk took a different angle to the one I expected."

Mr Newman threw his arms in the air. "What sort of excuse is that?" he said. "Who is responsible then – no one?"

Sofia chose her moment to stick the knife in. "Oh no, I think Simon is taking full responsibility for the misunderstanding," she said. "He should have told us about the agreement you made. Isn't that correct Simon?"

"Absolutely," I said, knowing it was my only way out. "I will make sure I don't make the same mistake again, I promise you that!"

"Well Mr Newman," Peter said. "It appears the whole thing was a misunderstanding rather than anything more underhand. Perhaps if we ever do another story about your school, we could show you the article before we publish, to put your mind at rest?"

Mr Newman didn't say a word. It was a stich up, and I think he knew it.

"Thank you, Simon, I don't think we need take any more of your time," Peter said. I got up and left as quickly as I could, leaving them to pick over the bones and no doubt explain I was only a cub reporter, who was really a bit still a bit green. They would keep an eye on me.

Fortunately Sheffield hadn't told the others about the meeting and I was glad I didn't have to explain it to everyone. He, though, was eager to hear the details.

"We agreed it was a misunderstanding, so I grovelled and left," I explained.

"I knew you would talk your way out of it," he said. "You must have the gift of the gab."

All the reporters chatted until Katie stuck her head in the door a few minutes later and told us to fetch the papers from the basement. Sofia grabbed me as I walked along. "I tried to get hold of you about that story but you weren't around," she said. "You must be available until we put the stories through to the subs in case we have any questions."

I could have pointed out that she could have given me a call, but thought better of it. There was no point in arguing. What she said was Pravda.

"Were all the quotes accurate?" she asked.

"Yes but that wasn't the point."

"It was one hundred percent was the point," she said. "Breaking promises is one thing, but getting a quote wrong is something else. Just ask the Press Complaints Commission."

She walked back to her seat and I followed Sheffield downstairs to pick up my excess papers. To my great pleasure, my edition had just three copies left.

"Bloody Hell Turner," Sheffield said. "I've never seen anyone with that few."

One or two of the other reporters looked over, and quickly carried on with their own bundles.

Sheffield divvied up his bundle and plonked half in my arms. We walked upstairs and dumped on the bench in the newsroom.

"You must be doing something right," he said. "What's your secret?"

"Just honest hard graft this week," I said looking him square in the eye.

Chapter 25: Are you experienced?

The last remnants of stress dissipated from my pores as I settled comfortably in my chair and contemplated that I had an entire day before my next deadline. It was the quiet time, a chance to take stock before the inevitable flurry of activity. And yet, I was soon berating myself for not having enough stories. I had one solid lead about the council's shenanigans over the community hall. But even that needed a lot of work because of its libellous implications. So I needed to think of it as a slow burner, something to work on but not rely on - and certainly not something for tomorrow's back pages. There was Selina's sting operation too, but I had no idea when that might come off.

What I needed was a few simple story ideas - nothing spectacular, just ones that could be reeled off in a few hours. I scratched my chin and twiddled a pen between my fingers for a few minutes, staring forlornly at an empty inbox hoping something might drop in. Nothing did of course; I needed some inspiration.

Still, I consoled myself that I had a few hours before panic would set in. I was calm and relaxed, and thinking clearly for once. I leafed through last week's paper, looking at the 'county pages' for inspiration. My eyes were drawn to an advert on the bottom of page nine.

Homes needed for rescue animals.

Animal lovers are needed to home cats, dogs and other pets from Heaven's Door Animal Sanctuary in Longley. To make an enquiry telephone Longley 25262

It sounded perfect.

I rang and the owner, Susie, who was immediately friendly and welcoming, and agreed to meet at 2pm that afternoon. I planned to write a feature article about the sanctuary, something endearing about rescue dogs and cats. Everyone loves animals after all.

I booked a camera from the picturedesk and turned my thoughts to finding another lead.

Building on my success I leafed through the rest of the paper's adverts for inspiration. "Bingo," there was an advert about a restaurant that smoked its own eels. It was a bit commercial, so learning from past mistakes I checked the idea with Sofia.

"Would this be okay for a page nine feature?" I asked, dangling the advert in front of her eyes. She hadn't noticed me walking over and I saw she was working on the crossword again. This time I didn't pretend I hadn't caught her and instead stared at the puzzle on the paper. She grabbed the advert from my hand and read it.

"It should be okay if you make it about 'east end food heading west,'" she said. "Tie in all the stuff about how the restaurant smoke the fish themselves and it should make an interesting feature."

I was relieved to have story ideas for the back two pages and rushed to my desk to give the restaurant owner, Joe Green, a call.

Like any savvy businessman, he jumped at the opportunity once I'd explained that it was essentially free advertising.

"The story will fill most of the page, so it is worth about ten times what you forked out on that advert," I explained. "What did that set you back, fifty quid?"

"More like a hundred," he said. "Will I get to see the story before it is published?"

"Oh no, that is the one difference between Editorial and Advertising departments. If I find a fly in your mash, I will have to report it."

He laughed nervously because we both knew there was more than a little truth in my jest.

"Don't you worry about that," he said. "I'll get the chef to pick them all out before you arrive."

The day was panning out well, and both the stories looked easy on paper. Len had overheard me arrange the restaurant interview for 4pm, and waved his hand in the air to catch my attention after I had put the phone down.

"You can use the same camera for that story," he said saving himself a job. "Get someone to take a picture of you and the owner, but make sure it's like this…" He lifted his hands to face level and pretended he was holding a knife and fork over a plate, then smiled a cheesy grin.

"Get the owner holding the plate and you hold the knife and folk," he explained. "And get the restaurant sign in the background. You should be able to do it without too much difficulty. Got it?"

"Yes, got it," I said still trying to unpick what he had said.

It was pleasing to have found a new source of stories right there in the paper's adverts, but I wondered why no one else had ever mentioned it. Thinking I might be onto something new, I whispered the idea to Sheffield who rifled through the paper looking for something he could use.

"You were dead lucky," he eventually replied. "I have nothing but adverts for plumbers, electricians and furniture shops for my patch."

It was just before noon, which gave me time to check the district council's website for planning applications. It was tedious, but the newsdesk liked lots of two sentence planning nibs because so many people were affected by home extensions, new shop lighting or signs. But I felt like giving the guy who published the stuff a call because nine times out of ten there wasn't quite enough detail for the nib. Each one needed to explain 'who, what, when and where.' So I spent an hour sifting through and only found a few which ticked all the necessary boxes:

Plan to Extend Home

Dr and Mrs Parsons of Westmead, Green Lane, Appleton will be building a two-story extension to their home along with a garage after planning permission was granted by South Somerset District Council on Thursday Oct 3.

New Work Studio Planned

Mr and Mrs Jones, of The Mousehole, Longley, applied to South Somerset District Council this week to build a single story work studio adjoining their home.

While I was typing them out, a court story dropped in my inbox. I clapped my hands together in delight. Things were going well.

"What's happened?" Sheffield asked looking worried.

"Some court copy just landed."

"Katie says I can only use it for one lead a week," he bemoaned. His patch generated a lot more court copy than mine, so he had to be restricted.

"I've never had more than one," I said.

But on closer reading, my hopes for Monday's page seven lead were dashed because the case was at the pre-hearing stage, which meant I could only report the basics or potentially be held in contempt of court.

"I spoke too soon – it's only a nib," I told him, my heart sinking.

"Thank god for that," Sheffield said grinning. "I thought you were turning into Colin. I'm still searching for page 11."

I typed up the court story nib, saving it with the others to be filed with lead stories the next day:

Man on rape and child-sex charges

A Bishopswood man appeared before magistrates this week facing allegations of rape and sexual offences against children.

The 21-year-old electrician was charged with five sexual offences against children aged under 16 between February and May…

Sheffield was starting to fret over finding a story for his back pages, so I left the office without saying goodbye. I stopped at a petrol station on the way and bought a cheese sandwich which I ate while driving, crumbs of bread scattering into the foot well as I motored along. I was feeling pretty smug and convinced myself that my good start to the week was down to growing experience. There was light at the end of the tunnel after all.

Heaven's Door animal sanctuary was situated on a large plot of agricultural land, which had been turned into a home for a variety of abandoned animals. As I arrived, I could see donkeys and ponies meandering in several paddocks as well large cages full of cats and dogs.

Suzie ushered me into her office, which was a converted portakabin, where I sat down on a comfy leather sofa. She sat across from me on the other side of a rectangular glass table. A beautiful cross section of an oak tree formed the table's stem, its rings shining beautifully through the glass.

The sanctuary had been initially set up to rehome cats and dogs that were abandoned after Christmas, she explained. But numbers had grown every year and it now housed hundreds of animals ranging from abandoned moggies to peacocks and lizards.

"A lot of the problem is that people find it hard handling the stress of organising children and pets after Christmas. So they come to us quite literally in tears, asking to take them off their hands – the pets that is," she laughed. "But seriously, the numbers coming through has definitely increased, and we are full to bursting point. But it's not just cats and dogs; we had a turkey handed in after it was found wandering around the cemetery. She was found by one of the crew from EastEnders, who were filming an episode down here. I imagine it's the sort of thing you will want to write about, so I'll take you to see her later."

It was exactly what I needed. And I was starting to enjoy the job for the first time. Not just as I looked back on events while chewing the fat down the pub with Sheffield, but actually in real time as things happened.

We went outside where she introduced me to Lucy, one of the animal carers. She had the most beautiful big blue eyes, so I snapped a couple of photos of her holding abandoned cats. A bit of glamour never harmed the paper, Len always said. Then we moved to the Turkey enclosure and Susie headed back to the office.

"We call her Kat Slater after the character in EastEnders," Lucy said kneeling down next to the huge creature, which stood head high as she crouched.

I took a few snaps of the two together, which was tricky because the bird had a habit of darting its gaze away from the camera just as I pushed the button. So I had to keep circling round Kat until I finally had a shot of the two locking into the lens. Job done, I thought, and said my goodbyes to Lucy and Susie.

I had half an hour before the smoked eel interview, so I nipped into Appleton for five minutes to check the notice boards for nibs and jotted down a nib in the news agents.

Music for your little ones

A children's group is offering parents the chance to give their toddlers a musical morning.

Music with mummy is a lively approach to music for children under three....

It was 3:45pm so I drove to the restaurant which was a couple of miles away. I wasn't rushing between jobs, which was a good sign. And I managed to scoff down the rest of my sandwich as I drove through the windy country roads. One hand on the wheel, and occasionally steering with a knee, the police wouldn't be amused if they saw me. But they were in rare supply in deepest Somerset and there was no CCTV to catch me either.

Green Forest restaurant was set in a former boat builder's yard on the outskirts of Appleton. Judging by its location, I reckoned it needed good food to attract people from the town centre. There was little passing trade down the country lanes, so word of mouth must have been critical to success. I parked up and walked into the restaurant, dusting down the crumbs from my suit trousers before I got there because I didn't want to make a poor impression.

Joe Green was one of the tallest, thinnest men you'd ever be likely to meet. His six feet six inches height was only exaggerated by his lankiness, and he towered over me like a giant as he reached out a slender hand to shake mine. His red hair was pushed forward in a Caesar style haircut. Long red sideburns were carefully maintained.

"Good afternoon Mr Turner," he boomed in a confident base voice. "I am so pleased that you could come."

We sat in the restaurant, which was being set out for the evening. There were about twenty tables, and perhaps sixty places set. Not bad for a Thursday night in the sticks, I contemplated.

Joe clicked his fingers to grab the attention of a member of staff, who trotted over and dutifully asked how he could help

"Could we have a plate of eel and organic vegetables?" I asked. Joe nodded and the waiter disappeared with my order.

Mr Green explained that he'd set up the smoker after travelling to Holland in his youth where he had worked as a waiter and learned about continental dishes. The waiter appeared a few minutes later and placed a plate of smoked eel and new potatoes under my nose.

Mr Green smiled as he waited for me to try it.

I took a large mouthful – it tasted light and nutty; not at all what I was expecting. I took another bite and was tempted to eat the whole plateful.

"Delicious," I said "Quite a subtle flavour."

"It's a delicacy in Holland unlike Britain," Mr Green explained. "They smoke it a different way, using hot smoke which is much quicker. It gives it a mild, nutty flavour which is quite distinct from the eel and mash you get in the East End."

He explained about the life cycle of the eel, which seemed very similar to the salmon; it would start its long journey along the river to the sea where it would live for several years before returning to the river it came from to give birth. I jotted it all down and took another couple of mouthfuls.

"I'll need to take a picture by the sign at the front," I said, remembering just in time to leave something on the plate.

"Don't they feed you at The Sentinel?" he joked, seeing my hunger.

"Nothing as good as this," I said. "I can see why people would come and visit."

I asked if the waiter could take the photo just as Len had requested. Mr Green had to bend at the knees to get in the picture, and gave a crocodile smile as we posed with the food, his ginger hair shining in the winter sun.

"Perfect," I said looking at the digital photo on the back of the camera.

Then just as I was about to leave, he popped a letter into my hand. "This is for you," he said.

195

I thanked him, assuming it was a voucher to eat at the restaurant, and put it in the glove compartment where I promptly forgot about it and left.

Chapter 26: Night terrors

The arsonist must have been waiting for me to return home, because my flatmate raised the alarm just a few minutes after I'd parked up.

"Someone has torched your car," Jenny screamed and banged on my bedroom door.

I opened it to see her startled face staring at me from the dark corridor.

"You mean my brown Vauxhall?" I asked dozily, the facts yet to fully register. The idea seemed preposterous because why would anyone target such an old banger, which I had deliberately chosen because of its worthlessness.

"Yes," she shouted. "I watched a man throw something through the window and the whole car exploded. Come take a look if you don't believe me." She was terrified and close to tears.

"Show me," I said still not believing.

She grabbed my hand and led me to her bedroom window, which overlooked the street below. Only then, when I could see my car blazing - huge flames leaping from the windows - did I fully comprehend. As we watched, the petrol tank exploded, lifting the car a few feet in the air and throwing flames in all directions.

"But who on earth would do that?" I said to myself. The explanation quickly dawned on me. "Ripley," I said under my breath.

"Who's Ripley?" Jenny cried. "You know the guy who did this?"

"No. I mean forget it," I said. "I was just thinking out loud."

"Look there's someone there!" she shrieked pointing to someone getting onto a motorbike further up the road.

Within seconds, I'd sprinted along through corridor, down the stairway and crashed through the front door. With Jenny trailing behind, I rushed around the block to head him off. But I was too late, the bike had left. I could hear him changing up the gears in the distance as he made his getaway.

I walked Jenny back to the car, which was still spouting flames. "I didn't get a close look," she said. "But I saw him run up the road after he'd set fire to your car."

"What was his build?" I asked.

"He was short and stocky, that's all I can say."

That was Ripley's frame, but surely he wouldn't be so stupid as to do it himself. It must have been one of his men, I thought.

"Sorry Jenny. It was probably someone getting revenge for a story," I said. "I'm just sorry you had to be involved."

"It's not fair Simon," she said. "I shouldn't have to go through this while I'm pregnant."

I'd have to look for a new place and promised her I would start straight away. The police arrived a few minutes later, sirens blaring. Then a fire wagon turned up, screeching to a halt in front of us. A crew started to hose down the car, leaving a pile of burned out rubble. They set up a cordon and moved us further back.

A police officer snapped off some questions at me after learning I was the car's owner.

"Can I see the contents of your pockets?" the constable demanded.

I pulled out some keys, a wallet and a few receipts. He asked me to hold up my hands and inspected them with a torch.

"My flatmate was a witness," I said. "She saw someone throw something - a petrol bomb - through the window from her flat." I pointed to the room above.

"What makes you think it was a petrol bomb?" the constable asked.

"I assumed it was a petrol bomb because the car exploded in flames," I said.

He gave me a dirty look, then walked around the crime scene. I could see him look above a neighbouring hardware shop.

"What have you spotted?" I asked.

"CCTV," he said pointing at an installation inside the shop. "We should have the whole thing on there."

"That's brilliant news," I said. "When will you know?"

"I'll check it with the owner first thing in the morning."

We gave our details and he asked us to provide statements at the police station the next morning. We were left alone after that so Jenny went back to the flat. I rang Sheffield and he rushed over to check out the scene.

"Who do you think did it?" he asked, marvelling at the wreckage.

"I'd bet my mortgage it was one of Ripley's men," I said.

"In revenge for one of your stories?" he said.

"More of a warning to keep my nose out I'd guess," I said. "He's rumoured to have a financial interest in The Lodge."

"Your front page must have cost him a fortune," he said. "Why else would he take such a risk? This could be another great a story, if you want to run it?"

"They have CCTV from that shop," I said pointing toward the glass window. "So if they get a still of the suspect, I can lead on that."

With the fire still smouldering, I said goodnight and headed back to my room. I locked the door and fell into a feverish sleep.

It was a recurring nightmare I'd not experienced since my final exams at university, and before that when I first started secondary school. But unlike the past, where I'd been fleeing in terror from two thugs in a Victorian style coach and horses, this time they were hunting me in a cream Seventies style sedan.

One man was short and stocky and the other was tall and thin. Both were pale faced and expressionless. As I ran from them, I watched in horror as their car drove past me, then pulled to a stop. Cloaked in black and wearing top hats, they jumped out of the sedan and rushed at me holding wooden coshes. I picked up a fist sized rock from the floor, and tried to throw it at the short fat man, but my arm slowed to a snail's pace and the rock dropped pathetically to the ground. I turned to see the tall one was on me - his cosh raised ready to crash down. I clenched my fist and threw a punch but again my arm slowed to a crawl and puffed gently against his face. Then they were on top of me reigning down blows.

Soaked in sweat, I woke with a jolt. It was 7am.

Pulling on my dressing gown, I walked down the corridor to the bathroom, picking a towel from the back of my bathroom door on the way. The shower burst on, and I pulled the curtain across me. My feet were freezing on the concrete floor, and my body shook violently as cold water sprayed onto the top of my head and ran down my body. A couple of minutes was all I could take. I dried myself and walked back to my room feeling human again.

At least I was running early. I dressed, stuffed down some toast and walked briskly to the police station.

The sergeant was expecting me, and took me straight through to the interview room where I was met by a thin, pitted faced investigating officer.

He said "hello" curtly and I sat down opposite him.

"I'll be recording your statement on tape," he said referring to clunky device on the table between us.

"Fine," I said joylessly, still bleary eyed from my sleep.

He clicked the record button and it whirled into life like an Eighties style cassette deck. He moved his face towards a mic which was attached to the recorder via a lead. But just as he was about to speak, the cassette screeched and then jammed.

"Dammit!" he said banging his fist on the table. "Sergeant, the tape has stuck again!"

The sergeant, who had been hovering nervously in the background, ejected the tape, pulled out a pencil from his top pocked and inserted it into the spirals in the centre of the cassette. He twirled the pencil gently in both directions to release the jam and then put the cassette back into the recording device.

"That takes me back," I said to the sergeant. "It's just like my old cassette recorder at school."

"It is exactly like that," he said.

"When you are quite ready," the pitted faced officer said and the sergeant retreated into the background. The pitted faced policeman clicked the record button and the machine whirled into life.

"Inspector Lane of the Yeovil Police, interview with Simon Turner," he said, and then read out the case number.

"Please confirm your name." he said to me.

I leaned over so my mouth was about six inches away from the mic. "Simon Turner," I said.

"Occupation?" Inspector Lane asked.

"I'm a reporter at The Sentinel," I said.

Like a duet as we leaned forward in turn speaking into the mic as the interview progressed.

I recognised the line of questioning: "who…?", "what….?" "Why….? When…?" and "where….?" and answered each question honestly until he came to the final one.

"Do you know why someone might want to set fire to your car?"

"I'm a reporter so I must upset a lot of people. There could be dozens of folk with a motive," I said.

"Could you provide names?"

"I wouldn't like to point the finger, but you have CCTV pictures so you can see for yourself."

"Interview paused 8:15am," he said hitting the stop button. "We don't have any CCTV pictures, so if you don't mind just answering the questions."

"But the policeman said there was a CCTV camera above the shop?" I protested. "He said he would be talking to the owner this morning."

"Yes we had hoped that there would be some images but there was a technical problem," the inspector said dismissively. "Unfortunately none of the footage is usable."

I was hit by a wave of disappointment, then anger. My antennae was up - it felt like I was being conned.

"Ask me the previous question again," I said raging.

"Who might have a motive for doing this?" he repeated after restarting the recorder.

"Chairman of Appleton Council Tom Ripley," I said.

He leaned forward and stared at me for a few seconds. "What would be the motive?" he asked.

And there was my problem. Unless I told him everything Selina had confided in me, I had very little to go on. Just that we didn't get on. Hardly motive for a Molotov cocktail.

"Sorry you are right," I said backtracking. "I take that back. I have no names."

From that moment on, I just wanted to leave. It felt like a charade and I wanted to get it over as quickly as possible. The inspector was only too happy to oblige.

"Interview completed at 7:32am," he said after a few more pointless questions, and then stopped the machine.

"We will be in touch if we learn anything," he said.

I marched out of the police station still raging at the injustice. I had a few minutes to kill before work, so I decided to get a coffee at the café to settle myself down.

As I walked, I imagined Ripley's power spreading like fog across the countryside, suffocating swathes of people from Yeovil to Longley. Councillor Malcolm was an island of high ground and so was Lady Fothergill. But most of my patch was enveloped in his choking white mist.

Every step made me more determined to exact revenge, and by the time I'd reached the café, I had a clear picture of what I was going to do. I pulled out my note pad and gleefully wrote a letter:

Dear Sentinel,

I am writing to inform you that a great injustice is being done to the people of Appleton over the sale of land at Alma Court and Breakers Gate.

The council chairman has perpetrated a fraud on the people of the town by failing to add clauses called 316 agreements as part of the sale to Compton House Ltd.

These agreements, which limit the number of houses that can be built on a plot to protect our heritage, were included when the land was bought by Appleton council. The failure to include them in the sale to Compton House, part owned by

Chairman Ripley, means the land was under-priced. The result is that the chairman is set to make a fat profit from the development of the land.

Chapter 27: Fake letters

My mind was still whirling with thoughts of revenge as I walked into the office. There was the usual din of reporters at work, and Sheffield gave me a sheepish look from his side of the desk as I sat down.

"What is it?" I asked.

"I may have let slip about your car," he admitted.

"Oh, you may have spoken too soon about that," I said. "The police say there aren't any CCTV pictures, so I won't be running a story."

"I'm not sure if the newsdesk will agree."

He nodded in their direction, and I looked over to see Sofia making a beeline for me. "Sheffield told us everything, you poor darling," she mocked. "Peter has decided to run it on local radio. He thinks it will be good PR for the paper, showing us as the victims for once. Showing what lovely and humans we are." She shrieked with laughter at the thought. "Anyway, it will be good for people to see there are two sides of the coin. We might even get a few more locals ringing in with stories. The thing to do is link the car bomb to your splash... So people buy your edition next week, see?"

"But we've got no evidence of that," I said hesitatingly.

"Oh don't worry about that," she said. "This is radio, not print, so you can get away with a lot more. Just say it's something you are investigating. Keep it vague - we don't want you in court for slander, do we?" She snorted laughter again.

"No," I said.

"Peter says he will pop his head round the door and grab you in a few minutes, so you better work out what you are going to say before then."

She walked back to her desk still grinning at the turn of events, or my impending humiliation on radio. Or possibly both.

"What the hell was so funny?" I whispered to Sheffield once she was out of earshot.

"Sofia and Katie were making a joke about your car," he explained. "They said you should inform the insurers, but they might say that it's worth more now that it's melted down. They were cracking up about that."

"Oh hilarious," I said. "I do wish you'd kept quiet. Now I've got to go on radio and make an idiot out of myself."

"Sorry," he said.

I was still trying to work out what to say, while remaining on the right side of the libel laws, when Peter strode confidently into the newsroom and gripped me by the shoulder.

"Has Sofia briefed you on what to say? Oh good," he said without waiting for my reply. "Well done for getting this story. I have arranged an interview with South Somerset commercial radio. Have you done radio before?"

"No," I said.

"No matter - you just need to explain exactly what happened last night and why you think it is linked to your splash about The Lodge."

"I'll do my best," I said.

207

"Don't worry it's only local radio. But you did learn about libel and 'fair comment' on your course didn't you?"

"Yes," I said lying. We might have had one or two lectures about it, but my course was too short to get any real insight.

We sat down at a table in his office, which had a digital radio operating system set up and ready to use.

"It's an ISDN line," Peter said proudly. "It gives the highest quality sound, which is what national radio demand. Local radio aren't too worried though. I haven't had much cause to use it recently, so I may be a bit rusty operating it. Just stick with me if I'm a little slow."

He grabbed a set of earphones and stuck them on my head, a microphone dangled awkwardly in front of my mouth.

"I'll start the machine so hopefully all you have to do is speak," he said placing another set of earphones over his head and positioning his fingers next to a red switch on the ISDN box.

It took about five minutes before we were called, which was enough time to jot down a few key lines which I could link to.

"Hello is that Simon Turner from The Sentinel?" came the reassuring tones of a woman's voice down the line. Peter flicked a switch and gesticulated at me to talk.

"Yes it is," I said. My heart started to pound.

"Okay, the presenter, Kim, is speaking to another guest at the moment, so you will hear them speaking for a couple of minutes then he will ask you a few questions about your car. Okay?"

"Yes, should be fine," I said.

Voices from the radio show came through my earphones. "....So Mr Storani, could you tell me a bit about the air pollution warning for Somerset today?" Kim asked.

"Somerset is experiencing high air pollution levels today and probably will again tomorrow," the scientist said in an Italian accent. "So we are advising vulnerable individuals about the actions they can take to reduce the risks."

"Who are the vulnerable groups, and what is your advice?" Kim said.

Spotting a page seven story, I pulled out my notepad and started frantically jotting down the quotes.

"People with cardiovascular or respiratory illnesses are particularly susceptible to air pollution," Mr Storani continued. "So when levels of pollution are high, we advise they should reduce physical activity when they are outside."

"How worried should we be?" Kim asked.

"Most people will not experience any symptoms, which is why we are advising action for vulnerable groups only. However, if anyone experiences shortness of breath, we recommend they reduce physical exertion. People with asthma may need to use their inhaler more often."

"And where is the pollution coming from?"

"This pollution for this episode is coming mainly from the continent, although local traffic is adding to the pollution. It is not uncommon at this time of year. Dust from the Saharan desert is exacerbating the situation on this occasion."

"Okay thank you for your advice Mr Storani from the Faculty of Air Pollution," Kim said closing him down.

"Last night the car of local journalist was fire bombed apparently in response to a story he wrote in The Sentinel about an alleged drugs den at a premises called The Lodge. My next guest is Simon Turner, The Sentinel reporter who broke that story.

"Simon, thank you for coming on the show."

I coughed to clear my throat. "It's my pleasure," I croaked.

"Can you take us through what happened last night?"

"I was in my bedroom after returning from work when my flatmate bashed on my bedroom door. She had been watching someone acting suspiciously around my car, and saw him throw what looked like a petrol bomb through the window. The car exploded and we rushed down to take a look, but he had disappeared."

"That is awful Simon, but what makes you think it was linked to a story in the paper?"

"We can't be sure of that, but it is one line of thought," I said. "As a journalist you can upset a lot of people."

"I'm sure that's right. Your editor mentioned a story about a brothel called The Lodge, which you ran last week?"

"It was on the front page of my edition. Residents in Appleton and Longley called for its closure following allegations of drug dealing, so I ran that story."

"And you think that might be linked to what happened last night?"

"We really don't know at this stage, but I will be investigating," I said.

"Okay, well keep us informed how things develop," he said moving to the next story.

Then the producer spoke to me again. "Thank you Mr Turner, we very much appreciate you giving us your time today. I'm sure you are very busy."

"That's fine, and thank you," I said. The producer said goodbye and I nodded at Peter to end the call. He flipped the off switch and I took the earphones off.

"Thank you Simon, I'll let you know if there is further interest," he said warmly. "You've really turned things around on your patch. When you first got here you were really struggling and now the paper is selling really well. It is quite remarkable."

I didn't think I deserved any praise for having my car petrol bombed, but I got the feeling that's the way things worked in newspapers.

"Thank you," I said as I got up and walked back to my desk. Just maybe my job was getting more secure.

Katie beckoned me over as soon as I walked in. "Did you interview the animal sanctuary people?" she demanded to know.

"Yes, yesterday," I said relieved I could give a positive response for once.

"Good, then put it through in ten minutes – I need it for a county page."

"I was planning it for my page 11," I said.

"You can do the eel story for that."

"I was going to use that for page nine," I protested.

"You've got all day to find a page nine," she said. "Ten minutes then."

I exhaled loudly in protest and walked back to my desk.

Ten minutes was not nearly enough time to write a decent article particularly as I hadn't thought the story through. There was no time to think up a decent introductory paragraph – so I just made it up as I typed:

Animal sanctuary full to bursting point

A huge surge in abandoned animals has left staff at an animal sanctuary desperately trying to cope.

Susie Sweet, owner of Heaven's Door in Longley said that people find it hard handling the stress of organising children and pets after Christmas.

She said: "A lot of the problem is that people find it hard handling the stress of organising children and pets after Christmas.

"The number of animals coming through has definitely increased, and we are full to bursting point. But it's not just cats and dogs – we had a Turkey handed in after it was found wandering around the cemetery."

Ms Sweet started the sanctuary twenty years ago to house unwanted cats and dogs. It is now home to a vast array of different animals......

Katie called for the copy as soon as the ten minutes were up, so I filed it immediately, wincing at the way I had written the first quote. The repetition of the sentence above it was embarrassing; like a joke article.

"What was that all about?" Sheffield asked.

"Katie nicked my page 11 for a county page," I said. "Remind me to never again let the newsdesk know when I've got a couple of stories in the bag in future."

"Will do boss," he said trying to repress a grin.

At least I had some time to properly write up the eel story. I tinkered with it for half an hour before filing it along with enough nibs to fill the page:

Whale of a time for eel smoker

Historically a delicacy of London's East End the humble eel has gone West to star on the menu of Somerset's top restaurants and most exclusive of tables.

The change in the fish's fortune comes as no surprise to Joe Green who started an eel smoker in the Nineties after travelling to Holland.

Mr Green said: "It's a delicacy in Holland unlike Britain. They smoke it a different way, using hot smoke which is much quicker….."

Fortunately, the radio interview had given me a story for a page nine. And a quick look at the Faculty's website gave me the background I needed about the health effects of air pollution. The press office even emailed me a map showing different concentrations of smog around the country. But I knew the Sofia would not accept it as a page lead unless I had some quotes from locals.

"Do you know anyone with asthma?" I asked Sheffield over lunch. He was sinking his teeth into a homemade cheese and onion sandwich, which he ate every day without exception.

"No. Why?" he said after gulping down a bolus.

"I need an asthmatic for an air pollution story I heard while I was on the radio. You could probably use it as a story too."

"I will!" he said. "You could try ringing the GP surgery. Email it to me once you've written it."

I leafed through the phone book to find a number for the Breakers Gate GP surgery and called right away. The receptionist was efficient to the point of rudeness.

"Breakers Gate practice," she said.

"I am writing a story about air pollution and would really appreciate it if I could speak to a patient who is suffering from the smog we are apparently experiencing?"

"We can't give you any names because of patient confidentiality," she said quickly.

"Then could I speak to one of the doctors about the pollution please?"

"I will let the GP practice know," she said. "They will call back if they can help."

"Thank you," I said and she hung up.

"I'll have to go down there," I said to Sheffield.

"Where?" he asked.

"The GP practice - I'll have to catch one of their patients on the way into surgery."

"Good luck with that," he said. "And don't forget to send me the story when you've finished."

I signed out one of the pool cars and drove to Appleton, parking in the surgery car park when I got there. The practice was set up in a single story building backing onto a housing estate. I sat in the car surveying the scene for a few minutes, hoping to spot an asthma patient going in or coming out of the reception. A steady trickle of people walked to and from the surgery, but none of them was gasping at their inhaler.

I got out of the car, smartened myself up and waited for the next patient to appear. A minute or so later, an elderly gent walked out of the surgery's glass door and headed towards me. He was wearing a green felt fedora hat and holding a walking stick in his right hand.

"Excuse me," I said as politely as I could. "I work for The Sentinel and I'm trying to speak to people who are suffering from the smog, which has blown in from the continent. Have you heard the warnings?"

"No," he said looking bemused.

"Are you experiencing any health symptoms?" I asked.

He looked at me blankly. "None of your business," he said gruffly and walked off.

Likewise, the next patient, a mum pushing a pram, said she was in "too much of a hurry" to talk to me. And the third person I stopped was so terrified at the prospect of being in the paper that I had to apologise to her for suggesting the idea.

But I didn't get disheartened. I knew it was a numbers game. It was just a matter of time before I got lucky, which happened with patient number four.

"Yes I have been using my inhaler a lot more," said Megan Davies, a thin elderly lady with curly white hair. "It's all the Saharan dust coming over from France that's causing it I hear. That along with all the cars on the road."

She was quite a chatterbox and I had to be quite rude to end the interview. But I needed to speak to at least a couple more patients before I could write up the story. So I continued playing the numbers game until I had bagged four quotes, all saying slightly different things about the smog. That way they would hang nicely together in the story.

I was back in the office by mid-afternoon so I could write it up without too much of a rush:

Pollution warning for South Somerset

Warnings have been issued by air pollution experts after high levels of air pollution were experienced in south Somerset.

Health bosses advised people with lung and heart conditions to reduce exercise outdoors after air pollution from the continent was detected.

Dr Storani said: "Most people will not experience any symptoms, which is why we are advising action for vulnerable groups only. However, if anyone experiences shortness of breath, we recommend they reduce physical activity. People with asthma may need to use their inhaler more often."

Asthma sufferer Megan Davies, 42, visited the GP surgery in Cox's yard, Appleton, after suffering from shortness of breath.

She said: "I noticed I've been using my inhaler a lot more. It's all the Saharan dust coming over from France that's causing it. That and all the cars on the road...."

The newsdesk was blissfully silent after I'd put the story through, which I took for contentment. Sheffield was pleased to have a story idea for Monday, and I got to relax for a few minutes having completed my tasks for the day.

But my meditation was interrupted by a phone call.

"News?" I said after picking up the receiver lazily.

"Mr Turner? It's Doctor Simmons. You rang the surgery earlier about air pollution?"

"Yes, thanks for getting back to me," I said instantly waking up. "I've filed the story now but perhaps we can chat about the air pollution anyway? I might be able to put together a follow up story in next week's paper."

"I can't see the point in that unless we have a huge wave of people come into the surgery over the weekend," he said. "But as it happens I would like to speak to you about a different matter, if I may?"

"Of course," I said, my ears pricking up.

"What are your thoughts on the council's sale of Breakers Gate to Compton House? You must have heard rumours about proceedings?" he asked.

"I have heard certain things, so I am investigating," I said. "It seems very odd given they bought Alma Court and Breakers Gate for the same purpose – to build a community hall. Then dropped the idea."

"May I speak strictly off the record?" he asked.

"Of course."

"I can tell you in confidence that the practice has come under tremendous pressure to move since the land was sold to the chairman."

"What sort of pressure?"

"This is totally off the record?"

"Yes it is."

"Then I can tell you that certain financial inducements were offered to sell the lease."

"Exactly how much are we talking?"

"One hundred thousand pounds – rejected of course."

"I assume this was done above board, as part of a financial package?

There was no reply.

"Then it was offered in cash terms as a bribe?"

"Let's just say that if a doctor had been identified who might be able to influence the sale of a lease, then a cash inducement might seem logical in certain quarters."

"You mean Ripley tried to bribe you?"

"Dependent on result of course."

"What did you say?"

"I told him what he could do with the money. But I am telling you this in the hope that you support the surgery if we come under pressure to move."

"You have my support, I promise," I said.

As soon as I'd put the phone down, I added the bribery claim to the fake letter I'd written:

…..The doctors' surgery in Breakers Gate has since been bribed £100,000 to sell the lease - an offer which was rejected.

I suspect the Ice House, a worthless piece of brown field land, will then be used to build the community hall. It's a three card trick which is making Ripley and his cronies a fortune at the expense of the taxpayer.

Yours

A concerned resident

I slipped the letter into the envelope, sealed it with a lick of my tongue and popped it into my jacket pocket for posting that evening.

Chapter 28: Yews

A dazzling array of whitened teeth flashed at me from a line of seated councillors. They laughed in unison.

"Ha, ha, ha, ha…."

I grabbed a copy of The Sentinel from the desk in front of me and looked at the front page – it was blank.

In desperation, I leafed through the rest of the paper – all the pages were blank.

"Oh my god!" I said staring in disbelief.

"Ha, ha, ha, ha, ha…"

Then I was on the floor, Ripley standing over me laughing, sneering.

"Get your arse back to London," he snarled, the heel of his boot grinding away on the top of my head.

I woke bolt upright, drenched in sweat and immediately took a swig of water from a glass I kept on the floor next to my bed. It was 8am.

Carl Gustav Jung, the Swiss psychiatrist of some renown, advised people to listen to their dreams; that much I had learned from the psychology modules of my business degrees. So I didn't dismiss the nightmare out of hand, especially since it was the second night terror I'd had in two days. I lay in bed analysing it for a kernel of truth.

It was obvious, I thought, I needed more page leads.

I jumped out of bed, threw on a few clothes and grabbed the keys for the pool car which had been given to me on semi-permanent loan until I'd bought a new one.

It was best to get out of the flat in any case: Josh and Jenny would be on at me about the car fire, trying to get me to move out before I was ready.

Despite all of this, the lazy side of my character took over as I contemplated the tactics needed to secure a lead, and I therefore settled on driving through Appleton hoping to spot a story from behind the wheel, rather than walking door to door asking questions.

But I was lucky that day.

A few weeks earlier I wouldn't have twigged it as a story at all, but by that stage in my career I had just enough news sense take a second look at the lumberjack, who was busily sawing down a huge specimen of some unknown variety of tree in the town's cemetery.

The story clicked, I slammed on the breaks and reversed up next to the cemetery gates. Fortunately for me, he was still half way through dismantling a row of the impressive specimens, which ran along one side of the main cemetery building.

"Man chops down line of stunning trees;" I thought to myself. "Must be a story!"

My only concern was broaching the lumberjack while he was wielding a roaring chainsaw.

He was standing to the right of five decapitated tree stumps, and was busily slicing the felled timber into shorter more manageable sections for removal. Another six trees lay untouched to his right, which were destined for the same fate.

221

I snapped a couple of photos from a safe distance, just out of sight, while he sawed the timber with short bursts of the machine. Then I walked over to him, smiling and waving a hand to indicate I wanted to chat. He flicked a switch and the machine coughed to a stop.

"Morning," I said, my camera and notepad well hidden from view, so as not to spook him. I would have to jot it all down later. "Just wondering why the trees are coming down?"

"It is council work," he said dismissively, making it all too clear he didn't want to chat.

"They've contracted you to cut them down then?" I asked a little impertinently.

"The arborist has condemned them as unsafe. They are all coming down," he said curtly. I imagined he might be feeling guilty about culling them all.

"What's wrong with them then?" I asked.

"Ask the council, I'm just here to lop them down."

He fired up the chainsaw, and continued to systematically tear up the timber.

The wood looked healthy, but I was no expert. My antennae was up, but perhaps there was a disease invisible to the uninformed eye. No matter, though, because someone would complain about the felling and that would be my story.

I decided to sit tight and wait for someone to walk by who I could interview. Preferably someone passionate about trees. The lumberjack stopped for lunch, which he ate in a van parked in the cemetery grounds. Twenty minutes went and I was beginning to wonder if I was wasting my time. Then a smartly dressed woman walked through the cemetery gate with a border collie on a lead. She was elegant, with long dark hair and walking briskly at almost powerwalking speed.

I pulled out my reporter's pad to show I was there in an official capacity, holding a pen to the page as if ready to write and put on my friendliest smile.

"I'm writing a piece for the local paper about these trees," I said as she came close.

She smiled sweetly and stopped next to me. "They've bloody ruined the place," she said angrily. "It's total vandalism. Whoever agreed to this should be strung up."

Her collie sat obediently beneath her feet, so I leaned down and gave it a pat.

"Did you know they were for the chop?" I asked.

"No I bloody didn't, or else I would have taken legal action to stop it," she said. "Yew trees take hundreds of years to mature - we will never see the like of them here again."

We were getting on well but she balked when I asked her age for the paper.

"None of your business," she said emphatically. "Damn cheek – I'm not having you put that in The Sentinel."

But she agreed to have her photo taken. I got her to pose in front of one of felled yews, with the other tree stumps lined up behind her in the shot. The collie sitting happily beside her.

"When's this coming out then?" she asked after I'd thanked her.

"Should be in next week's paper," I said.

"I'll keep an eye out then," she said, and gave me a backwards smile as she walked off. Her teeth perfectly straight and brilliantly white.

The council offices were officially shut on Saturdays but I knew that Alderman worked the mornings so he was prepared for the week ahead. I rang him and sure enough, he picked up the phone straight away.

"I'm at the Appleton cemetery," I explained "watching a lumberjack cut down a line of beautiful old yew trees."

"Yes," he said cordially.

"I am wondering if the town council gave the go ahead for it. I don't remember hearing anything at the council meetings."

"It was decided by the council's amenities sub group," he said curtly. "They agreed to cut down the trees on advice from the council's arborist. As it turns out, there are quite a few residents who want them replanted. So the council will be taking views on replanting at a future meeting."

"Was any of this agreed at the public meeting?" I asked.

"The subgroup sits in closed session," he said.

My antennae was up again. I learned to be suspicious of any decisions done in closed session. It also seemed a very good deal for the arborist. He would order the council to cut down trees, and the council would ask him to replant them.

"So who is this arborist?" I asked, almost thinking out loud.

"That's not the point here; the work needed to be done because the trees were diseased."

"Of course," I said trying to control my anger at the refusal to answer. "But I'd like to know his name - otherwise I will write that the council has refused to give it, which might seem odd to residents."

"It's Cllr Cummings," he admitted.

Chapter 29: Blue Monday

Monday morning was largely spent looking forlornly at my mobile phone, wondering why Selina hadn't returned the calls I'd left over the weekend suggesting another date. 'Surely, she could send a text?' I thought feeling sorry for myself.

The first call I'd made to her on Saturday evening was fair enough and perhaps even the second, later Saturday night, was excusable considering we'd spent the night together. But the third message, on Sunday morning, asking why she hadn't replied was embarrassing, cringeful even. In short, I had probably blown it. I had every confidence that she still wanted to set up the sting, but the chances of anything more romantic seemed over.

For once I was glad when Sofia waved me over to the newsdesk because the walk of shame shook me out of my unhealthy introspection. She was in the deputy editor hot seat that day because Katie was out of the office.

"What happened to the animal sanctuary story?" she asked looking disapprovingly at the copy on her screen. Katie had sent it to the subs the day before so couldn't be called back for editing.

"I was only given ten minutes to write it up," I explained.

She shook her head – a sloppily worded story like that would never have got past her radar. But Katie was less of a perfectionist.

"You really must get used to bashing these stories out more quickly," she said adamantly. "But at least you can do a follow story next week about the turkey. Something like 'EastEnders moving West for

Christmas.' Make sure you do a good job this time – or the sanctuary will stop doing stories with us."

It was a better outcome than I'd been expecting as I'd marched across and I'd even got another story idea out of it. This time I would try to keep it for my edition though.

My page seven story had been whirling round my head since Saturday afternoon, and it only took me a few minutes to write up. But I waited until just before deadline to file it, just in case Sofia was short of county pages:

Cemetery visitor wants Yew trees back

Residents have blasted a council for vandalising a row of mature trees in a cemetery.

Dog walker Nigella Penman 'would have taken legal action' if she had known about the plans, which were rubber stamped by the Appleton council on the advice of their arborist.

But now the council says it will perform a Yew turn and replant the trees after complaints by residents.

Ms Penman, of Hendon Hill, said: "They've ruined the place. It's total vandalism in my view. Whoever agreed to this should be strung up. Yew trees take ages to grow - we will never see the like of them here again."

The trees were cut down after council arborist and Appleton Council deputy chairman Pat Cummings said they were diseased.

Appleton spokesman Sean Alderman said they would probably now be replanted.

He said: "As it turns out, there are quite a few residents who want them replanted. So the council will be taking views on replanting…"

I was just started to relax when Sheffield shook me out of my slumber. "I thought you said there was something wrong with your Pet Cemetery story?" he said after filing his page seven story.

"Oh god, thanks for reminding me! I'd forgotten all about that mistake." I said.

"That's my point," he said. "It looks like they've corrected it. The story reads fine."

I opened the page and scanned through it. Sure enough the line saying the plans had been 'approved' had been changed to 'revived' and the next sentence changed from saying the council "had approved" the scheme to "were to approve" it at the meeting that week.

At first I was relieved, but then I became furious that Sofia hadn't told me the page had been corrected.

"She lied to me about it then!" I said angrily to Sheffield.

"I can't believe they let you think you'd made a fool out of yourself when they'd corrected it," he said, which made me all the more angry.

I marched over to the newsdesk with the paper in my hand.

"I thought you said this couldn't be corrected because it was already set at the printers?" I said barely able to conceal my bitterness.

"Yes that's right," Sofia said.

"But it has been corrected!" I said.

"Yes, and aren't you lucky?" she said. "You must be the first reporter to complain that you've had an error corrected, Simon."

"But you might have told me," I said.

"Well maybe next time you won't make the same mistake, so I won't have to ask the subs to ring up the printers and do us a favour."

"Oh, I see," I said realising the effort involved. "But I would have learned the lesson if you had told me."

"Maybe," she said and turned her gaze to the crossword she was finishing.

I walked back to my desk still furious at the strategy.

"So what did she say?" Sheffield asked after I sat down.

"It's a training policy – learning through humiliation," I said.

It was the end of the day before I'd fully calmed down. But just as I was thinking of heading off, a bunch of mail was dumped on my desk. I sifted through it looking for the fake latter I'd sent on Friday evening.

"Bingo," I said to myself after spotting it between the usual banal batch of press releases about car boot sales and church bazaars.

"What's up boss?" Sheffield said looking over, his hands full of letters for his patch.

"Just got a few nibs I needed for page seven that's all," I said not wanting to reveal my hand. "Did you get anything?"

He handed a letter over the partition. "This nutter thinks he's being poisoned by aeroplane 'chemtrails'," he said. "There's some weird stuff about it on the web, so I will probably write it up for page five."

"Just checking through the rest of my letters now," I said thinking that perhaps this was the time to reveal the fake letter story.

"Wow - what do you make of this?" I said, passing it to him.

He studied it for a few moments before the contents hit home. "Bloody hell you've got a secret mole! Like the guys in Watergate," he said. "This is totally dynamite."

It must have been the awful lie, but I felt a nothing but guilt at the adulation he was sending in my direction. It was unkind to play him along in such a way.

"This is so totally going to be a big story," he added.

"I guess you are right," I said almost apologetically, and grabbed the letter back off him. I walked over to the newsdesk with it to show it to Sofia.

"This just came through the post," I said dropping it on her unfinished crossword.

"Oh my Lord!" she said, after a few moments, her eyes lighting up after reading the text. "This is your splash for sure. You'll need to give the council a chance to reply, but leave that till first thing on Wednesday morning, otherwise they might slap an injunction on it."

"Okay, will do," I said pleased my plan was working, even though it felt like cheating.

"How are you set for the rest of your pages?" she asked.

"I have an Appleton meeting tonight so hopefully I'll get pages five and three sorted then," I said.

"Speak to me about it in the morning," she said. "I will need to check this story with Peter but it should be okay to run. Just don't mention it at tonight's meeting – got it?"

"Yes, got it," I said, annoyed she was still treating me like a cub reporter.

"Oh, and you will need to ring the surgery to get a response to the bribery allegation. But I'm sure you knew that?" It hadn't occurred to me, but I nodded and went back to my desk.

Chapter 30: Appleton meeting

"Order, Order – will members of public come to order!" Ripley demanded, slamming his gavel on the desk with a hard thwack.

I slipped into the room as the command was given, and quietly sat down at the press desk relieved to have escaped his notice.

Ripley looked at the agenda on the desk in front of him, then scanned the thirty or so residents attending the meeting – it was another big turnout.

I scanned my copy of the agenda, looking for potential stories and wrote down my thoughts next to them:

Item one: Council Clerk - *might be interesting.*

Item two: Sports Centre - *perhaps a dull page lead or a short story.*

Item three: Alma Court – *page lead.*

Item four: Breakers Gate – *page lead.*

Item five: Ice House – *page lead (although might have to combine with the two above).*

Then there were the usual bits and pieces on Paths and Walkways, Grants and Housing applications, which usually only made nibs.

Cllr Malcolm was sitting at his desk on the far side of the table, poker faced. But he gave me a little wink as our eyes met across the floor. I smiled briefly at him, to acknowledge contact.

"Order!" Ripley growled, again bringing the gavel down with a loud bang.

The room hushed.

"Item number one is about Sean," he said calmly. "As Chairman, I am probably best placed to speak on this?" He looked to the desk of civic leaders. They nodded obediently in unison. "Sean has been town clerk for five years and as I am sure we all agree, he has excelled at all his duties. Put simply, we are lucky to have him."

"Hear, hear," the councillors murmured in unison.

"Thank you," he continued, showing just a hint of a smile. "I am sure that no two days in the job are quite the same, and the demands have changed considerably over the years. Government departments now produce a steady flow of documentation on issues such as racial equality and ladies' rights." He looked around the table with a disapproving expression and got the head shakes he was after. "In addition, there is ever more human rights documentation including disability rights. And there is the issue of the press…." He glared at me with a disgust for a few moments. "In short, the job is no longer tenable as a contracted position, so the council has decided to make Sean a full time employee. We look forward to working with him on that basis. His pay will remain unaffected although he will now be entitled to some hard earned holiday, and a pension. Congratulations Sean!"

'Hear, hear' cheered the councillors, although the public benches were deathly quiet.

Alderman, who was sitting at a desk on the other side of the council table, was writing down the comments without acknowledging they were about him.

"Sean, would you like to add anything?" Ripley said looking across at him.

It was the first moment I'd realised he was a shy man rather than aloof, as I had always taken him to be. It was obvious he would have preferred just to carry on jotting down the minutes, not speaking at all, but under pressure from Ripley, he was forced to say a few words. He cleared his throat as if it was a great effort to use his vocal chords.

"I am very grateful," he croaked. "Residents can now visit me at the Council Office five days a week before midday to discuss issues, although I can arrange other times if those hours are inconvenient."

"Thank you Sean," Ripley said, satisfied at the response.

"Item two. Sports Centre: As many of you will know, this has been in need of a revamp for many years. More recently the council has been considering the case for upgrading facilities and today I can announce that the county council has set aside £10,000 to study how an upgrade would benefit the community. Perhaps the member for Leisure and Tourism would like to add a few words?"

This was one of deputy chairman Cummings's posts, although I had not realised it until that moment. "If the study gets the green light, the sports centre could get three million quid worth of funding for improvements including an outside swimming pool, new changing rooms and a car park," he said. "A consultant will now carry out a feasibility study which should take three or four months before we have some conclusions."

I smelled a rat but perhaps I was getting paranoid. It would do for a story in this week's paper, but I noted it down as something that needed a little more digging.

"We look forward to you presenting the consultant's report to the council," Ripley said, smiling at Cummings.

"Item number three: Alma Court," he said. "This will be of great interest to many on the council and to the public by the look of today's gathering."

My eyes darted around the people in the room who were listening intently. I hoped they were Malcolm's allies.

"County councillor Malcolm has received letters from a number of residents about this issue and has asked me to add this, and the next two items to the agenda so we can debate the concerns that people might have," Ripley said. "We have been criticised, unfairly in my view, about doing this work behind closed doors, which we had to do because of the sensitivity of the deals. Does anyone else on the council want to say anything on this issue?"

Cummings took his chance to leap in. "We needed to secure the site for the town; simple. Alma Court is a strategic site, which will help us with much needed car parking and cut future housing costs. For reasons of commercial confidentiality we had to conduct the purchase and sale in closed doors sessions."

"You mean in the pub," someone shouted from the middle of the public seating.

"Quiet please," Ripley demanded as a ripple of laughter rang out. "This is a serious matter and serious accusations have been made. We have agreed to hear from a member of the public on this issue. Mike Tomkins, if you would like to address the council?"

Mr Tomkins, tall, wiry and unshaven, stood up in the front row, turning side on so he could address both the council and the public.

Lady Fothergill was sitting next to him wearing a brown fur coat and matching fur lined gloves.

"Many of us residents would like to know whether the sale of Alma Court to Compton House was done fairly, under competitive tendering?" he said nervously, with a tremor in his voice.

Ripley looked round the table to see if any councillor was going offer an answer, and when none was forthcoming, spoke on their behalf. "The purpose was to secure the sale for the community," he said softly. "Any advertising of the deal would have risked losing the site for the town. We were very lucky that the country council were able to offer us such a good price when we bought the land, and a sizeable profit has been made over its sale." He looking round the room, pausing for a moment. "Are there any more questions about Alma Court?"

Mr Tomkins shook his head and sat down.

"Item number four: Breakers Gate. Mr Tomkins?"

He stood again. "The sale was again done behind closed doors, so how do we know that the proper clauses were included. Section 109 and 316 for example?" he asked.

If Ripley was surprised, he hid it well. "All the documentation is kept by Mr Alderman in the council offices," he said patiently. "I can assure you that everything is legal and above board. But I suggest you take a look for yourselves if you doubt it. But I must say the council would not take kindly to any malicious accusations about this issue, which could very well be damaging to members. We would seek legal action if that is the case."

Tomkins sat down, defeated, and Malcolm buried his head in his hands.

Cummings chose the moment to speak. "The surgery will continue to be let to the GP surgery for at least two years, at which point we will consider whether it might better be moved to another location. But the point is, the town is now the proud owner of these two important sites and will benefit from any future development."

"If I may move the next item?" said Ripley.

"You may indeed Mr Chairman," said Cummings.

"Item five then: The Ice House - Mr Tomkins, any thoughts on this one?" he mocked.

He shook his head, prompting Lady Fothergill to jump out of her seat, throwing her arms in the air in disgust as she did so.

"I don't care what you think, this was yet another grubby deal done in secret," she yelled. "We are all wondering who is benefitting the most – the chairman who's selling this derelict piece land, or his deputy who will no doubt be furnishing the hall when it's built?

"Lady Fothergill, I would thank you to keep your conspiracy theories to yourself or you will be hearing from the council's solicitors," Ripley shouted angrily.

But Lady Fothergill wasn't finished. "Oh that old trick, it won't stop me Mr Ripley," she said staring at him squarely in the eyes. "You have been threatening legal action against anyone who raises concerns about these deals for years, and I have yet to see you take anyone to court."

"May I just intervene," demanded Cummings. "The public should know we are very lucky to have the chairman working for the community. He has done so much for this town. And as a businessman myself I have to say there are times when negotiations have to be done in private. This has nothing to do with any self-interest, we only have the town's future interests at heart and I would ask residents to trust us."

"Hear, hear!" rang out across the council table.

Lady Fothergill sat down and Ripley scanned the room for more speakers. No one raised their hand.

"I suggest we move onto item number six: Paths and Walkways," he said with just a hint of triumphalism.

Chapter 31: Super Tuesday

I was excited that a big splash was just round the corner, but I still had a lot of work, and writing, to do before I could celebrate. And the paucity in variety of stories the night before left me fretting about whether I would be able to fill all the pages. I was in luck that morning, though, because a trader rang as soon as I walked in through the office door.

"It must have been an inside job," she said adamantly and without any explanation.

"What must have been?" I asked, tucking the phone under my chin and grabbing a note book as I sat down. Sheffield winked to say hello and I nodded back.

"Have you not heard yet? Really?" she said rather melodramatically. "I thought the press were always the first to know about such things?"

"I'm afraid not. We rely on people such as yourself ringing them in."

"Oh I see, well that is very disappointing. I assumed you would be well abreast of things, she said disparagingly.

She introduced herself as Jean Farer owner of the Organic Movement food shop in Appleton. I'd met her doing my rounds on the first day in the job, and she'd promised to call if she ever had a story. She was raging because her shop, along with two others in the town's miniscule shopping mall, had been burgled overnight.

"It must have been an insider because hardly anyone knows the code to the shopping centre," she explained. "They disabled the alarm and walked straight in."

The three shops had been raided for cash; each with their tills busted open. "It's awful, I can't trust anyone, that's the worst thing," she added.

I was wondering why they would leave cash in their tills overnight, but thought better of mentioning it. I was no shopkeeper after all.

"Do you have any ideas about who's behind it?" I asked. She refused to point the finger, or reveal who had access to the codes, but continued to rage about the injustice. There was also a frosty silence when I asked who on the council was aware of the codes. I had my suspicions about who was behind it of course, but nothing I could put down on paper, or mention over the phone. She gave me the numbers of the other shop keepers, and I got a few quotes from them to bulk out the story. Then I rang Alderman, who came back to me with a quote from the council five minutes later, predictably blaming 'local yobs.'

Any other week and the story was good enough for my splash, but I filed it for page five along with a library photo of Jean smiling outside her shop:

Shops left fuming by three-in-one burglary

Shopkeepers are furious after thieves broke into three shops in the Gainsborough shopping centre in Appleton.

They stole cash from businesses Organic Food Movement, Historic Clothing and Short and Curly's hairdresser on Monday evening.

Jean Farer, of Organic Food Movement, claimed it was "an inside job."

She added: "It must have been because hardly anyone knows the code to the shopping centre. They disabled the alarm and walked straight in…"

I'd filed it an hour early, which gave me time to plan the rest of the paper. The Appleton meeting had given me a lot background for my splash, so I pencilled in Town Clark Goes Full Time for page three, and Plans to Revamp the Sports Centre for page two.

But first I wanted to ask Dr Simmons about the Fake Letter bribery allegations. So I rang the surgery, and this time got a far friendlier reaction.

"Of course Mr Turner, I'll put you straight through to Dr Simmons," the receptionist said as if she had been expecting my call.

I told Dr Simmonds that there had been a development in the story, that it was a tricky situation, but I needed a quote from him, or the surgery. "It's an amazing coincidence," I explained. "But after our conversation last week, a letter came through the post making all sorts of allegations against the council about Breakers Gate, Alma Court and The Ice House."

"This is a piece of serendipity," he said almost too casually.

"Exactly what I thought," I continued. "But the most incredible thing is the letter mentions the bribe you said the council made to facilitate the surgery's moving out of Breakers Gate."

"The letter mentions 'a bribe' – actually used those words?" he said in surprise.

"Yes that's right," I said, sure he was about to twig.

"Can you tell me who wrote the letter?" he asked.

"It was anonymous – a whistle blower."

241

"But it makes no sense."

"Why not, you told me yourself you had received an offer."

"Yes that's right," he said. "But firstly, hardly anyone knows about that apart from you and I, and no one who knows would have the motivation to send a letter to the paper about it. And secondly, no one refers to it as a bribe. An offer, yes, but apart from our conversation, I have never known it be called that."

I quickly reassured myself that if I'd made the leap of logic about it being a bribe, then others would too. "But a bribe is what it was," I said. "So it is hardly surprising that a whistle blower would use that language."

"But it would be out of character for the other doctors to write such a letter. I know them too well," he insisted.

"But what about their families?" I asked. "Are you telling me they wouldn't speak to their spouses? Or even their friends?"

"I suppose you may be right," he said relenting finally. "After all I spoke to you about it, didn't I? So there is every chance another third party could have been made aware of it. I hope that is the source rather than someone at the surgery."

"Those are my thoughts too," I said feeling vindicated.

"So why are you telling me this?" he said. "I will see the story on Thursday no doubt."

"Yes, you will. But I need a response from the surgery about the claim that a bribe was made."

"Oh that's simple," he said. "You can quote me thus: 'ask the council.'"

I fist pumped the air with excitement. Sheffield, who was still scratching around for page five lead looked annoyed, so I quickly recoiled.

"Bloody hell, what's going on?" he said after I'd put the phone down.

"Just nailed my splash, that's all."

"The one about the anonymous letter?"

"Yes, the doctor's surgery just 'refused to deny' the bribery allegation. Peter will have to run the story now."

With my splash standing up nicely, I turned my thoughts to page three. But I was so far ahead of schedule that I decided instead to surf the internet for an hour or two. Sheffield was too busy searching for stories to chat, so I then went for a leisurely lunch. Then with just under an hour before deadline, I bashed it out ready for filing:

Clerk puts down full time roots

A Clerk has been made a full time employee of a south Somerset council because of the increasing demands of the job.

Appleton Clarke Sean Alderman, who had previously been a contractor, was given the salaried post in recognition of all the hard work he has done. For the first time he will have paid holidays and a pension.

Mr Alderman, 67, said the council office will now be open to the public five days a week.

Appleton Chairman Tony Ripley said: "Roger has been in post for five years and has excelled in his duties. Put simply, we are lucky to have him. No two days in the job are the same and the demands have changed considerably over the years.

"Government departments now produce a steady flow of documentation on issues such as racial equality and ladies rights…"

Sofia popped over to my desk just as I was about to put it through to the newsdesk. She was smiling, which instantly made me nervous.

"How's the splash coming along?" she asked flashing a set of perfectly aligned teeth.

"Oh pretty well, I've got a response from the surgery."

"That's good. Don't forget to ring the council first thing tomorrow, though."

"I'll come over as soon as I get it," I said.

"And what have you got lined up for page three?" she said.

"Still working on that one," I said, expecting a bombshell.

"We need a county page," she demanded. "Have you got anything from yesterday's meeting?"

"Nothing that is good enough I'm afraid – just a lot of background quotes, which I can use for the anonymous letter story and some stuff about the town clerk going full time, and a sports centre revamp."

"Okay but I need another ten paragraphs for your page five, so put through the sports centre story," she said, the smile having gone, and then walked over to Tim's desk.

I was learning, but I still had to sacrifice the sports centre story:

Sports centre revamp considered

Community leisure facilities could be in line for a massive upgrade if a feasibility study to develop a sports centre gives the green light.

Appleton Council is to finance a study into adding an outdoor pool and additional parking at the town's sports centre...

It was 4pm, just half an hour before deadline, before I finally had the confidence to file page three. And to my relief, there was no walk of shame. So with the day's pages wrapped up, I did what most of the other reporters did on a Tuesday afternoon and started working on my splash, ready for filing the next day:

Whistle blower accuses council of fraud

A south Somerset council decision to buy and sell land for community use was motivated by personal financial gain, a whistleblower has claimed.

An anonymous letter sent to The Sentinel's offices in Yeovil claims Appleton Council deliberately omitted special contractual clauses when it sold Alma Court and Breakers Gate to property developer Compton House. The omission means that Compton House, which is part owned by council chairman Tom Ripley, can build more homes than was originally envisaged.

The council has been criticised for buying and selling the premises 'behind closed doors' but says the secrecy was needed due to 'commercial confidentiality.'

The whistleblower said in the letter: "The failure to include them in the sale to Compton House.... means the land was under-priced. The result is that the chairman is set to make a fat profit from the development of the land."

245

The letter, signed 'a concerned resident' also accused a councillor of trying to bribe the doctors' surgery to move out of Breakers Gate so the land can be developed.

"The doctors' surgery in Breakers Gate has since been bribed £100,000 to sell the lease - an offer which was rejected. I suspect the Ice House, a worthless piece of brown field land, will then be used to build the community hall. It's a three card trick which is making Ripley and his cronies a fortune at the expense of the taxpayer."

Under Chairman Ripley, Appleton council had bought three sites for a community hall. These were Alma Court, Breakers Gate and Ice House, a light industrial site which was owned by Ripley.

Responding to the allegations, Appleton Council said in a statement: "QUOTE NEEDED."

It looked like the story was going to be longer than usual, so I asked Sofia if I could do a page two 'wrap around' using the quotes from meeting. I'd seen Colin do it a few times and it was a nifty trick because it meant I no longer needed a page two lead.

"That's fine," she said. "But make sure the whole story is no longer that 20 paragraphs. And don't forget to file a picture!"

Page Two wrap:

At a packed town council meeting on Monday, Chairman Ripley denied claims that key clauses had been left out of the contracts.

Resident Mike Tomkins said: "The sale (of Breakers Gate) was again done behind closed doors, so how are we to know that the proper clauses were included - section 106 and *316 for example?"*

Chairman Ripley threatened legal action against the claims.

"All the documentation is kept by Mr Alderman in the council offices. I can assure you all the documentation is legal and above board. But I suggest you take a look for yourselves if you doubt it. But I must say that the council would not take kindly to any malicious accusations damaging to members. We would seek legal action if that were the case…"

Chapter 32: Splash

"The council will sue The Sentinel if it prints these false accusations, which are obviously malicious and very damaging," Alderman told me over the phone on Wednesday morning.

I'd phoned him first thing and he had got back to me within half an hour, reinforcing my view that he had a hot line to Ripley.

I walked over and told Sofia who looked worried and made a beeline for Peter's office. I sat at my desk and waited for her to come back.

Five minutes later, Sofia returned to collect me. I was seated directly opposite Peter who was sitting at his desk. Sofia was standing next to him with a hand on the top of his chair.

"Sorry, we can't run the story, Simon," he said gruffly. "The paper just can't take the risk of being sued. It could break us financially."

Sofia weighed in to support him. "The thing is, we have no proof that anything that the whistleblower said is true," she said. "The judge would throw the book at us if it's taken to court."

After all I'd been through, and all the risks I had taken, I felt betrayed by their lack of guts. Surely it was their turn to take a risk, I thought. Anyhow, I wasn't going to give up without a fight.

"But what about the non-denial from the doctors' surgery - that's evidence isn't it?" I insisted.

"It's hardly strong evidence though, Simon," said Sofia. "The onus would be on us to prove beyond reasonable doubt in court that the claims are true. That's the law."

"Okay I think we are done here," said Peter cutting me off

"One moment," I said desperately trying to think. "The story was raised at the council meeting last night."

"The anonymous letter was mentioned?" asked Peter.

"No, but a member of public asked if the correct clauses were in the contract because all the deals were done behind closed doors. He asked how were residents to know everything was above board."

Peter looked at Sofia for a moment, and then back at me.

"I don't know Simon, it still sounds a bit weak. What exactly did he say?"

"He asked if section 316 clauses were in the contracts. That's exactly what the anonymous letter goes on about – section 316 being missing from the sale. Lady Fothergill then asked who was benefitting, councillors or the town. Ripley denied there had been any wrongdoing."

"It sounds like the person who wrote this letter has also been in touch with Lady Fothergill," Peter said looking at Sofia. "Write it up Simon, I'm going to print it!"

The newsroom door slammed shut with a bang as Sofia came back into the newsroom. I'd left Peter's office first and was already sitting down.

"Congratulations Simon," she said furiously. "But next time perhaps remember to tell me that you debated the story at the council meeting It would have spared me the embarrassment of making a fool out of myself in front of the editor!"

Chapter 33: Attack

The attack took part in two stages. First, a common house brick was thrown through my bedroom window, spraying razer-sharp splinters of glass in all directions, which caused lacerations to the side of my face. The brick itself only missing me by a whisker, landing in the middle of the room as I sat at my desk reading. I jumped up and was still staring at the window in disbelief when the Molotov cocktail came crashing through, lighting the curtains and spewing a blanket of flames over the mattress.

Lucky not to be on fire myself, I rushed to the kitchen, filled a bucket full of water and chucked it over the bed, which dampened down the flames considerably. I repeated the process, this time dousing down the curtains, by which time my flatmates had come out of their bedrooms to see the commotion. They watched me extinguish the last remnants of the fire with a third bucket, causing great vapour clouds to billow out of the mattress.

"Call the police," I told Jenny, who was standing speechless next to me. Josh walked over to the window and peered out, looking toward the street below.

"There's someone standing below!" he shouted in horror, pointing a finger directly downwards.

A red mist must have descended because without thinking, I sprinted along the corridor, down the stairs and around the side of the house to confront him.

A motorcycle was pulling away as I got there, wheels spinning in a desperate attempt to escape. Dressed in black leathers and wearing a full faced helmet, the bike came towards me. I leapt at the rider and, rather like a failed rugby tackle, caught him a glancing blow to his shoulder with my right hand. The impact caused the bike to jack-knife and slide into the pavement. Seemingly unhurt, the rider sprang up and started to run down the street.

I began a foot chase. My instinct was to sprint after him at top speed, but I had been better at middle distance running at school, so I slowed to mile pace.

He started pulling away from me as we rushed down the street. First he was 30 metres ahead, then fifty and after a minute more like 75. As long as I keep him in my sights, I reasoned, there was every chance I would catch him. He looked back at me every few seconds, and I could see the growing alarm as the gap started to close. After ninety seconds there was 50 metres between us; two minutes and I was just ten metres behind him. He was breathing heavily by that stage and must have known it was only a matter of time before I grabbed him.

He was roughly my height but a lot bulkier, so the more tired he was the better. He ran past the entrance to the railway station on his last legs. I slowed to his pace, considering my options. Better to tire him out a little more before I rugby tackled him. Then, when I was on his coattails, he swivelled round once more to see me baring down on him, and almost lost balance in shear panic. I could see his face under the helmet visa – sinewy, dark; a stranger.

Putting in a last desperate burst of pace, he veered off the pavement and down an embankment to the railway line. I slowed to a jog and followed, spotting a sign as I went past. It was warning of something – could it be electrified?

He ran over the track, and clambered up the bank on the other side, looking over his shoulder one more time to see if I was chasing.

But I had given up. Whether it was the prospect of stepping on a high voltage cable, or tackling a thug who might be carrying a knife, I stopped and watched him go. His day would come, I told myself.

Trudging back, I took a look at the warning sign and cursed when I realised I'd misread the final word:

Danger: trains approaching

Trespassers will be **prosecuted.**

Four fire crews were parked up by the time I got back to the flat, and Inspector Lane was speaking to Jenny.

"I lost him at the railway line," I said as I approached them.

"Did you get a good look at him?" Inspector Lane asked.

"He was wearing a motorcycle helmet, leathers and a helmet – about my height and well built. That's all I can say," I said.

He relayed the message through police radio.

"Could you pick him out in a line?" he asked.

"I only got a glimpse through the visor so I doubt it," I said.

He seemed all too easily content with that. We ran through the details of what had happened; the usual 'who, what, when, where and why,' and he promised to be in touch if he needed anything else.

"Have you got anywhere to stay tonight?" he asked.

"I can stay at a mate's house," I said, but stopped short of telling him Sheffield's name.

Chapter 34: Legend

"Your edition sold out by 9am!" Peter blurted as I walked into the news room on Thursday morning. He had been waiting at my desk to give me the good news along with Katie and Sofia. "Really well done!" he enthused.

To stop the rumour mill going into overdrive, I'd telephoned Katie at 6am to tell her about the arson attack. So it was obvious that they all knew about what had happened the night before. I didn t need to explain how I'd got the lacerations on the left side of my face. Or rely on Sheffield to keep the secret.

"Thank you," I said to Peter who was grinning broadly. I looked across at Sofia and Katie who were less impressed.

"Katie told me about what happened last night," Peter added. "Are you okay?"

I nodded.

"Good," he said breaking out into another smile. "Then I think we can make some mileage out the story. Radio, perhaps even local television. And of course you can use the experience for a back page this week."

Katie was peering at my lacerated face, which I'd gently washed out with salt water the night before. It was starting to scab over.

"Get Len to take a photo of it this morning while it's still inflamed," she said. "It will make a great picture story."

"You can use it for page 11 or even page nine," Sofia added.

"Where are you staying?" Peter asked.

"Sheffield agreed to put me up on his bedroom floor until I find a new place," I said.

"Great teamwork," Peter said to Sheffield.

Curiosity fulfilled, they left Sheffield and I to collect the papers from the basement.

"I loved that," he said as we walked down the steps. "Katie and Sofia looked jealous at the way Peter was treating you. Jealous!"

"That's bad," I said. "You know what they can do to us."

"Not anymore; not to you at least," he said. "I bet you could tell them to get stuffed now – Peter would back you."

I was on the verge of levelling with him, particularly since his bundle of papers was larger than ever. But the time wasn't right, so I thought better of it. We split his stack in two and carried it to the newsroom.

Peter arranged half a dozen interviews within an hour, and called me into his office to rave about one he'd set up with regional television.

"We don't often get on the tele," he explained. "It's a real coup. They were really interested in who might be behind the attack on your home – I hope you understand that will be their line of questioning?"

"Yes of course," I said.

"Good, but let them make the link to your front page story. You just stick to the facts. Okay?"

"Yes got it," I said.

We sat in his office for the rest of the morning while I gave interviews with regional newspapers and local radio. Then Peter drove me to the television station's headquarters in Bristol for a Down the Line interview.

"This will be live," he explained on the way over. "You will hear the questions but won't see the interviewer."

The producer sat me in a chair facing a camera and slotted an ear piece in my right ear. "You'll be speaking into the camera," she said. "I'll count down from five so you'll know when the questions are coming. Okay?"

"Okay," I said, feeling butterflies in my stomach.

"Two minutes," she said to the television crew. I waited, trying to relax and remember my lines.

"Three, two, one – you're on," she said and nodded at me.

The voice of a male presenter came down the line; smooth, cultured and clear as if he was standing next to me.

"The home of a local newspaper journalist was firebombed last night just hours before the paper ran a story about council corruption. Sentinel reporter, Simon Turner, then gave chase to a suspect. Thank you for joining us today, Mr Turner. In your own words, could you explain what happened last night?"

I took a deep breath and started to reply; nervously at first, then relaxing a little.

"A petrol bomb was thrown through my bedroom window. I managed to put out the flames with a couple of buckets of water, then gave chase to a man we saw outside the flat."

"You think he was the arsonist?" he asked.

"He was spotted by my flatmate, and drove off as soon as he saw me. So yes, I would say he was the main suspect."

"And did you catch him?"

"No I lost him at the railway station. He ran over the lines and up the bank opposite."

"But did you get a good look at him?"

"Not a close look, but he was about my size, five feet eleven; a white guy with a thin face. But quite stocky, as if he was a bodybuilder."

"The million dollar question is: do you think the attack had any link to your front page story? Could you remind us what that was again?"

"We received a letter from a whistleblower which accused the council of using special clauses in contracts to manipulate the value of property for their own gain. But you will have to ask the police about the possibility of a link."

"Okay we will do. Were you hurt?" he continued.

"No – just a few scratches."

"And will this put you off journalism?"

"Not at all. If the person who is behind this is listening, then I would like to tell him that I am going nowhere until he is behind bars."

"I think we would all echo that message. Thank you Mr Turner," he said. "I am sure all our listeners will hope you are successful in that endeavour."

The line went dead and the producer ushered in another guest, thanking me as we switched seats.

"You might end up doing a lot of this over the next few weeks," Peter said as we drove back to the office. "Is there anything you need to make life easier until things quieten down?"

"It would help if Sheffield and I could team up on some cross border stories," I said sensing an opportunity to help each other out.

"I'm sure Katie will be fine with that," Peter said as we speeded along. "Just say I've given the go ahead if there are any problems."

It was a moment to treasure, the tide was turning.

We got back mid-afternoon, so I still had time to get page 11 sorted and stop the usual panic on Friday morning. I'd decided to use the East Ender turkey story for page 11, but was dreading ringing Susie Sweet after the hash I'd made of the feature the week before.

"The girls said they were a little disappointed with the story," she said when I phoned. "They were asking why you repeated the sentence twice in the same article? I said you were probably only given half an hour to write the story."

I felt a prickly heat of embarrassment on my neck and my cheeks flushed red.

"Five minutes more like," I said feebly.

"Oh well, I'm sure you'll have more time for this story," she said being more generous than I deserved. I moved on quickly.

"This one is about the EastEnders turkey," I said. "My boss suggested a story about EastEnders moving West for Christmas?"

She laughed as if all was forgiven, and we chatted for ten minutes while I took down the quotes I needed.

The story was ready for filing that afternoon, but I tinkered with it until the next morning, terrified I'd made a clanger somewhere:

East End Turkeys Move West

A character from the hit television series EastEnders is moving to the West for Christmas, say staff at Heaven's Door animal sanctuary.

The bronze turkey has been moved into the sanctuary after the crew from EastEnders found it running around the cemetery near Longley.

She was named Kat Slater after one of the female stars of the show....

That left me the rest of Friday to write up the arson attack for page nine. As per my new strategy, I waited till just before deadline to file it, giving Sheffield the by-line because it couldn't look like it was written by me:

Reporter's home set ablaze

An arsonist set fire to a Sentinel reporter's home just hours after the paper went to press.

Appleton and Longley journalist Simon Turner was relaxing at home in Yeovil when a Molotov cocktail was thrown through his bedroom window.

He chased the suspect to the railway station where he escaped by running across the line and clambering up the bank opposite...

Once Sheffield had filed his copy, we ducked out of the office and went for couple of drinks at his local.

"There's something you need to know," I said after I downed the first pint. The place was packed out and the duke box was blaring out cheesy Eighties music.

"But it's something I need you to keep to yourself," I shouted over the din.

"No problem boss," he said, moving closer so he could hear me.

"Some of the stories I've been writing, not all of them," I said.

"Yes boss?"

"Like this week's splash, and that story about Ripley's shop being vandalised."

"Yes?"

"They were done by me - I wrote the letter, I vandalised the shop."

Chapter 35: Set up

James Rutherford was a smallholder. Not that there is anything wrong with that of course. In fact, I would say, such a living breeds the best of human qualities; stoicism, independence, understanding of nature just to begin with. No, the trouble with Mr Rutherford was not his vocation, though the isolation may have made him a little eccentric, it was that he had a little secret.

Rutherford was in his mid-thirties and fit as a fiddle. He lived in the wetlands just outside Bishopswood, which harboured some of the rarest bird life in England. Bearded reedlings nested in reed stems near his farm, and otters regularly visited the location. There were good numbers of water voles and the reed beds came alive with bird song in the spring. You could often hear the booming calls of male bitterns and the zing of dragonflies flying past as they chased butterflies which were abundant until late summer. He loved his farm and would go to any lengths to keep it. Who could blame him?

So when the chairman came calling one afternoon, he didn't need much persuading, just a gentle reminder that he didn't have planning permission for the caravan he lived in. It could be impounded within a week, with just one call to the right person.

And so Mr Rutherford was given my telephone number, a phial of white powder and told to ring me about a photo he had taken of the 'Beast of Bishopswood.'

To everyone's amusement, he'd told the story to friends down the pub. But the tale had made its way back to Ripley, who thought up a clever way of using it against him.

The story sounded ridiculous; an urban legend if ever there was one. But I realised that if the photo was half decent I could run it as a page lead. In fact it sounded ideal for page seven - a gift of a story.

So on Saturday morning I drove to his smallholding after he'd phoned me first thing. He sounded a little excited, or was it nervous? I didn't bother to ask where he got my number from, although I thought it quite curious. In truth, I was just happy to get the call.

"I have it here in my hand, a picture that solves the mystery of the Beast of Bishopswood," he'd assured me over the phone. "Come over and I'll show it to you. And if you like, you can run a story in The Sentinel about it."

It wasn't the first time the Beast of Bishopswood had been reported in The Sentinel. There had been sightings of this mythical creature two years earlier by a family visiting the area. Some locals were convinced that a pack of panthers or lynx were living in the woods, and feeding off sheep. A few lambs had disappeared that year, as they had the year before, and they would tell you it's 'the beast that's had them.'

I was a sceptic, not least because the description was remarkably similar to a fox: "tanned appearance, belting across the misty morning farmland," one of the visitors had said in the story. But I was not going to let minor details stand in the way of a good article, and I was looking forward to meeting Mr Rutherford that morning.

He was standing at the gate waiting for me as I arrived. Long salt and pepper hair, thinning a little on top, still curled impressively down his back. Hairs were spouting from his nostrils, his teeth were stained from too much smoking, although perfectly straight. He was friendly enough, waving at me and smiling as I parked outside his front drive

"Lovely time of year isn't it?" he said in a surprisingly cultured voice as I drew close to him. "It's just such as shame that it is not safe out there in the wilderness."

 I had no idea whether he was joking or being deadly serious, but I laughed anyway. "I won't take up much of your time seeing as it is Saturday," I said. "I'm sure you have lots to be getting on with."

In truth, I was thinking more of myself than him – the local pub was showing a rugby match and I fancied watching it with Sheffield. He hadn't spoken to me much since I'd confessed the true source of my recent success, and I wanted to get him on side as best I could.

Mr Rutherford and I were sitting in his living room, which was crammed full of functional objects fashioned out of off-cuts of wood. The stair rail for instance was carved from a small tree trunk while the seats we sat in were cut from oak stumps. A dozen or so watercolours decorated the walls, and it was natural to assume he was the artist. A quick perusal of one revealed his spider-like signature in the bottom right corner.

He pulled out an ordnance survey map from a bookshelf and placed it on the coffee table. It was homemade - the rings of a tree brought out beautifully by a clear gloss varnish.

"This is my farm on the map," he said jabbing a finger at a small square. "You see the wetlands start just the other side of my land and stretch for miles. The whole place can flood for months in the winter – that's when they come into contact with us humans."

"The cats?" I asked just to be sure.

"Yes but these are no ordinary moggies," he said. They are about twice as long as a feral cat; I'd guess they are some kind of large feline - probably puma."

"You have seen more than one?" I asked.

"Of course," he said as if it were a stupid question. "Only one at any time mind, but I can tell they are different by the markings on their coats."

He gazed out of the bay window for a few moments as if he was lost in thought. "I have been an awful host," he said looking back towards me. "What would you like to drink?"

I asked for a soft drink so he went to the kitchen and poured me a glass of orange juice, handing it to me across the coffee table. I took a sip.

"Let me show you some photos," he said, then he picked up an album from a bookshelf and opened it on the table.

"Here's the first photo I took, about three years ago." He pointed to a brown smudge in the middle of a green landscape. My heart dropped. It wasn't good enough for a page lead. "It could be a fox," I said unable to hide my disappointment.

He flipped over the page of his photo album.

"Here's another, taken last week," he said encouragingly.

I peered at it across the table. It was a better, still probably a fox, or maybe a deer, sprinting across the wetlands. But just about good enough for a lead story, maybe.

I took a large gulp of juice. It tasted a bit sweet, like the powdered version I'd had as a child. "Do you mind if I borrow this picture for the article?" I said.

"Not at all, that's what you are here for isn't it?" he said. "I keep a camera in the tractor, so I was able to capture it in full flight. I've seen it many times - always in the distance. It runs as soon as it sees me."

I was jotting it all down on my reporter's pad when a haze started to descend. Like an out of body experience at first, I started floating and gazing down on myself through a thick fog. Mr Rutherford appeared to be smiling, still talking about something. I shook my head and my mind cleared for a moment.

"Let me pour you a drop of water," I heard him say. I said 'thank you' in slurred response, and he poured something into my glass. I drank most of it down in one.

He filled my glass again, and I drank some more, hoping it would help overcome my increasing sense of delirium.

After my third sip, my phone rang. I only just managed to answer coherently – it was Lady Fothergill.

"Simon, listen to me," she said. "It's a set up. Whatever you do, don't get into your car."

"Oh, right," I slurred.

"I'll be there in five minutes to pick you up!" she said and the phone clicked off.

I grinned at Rutherford, trying to gather my thoughts. He offered me another drink.

"No thank you," I said. "I'll be off now."

I stood up and he guided me to the door. "I will be bidding you farewell," he said, or something along those lines. I was stumbling outside just as Lady Fothergill screeched to a halt.

"Get in Simon," she demanded through the passenger window. I opened the door, collapsed into the seat and we sped off.

"You can stay at my place to sober up," she said. "There's the police car!" She pointed at a vehicle parked a few yards down the road.

"They were setting you up for sure," she added. "Luckily for you, Ripley isn't the only one with spies."

It took at least four hours for me to sober up enough to leave her home. "He must have drugged me," I said, sipping what must have been my sixth cup of strong coffee.

"It wouldn't surprise me," she said. "He must be desperate to get rid of you. You've got him on the ropes. Better watch out, Simon."

I checked my pocket, at least I still had my notebook and the photo of the Beast of Bishopswood. The day hadn't been a total write off after all.

Chapter 36: Death at a travellers' site

Sheffield was playing his cards millimetres from his chest, but I guessed he was making up his mind about whether I was some kind of a monster or not. I told him about the trap Ripley had set for me as we settled down for the night, but he just grunted "okay boss" and rolled over to get some sleep. It was infuriating.

He continued the act all weekend, avoiding any meaningful conversation. So I decided to confront him as we walked into work on Monday morning.

"What are you going to do about what I told you?" I asked firmly as we approached the office.

"About what?" he said nonchalantly.

"About what I told you the other day - about me being a journalistic fraud?"

"Oh that," he said casually. "I knew you were lying to me about something. I just couldn't work out what it was. I'm glad you told me."

"Glad I told you?" I said feeling exasperated. "I fake a load of stories and you are glad I mentioned it? Is that it?"

"It all adds to the Turner legend," he said turning to me and grinning. "You may even go down in history as inventing a new type of journalism - a kind of do-it-yourself version. You may be onto something."

To say I was relieved is an understatement, although alarm bells should have been ringing over the keenness he was showing.

"So you are going to keep quiet about it?" I asked as walked up the office steps.

"Oh yes, I'm going to be as quiet as a mouse about it, boss."

I had already written my page seven story in my head over the weekend, so it only took about twenty minutes to type it up. It was a picture story, so I wrote it with that in mind. And in line with my strategy of ensuring stories weren't pinched for the county pages, I saved it for filing until just before deadline that afternoon:

Big cat sighting inspire tales of the Beast of Bishopswood

This is the mythical Beast of High Ham, according to a south Somerset man.

James Rutherford, who owns a smallholding on the Somerset levels, snapped the 'puma' from his tractor as it sprinted across the landscape. He claims to have sighted several different big cats and always has a camera to hand in case he spots one.

Mr Rutherford said: "These are no ordinary cats. They are about twice as long as a feral cat; I'd guess they are some kind of large feline - probably pumas."

"[I only see] one at any time but I can tell they are different by the markings on their coats…."

I was just summoning up the energy to hit the phones for tomorrow's page five when Katie came over with a story. "We've had a tip off that there's been a death at a new age travellers site in Weaverly," she said.

It was between Sheffield's and my patch, so a great chance to share a story and the work that goes with it.

"Get yourself down there and write it up for a county page," Katie added.

Tim punched the air with delight and Sheffield groaned as the chance of an easy page five spiked.

"Actually," I said, quickly. "Peter says he is very keen for Sheffield and I to do some joint by-line stories between our boundaries. This one is perfect for page five."

Katie stared disbelieving at me for a moment. "Peter said no such thing," she said tersely.

"I'm so sorry," I said. "I should have mentioned it earlier."

"I don't believe it," she said adamantly.

"Okay, but we can go to his office to clear this up it if helps?" I said.

She was sharp enough to know I wouldn't bluff about such a thing. And knowing she was beaten, she said "fine" and marched back to her desk in a huff. Tim sunk his head in his hands.

"That was your finest moment," Sheffield grinned. "You showed her who the real boss is today."

It was going to have to be a lighting strike, I thought, because the travellers would probably chase us out of the camp once they realised what we were up to.

"Let's hit them by surprise, and get out of there as quick as we can before we get in trouble," I said to Sheffield as we drove there.

It was the first time I'd worked with Sheffield and I was taking the lead. I was ten years older than him, so I assumed the leadership position. After all, what could he do better than me?

We drove slowly past the tree lined road which the new age community had stationed their mobile homes on. It was a beautiful spot several miles away from the nearest village.

Further up the road was a farmhouse, and we pulled into the drive and got out, checking for dogs as we did so. The farm was situated on the top of a gently rising hill, which overlooked the new age travellers' site below. We could see the row of caravans stretching sideways along a valley.

"Let me do the talking," I said to Sheffield.

"Okay, boss," he said compliantly.

I knocked on the front door and a short, grey haired man with a ruddy complexion came out. His name was John Penman, and as he was keen to point out, he was one of a dying breed of 'gentleman farmers' which has survived the mass commercialisation of the industry. His 45 acres was small by modern standards and was split into a dozen or so fields. Instead of relying on modern fertilisers, the crops were rotated to provide the required nutrients. Yields were much lower, which is why it is a way of life at odds with the gigantic farming monocultures which cover much of the country. But then Mr Penman had made a stack of money on the stock market in the Eighties, so the farm was more of a hobby than a business. A dozen chickens were strolling about in the front garden as he opened the door.

"Good morning," I said as politely as I could. "We are covering a story about the traveller site for The Sentinel and wondered if you had heard anything last night?"

"If a giraffe has fourteen more than a walrus, and a squirrel has half as many as a pig - what are they?" he said looking down at a magazine he was holding.

"Pardon?" I said dumfounded.

"It's a crossword clue, been nagging at me all day - five letters."

"Teeth?" said Sheffield as if the answer were obvious - I would never have worked it out.

"Well done," Mr Penman said delighted. "Bright fellow, now how can I help?"

"We've had a tip off that someone at the travellers' site died last night," I said still reeling from Sheffield's brilliance.

"And you are wondering if we heard anything?" Mr Penman added.

"Yes, that's right," I said.

"One moment," he said and disappeared back into the house.

"How on earth did you get that?" I asked Sheffield.

He shrugged his shoulders, "It just comes to me. It's the way my brain works."

"It's some kind of genius," I said.

"That's what people used to call me up north – the 'daft genius'."

Mr Penman was back at the doorstep, this time accompanied by his wife, Mary.

"These two gentleman wish to know about the commotion last night," he said.

Mary, who was short and round with a rosy face, greeted us with a friendly smile.

"I was out in the garden last night at dusk," she said "just pottering as you do, enjoying the air, when I heard screams coming from the valley."

"Screams? Are you sure from this distance?" I said.

"Sound travels well across the fields so I could tell it was screams coming from the people at the site," she said. "I'd say they were women's voices – two or three of them. "Then about an hour later the police turned up with sirens blaring. About an hour after that they lit the whole place up with electric lighting, which they left on through the night. I could hear crying coming up from the valley intermittently during the small hours."

I was jotting it all down in my note book, which didn't seem to put her off.

"Are you going down there to speak to them?" Mr Penman asked.

"Yes, we'll be going down there next. Hopefully they are friendly." I said.

"They've always been fine to us," he said. "They keep to themselves mainly, but we do say 'hello' to each other. That's all though. We try not to make enemies."

"I guess we'll have to find that out for ourselves," I said.

"We'll read it in the paper no doubt," he said. "Good luck."

They waved us goodbye as I pulled out of their drive. But I knew we wouldn't get such a warm welcome when we arrived at the camp. Colin's advice on how to deal with tricky customers came flooding into my head as we drove down the hill. 'Keep the engine running and wear a good pair of running shoes,' he had suggested. I looked down at my feet – size ten Hush Puppy boots - not good for running.

"Are you a fast runner?" I asked Sheffield.

"Why," he said nervously.

"I just want to know if they'll catch me or you first."

"Me probably," he said. It was almost certainly true - he didn't look like the most athletic of reporters.

"Don't worry I wouldn't leave you if it comes to that," I said. "But if they do chase us out, just keep running until you get to the car. Don't go down, just keep running whatever happens."

I saw the colour drain from his face and I wasn't feeling any better.

"Don't get your notebook out," I added. "They won't say a thing if they see our pens out. Does that genius of yours extend to remembering quotes?"

"Yes boss," he said. "During the short hand tests I can remember 150 words in my head – that's more than anyone they had ever tested."

"One hundred and fifty, that's incredible! I can barely remember two sentences. That memory of yours will come in handy today - we'll write down the quotes as soon as we get back to the car."

Ideally we needed half a dozen quotes from the new age travellers to stand up the story. Plus the background from the Penmans.

With our notepads hidden well away, we parked at the site just short of the first caravan, got out and started walking towards it.

It was painted with multiple hearts, stars, moons and suns. Feeling self-conscious in a suit, I took off my tie.

As we got to the first caravan, I noticed a woman in her late twenties or early thirties sitting on a chair, weeping. We paused for a moment, but decided against speaking to her and walked on.

Two bull terriers were sleeping outside the next caravan, so we gave that a wide birth too. Each of the caravans were about twenty metres apart. That gave some privacy to the occupants but also lessening the risk of us being overheard by neighbours as we interviewed people.

A young man, probably in his mid-twenties, with long platted hair was sitting on the step entrance of the third caravan. He was speaking to a young woman. Both were wearing baggy combat style trousers. His were green, hers were red.

I interrupted them. "We've been sent down by the local paper to write a tribute piece about someone who lived here," I said. "Would you like to say a few words?"

"You mean about the girl?" he said.

"We have only been told that someone was found last night. No real details," I said.

"You should go and speak to Pudsey in the end pitch," he said. "He was a close friend of hers." He pointed to a large green caravan further down the line.

"We'll go there next," I said. "We were told the police lit the place up last night after she was found?"

"You really do need to speak to Pudsey," he said. "She went missing a week ago - we all wondered where she'd gone. Then last night, two of the women were out playing a game on the farmland – somewhere we don't usually go. In the fields over there," he pointed towards Mr Penman's bottom field.

He was smiling now, giving us exactly what we needed. I felt a pang of guilt for being so sneaky. He had no idea that everything he was saying would be used. "They were playing a game when one of them found her body in the field," he continued. "They looked up and saw her head still in the tree."

"She'd hanged herself?" I asked.

"That's right. She was depressed, but we didn't think she would do anything like that."

We thanked him and we started off towards Pudsey's caravan. But just as we left, I paused and looked back. "Nice to meet you," I said. "For future reference, I am Simon and this is Sheffield."

"I'm Jason," he said, which was enough to stand up the story.

Pudsey was sitting on the steps of his caravan as we arrived. He had spotted us some way off and didn't look pleased. I explained that we were trying to put together a tribute piece, but he wasn't buying it.

"I will not speak to you," he said angrily. "We need space by ourselves to get over this."

He was growing angrier with each moment, so we quickly backed off. "That's fine. We'll go then," I said.

"We need time and space to get over this," he shouted, and started to follow us up the camp.

The commotion woke the two bull terriers from their slumber. One bared its teeth as we walked past.

"Nice doggy," I said. Jason was grinning at the sight; suddenly I felt less guilty about turning him over.

"We need the space and time to grieve, can't you understand that?" Pudsey shouted as we weaved past the dogs.

We started running when one of the hounds began to chase us, with Pudsey in close pursuit. Then the dog was at my leg, grabbing my boot - its teeth sinking into the thick leather sole. I continued to run, like a man dragging a ball and chain.

By the time we got to the car, I was panting hard. I opened the door with the dog still attached to my boot. It was tugging against me but I managed to haul myself inside, and push on its head with the heel of my other boot. My right boot came off, and I slammed the door. Sheffield had circled round the car, and got in just before the dog could get to him. We wheel spun out of there, and I glanced in the mirror as we left to see Pudsey waving a fist in defiance.

Sheffield started scribbling down the quotes as we drove home back to work.

"Did you get it all?" I asked once he closed his notepad.

"Yes. Everything Jason and Pudsey said."

"Great, then if you send me the quotes, I'll write it up when we get back."

"Okay, boss," he said.

Word soon got round the news room about our adventure and while Sheffield was repeating the story of my lost boot for the third time, I put in a call to the police.

"The dead girl's name was Carrie Stephenson," he said. "You may have seen her around because she used to beg in Yeovil."

It was a huge wakeup call – the story was now about someone I knew, which made the breach of privacy feel all the more acute. But I bashed out the story anyway, while Sheffield was regaling our exploits:

Dead Body found on Travellers' Site

The gruesome remains of a new age traveller have been found on a field near the community where she lived.

The decapitated head and torso of the body of Carrie Stephenson were found near Drew Lane on Saturday.

Jason, who lives at the travellers' site in Weaverly said: "She went missing a week ago and we all wondered where she's gone. Then last night, two of the women were out playing a game on the farmland – somewhere we don't usually go; in the fields. They were playing a game when one of them found her body in the field. They looked up and saw her head still in the tree."

Close friend Pudsey who looked for her after she went missing asked for privacy.

"We need space by ourselves to get over this. We need the space and time to grieve."

Neighbours heard screening on Saturday evening after the body was discovered.

Mr Penman of Honeydew Farm, Bishopswood, overheard the cries while she was tending to her garden.

"I heard shrieks coming from the valley. The sound travels well across the fields so I could tell it was screams coming from the people at the site. I'd say they were women's voices – two or three of them.

"Then about an hour later the police turned up with sirens blaring out. About an hour later the whole field was lit up with lights, which they left on through the night. I could hear crying, sobbing, coming up from the valley...."

Chapter 37: Some explanation

It was time Sheffield and I had another little chat. After all, I had a lot more explaining to do, or so I thought. So after work on Monday, I turned down the chance to chew the fat with Bob, Bert and the others at Wetherspoon's and instead cajoled Sheffield into joining me for a quiet beer.

"You might be wondering why I kept you in the dark for so long," I started to explain after plonking our pints on the table.

"Not really boss," he said. "But I thought you'd get round to telling me eventually."

"Well you were right," I said, surprised he was one step ahead of me again. "But I didn't tell you because firstly, I was ashamed of what I had done, and secondly, because I didn't want to put you in a tricky position with the police."

"Forget it," he said taking a slurp of lager. "Anyone can invent a quote, which is why they get caught. But to actually do the story – that's genius. No one would think for a moment you'd do that. Not Katie, Colin or even Timmy."

"Well I'm not proud of it Sheffield, though," I said a bit worried that he was impressed rather than ashamed.

"But just so I'm clear, they are all real stories?" he asked. "It's just you haven't revealed your part in them, right?"

"Yes but that's a pretty big thing to miss out – we're supposed to be the 'eyes and ears of the people' after all," I said. "Not create our own stories to fill a page."

"So when did you have the idea?" he asked.

"It started when I smashed Ripley's shop front," I said. "That was not done on purpose. Well it was done on purpose, but not to get a story, if you know what I mean?"

"Not really boss."

"I mean I did it without realising I'd get a splash out of it. I just smacked the window."

"And turned it into a front page story?" he said.

"Yes but you understand it was done out of frustration?"

"If you say so boss," he said. "What was the next one?"

"It was the tractor story."

"You did that?"

"Yes."

"So you actually sprayed graffiti over the barn?"

"Yes, that's right. I broke in and drove the tractor onto the forecourt, then sprayed the words on the building."

Sheffield shook his head. "Unbelievable - what was next?"

"The anonymous letter was written by me."

"Okay, but you must have known about the dodgy contracts to write about them in the letter, so why go to the trouble of pretending to be a whistle blower?"

"Because I got the information by breaking into the council offices," I said. "I couldn't reveal that."

"You've been burgling the council too? Wow!"

"Not burgling, just searching for documents. The door was open. But that's the thing with all this stuff – you get sucked in. Once you've started, it's difficult to stop. It gets worse every time."

"Right, so what have you got planned next?" he asked.

It was the question I'd prepared myself for. There was the sting of course, and I could tell him about that. But I didn't want him to know about any other plans I was formulating because that would make him culpable in the crime.

"Selina and I are setting up a sting on Ripley. It's totally legitimate, but I'm waiting for her to call me to confirm. She says he regularly holds sex parties so we are planning to catch him red handed. Do you want in?"

"Of course," he said.

"Well let's do another joint by line. Only, she hasn't called for a while."

"Give her a ring now then," he said.

"I tried at the weekend but she hasn't replied, so I thought I would leave it a few weeks."

"Just call her, what's to lose?"

I didn't want to go into the details so just I dialled her number, fully expecting to get her voicemail. But to my delight she answered straight away.

"I'm so sorry I haven't been in touch," she said immediately. "But a girl went missing and I was doing everything I could to find her."

"Was her name Carrie?" I asked.

"Yes, you knew her didn't you?"

"It's a long story but I covered her death today with another reporter – that's what I'm ringing you about really - I've asked him to help with the sting."

"Simon! That wasn't the deal," she yelped. "I don't know the first thing about him. How can I be sure that I trust him?"

"You can. I promise," I said. "He is completely on side."

"I hope you know what you are doing for both our sakes. You obviously didn't with Carrie," she said with a hint of anger.

"What do you mean?" I asked.

"The word is Ripley stopped supplying Carrie drugs because you two were seen together. It was a punishment for being disloyal"

"We had a drink in town that's all. She gave me your name as a possible contact. That's all she did."

"Well that drink as good as signed her death warrant," she said.

"I thought she took her own life?" I asked as the full horror of what had happened dawned on me.

"She was a drug addict, Simon. She couldn't take it when Ripley stopped her supply. That's what everyone is saying. He as good as killed her."

A crushing feeling of guilt came over me, but I reconciled myself with the thought that I could never have predicted her death, so there was nothing I could have done about it.

"Do you still want to go ahead with the sting?" I asked feebly.

"It's made me surer that ever," she said. "Let's meet to discuss the plans, but somewhere where his spies won't see us. Tonight at The Fox near my place – just you and me. No Sheffield."

A date with the devil

Selina had been stewing on my decision to bring Sheffield into the fray, and was positively fuming by the time we met. "How do we know your friend won't blab about the whole thing?" she demanded to know. "He's a reporter after all!"

We were sitting next to a roaring log fire, which was spitting sparks like the incendiary words coming from her mouth. I moved the fireguard a few inches to stop them spewing onto the wooden floor.

"I'm risking my neck here and you are chatting with your mates about it," she continued. "That is totally unprofessional!"

"I'm sorry, but I had to bring him in," I explained. "He put me up after my flat was torched, and he would have twigged."

"Someone torched you flat? Who?"

"Ripley probably, but I don't have any proof. You see you're not the only one taking risks, Selina."

She sat back in her chair and let out a huge sigh. "Sorry, I had no Idea. If you trust this Sheffield guy, then I guess that's good enough for me."

"I do trust him totally," I said. "I've offered him a joint scoop for the story, which he wants. And it will be useful to have an extra pair of hands if things get tricky."

"I suppose so," she said. "The party is definitely happening. Ripley has already told me who to invite. He likes me to suss them out for him, what their weaknesses are - whether it's drugs, girls or even boys. You know - something he can hold over them later."

"You mean blackmail them?"

"You could call it that, but he never actually has to threaten them. He just reminds them of the night they spent with a hooker, and what their wives would do if they found out. They are pretty much putty in his hands after that."

"I don't understand why they take him up on the offer in the first place," I said. "Surely they know they are opening themselves up to a whole lot of trouble."

"Vanity I suppose. They are so grateful to be invited to his inner circle, to get into the boys club. Then I bring the prostitutes, the drugs, whatever is needed and bingo, he has something on them."

"And what does he have on you?" I asked flippantly

"My father;" she said fixing me with an angry stare, "he thinks I will stay in line because of him. He pretty much thinks he's got us all on a short leash. But you guys in the press, that's a different matter. He is terrified of you. And he's right to be. If we can get video recording equipment into the main dining room, you can ruin him."

"I'll need a few days' notice so we can get the devices?" I said.

"The party is this Saturday evening. Is that enough notice?"

It was tight, but I quickly worked out a plan. "I know a place in London. Sheffield and I can drive up on Saturday morning. We'll meet you at the pad at 2pm and set up the cameras. I will need to be at the party in case anything kicks off, so I'll lock myself in the spare drawing room."

"It's a deal," she said and placed her hand gently on top of mine.

Chapter 38: The fire

Carrie's face appeared in front of my eyes as I lay dozing in the darkness, her skin pallid white. She was smiling at me and looking straight in my eyes, just like the time we met for a drink. I thought I had forgiven myself for my part in her death, but it was clear that I'd just buried it deep in my subconscious. Guilt turned to anger, and anger to action. I looked over at Sheffield who was fast asleep and snoring loudly. I got out of my makeshift bed, dressed and left the house.

Rummaging through the glove compartment of the car, I pulled out the ordnance survey map of my patch and located The Ice House. It was surrounded by woods and farmland, so I figured I would park a short distance away and walk through the woods to minimise the risk of being seen. It might have been a bit melodramatic, but it seemed sensible at the time.

There was a small gym-style ruck sack and torch in the boot, but I needed to stop at a petrol station and buy some diesel - just a litre or two. I decided it was better if I drove out of town to reduce the risk of being spotted by a local, so I headed for the station I knew on the way to London. I checked my watch as I left - it was just after 2am.

It took about 20 minutes to drive there, buy a container and fill it with the diesel before starting the drive back to The Ice House. I knew the country lanes quite well by that stage, and I was sliding the car neatly around the bends as I hurried along.

When I got to within a mile of the building, I pulled into a layby and got out of the car. I stood still for a moment, listening for traffic - it was deathly quiet except for an occasional whistle as the wind rushed through the tree tops.

The leaves crunched underfoot as I walked through the forest, my eyes slowly adjusting to the half-moon light. Once I'd got to the perimeter of the building, I crabbed anti clockwise along the fence looking for an easy spot to get in.

The Ice House hadn't been used commercially for years, and was pretty well dilapidated. The fence was buckled and broken in several places and I walked through the first gap that appeared. Scores of shrubs had broken through the floor of the concrete yard, so I weaved my way through the greenery to the back of the building.

I shone my torch through a dusty window, lighting the contents of the shed. A pile of mature logs were stacked up against the wall on one side; next to them was a fork lift truck. I gave the backdoor a hard kick with the heel of my boot, and the lock gave way, causing the door to fly open and smash against the inside wall.

Great columns of traffic cones were piled so high on one side that they almost touched the ceiling, and hundreds of motorway maintenance lights, and signs, were stacked against the wall opposite. A pile of boiler suits were placed neatly in one corner next to several dozen steel toe-capped boots which were still in their boxes. A pneumatic drill was leaning against the wall beside them.

I emptied the diesel over the logs and onto the tyres of the truck. Then, taking a few steps back, I lit a match and threw it at the pile. The flame went out mid-flight and landed harmlessly on the floor.

I tried again, with the same result.

Walking up to the pile, I picked out a log still saturated with fuel and tried to light it by hand. Again the match went out, this time doused by the diesel.

"Jesus," I cursed under my breath.

I lit another match and put it to my rucksack; which burst into flames almost immediately. Then I grabbed the strap and threw it onto the logs. Within seconds, they burst into flames, and the fire quickly spread over the logs and onto the truck.

I dashed to the exit, pausing just a moment to take in the scene as I left - the place was an inferno; flames bursting out of the plastic cones and lapping the ceiling.

As I ran through the gap in the fence, the flames were billowing out of the windows. Turning for a final look, I stumbled and fell into the darkness, my eyes blinded by the light. Several loud explosions rang out as I inched my way to the car. It started up and I floored the accelerator, wheel spinning as I left.

Adrenaline had been replaced by pain as I pulled into the parking spot outside Sheffield's place. Caked in soot, my arms were grazed from the fall I'd taken. Blood trickled down my fingers

Sheffield was awake when I got back into his room, as if he'd been waiting up.

"Your splash?" he asked casually.

"Yes," I said.

"You'd better clean yourself up before my flatmates get up."

I chucked my clothes in a bin liner, tying the knot ready for disposal, and crashed into my makeshift bed.

Vibrations from my mobile phone woke me at 7am. It was Tim's turn to be on-call and he was angry.

7am: 'You need to get your lazy arse to The Ice House industrial estate in the Appleton, on the Longley road,' he said.

6:50am: 'As soon as you get this message GIVE ME A CALL!'"

6:45am: "'There's a fire on your patch, an industrial estate near Appleton called The Ice House – you know it? Emergency services just rang me; they are on their way down. Get your skates on and cover it."

I sent a quick text to Tim saying "got message – on way." Sheffield was asleep so I crept out for the second time.

The sun was just rising over the hills as I passed the layby where I had parked a few hours earlier. I pulled up outside the front of The Ice House and surveyed the scene.

Firefighters were dousing the building, which had almost totally disintegrated under the intense heat. Inspector Lane and Ripley were standing together looking at the debris. I made a beeline for them but seeing me approach, Ripley walked off briskly.

"You can understand if he doesn't want to talk to the press?" Inspector Lane said. "It's his yard that's been ruined."

"I suppose I do," I said enjoying the sweet taste of revenge. "Do you have any leads?"

He fixed a stare on me in such a way that I wondered if I'd somehow given the game away.

"Nothing specific, but let's see what forensics turn up," he sneered. "But you can tell your readers that if anyone has information about what caused the fire, they should contact the local police or Crime stoppers."

"So do you suspect arson?" I asked after jotting down the quotes.

"What makes you think that?" he said immediately.

"It's the line that we've been taking at the paper – that there has been a vendetta against Ripley."

"Well we are not ruling out anything at this stage," he said.

He wasn't being cooperative and I couldn't think of anything else to ask. So I put the question journalists are trained to ask when they might have missed something.

"Is there anything else you would like to add?" I said.

"Well my hunch is that since there's no electricity at the site, it's hard to see what it could be other than arson."

I took a couple of snaps of the fireman as they hosed water onto the top of the building. There were eight wagons lined up, so I snapped a photo of them. Then I snapped Inspector Lane silhouetted against the smouldering building and drove home. I had everything I needed for a splash and another page two wrap around.

Chapter 39: Midweek special

It was the first thing that caught my eye as I walked into the news room on Tuesday morning. Bright, white and with my name hand written on it; the letter must have been delivered overnight. I sat down at my desk and opened it hoping for something better than the usual inane press releases:

Council sorry for being the best Appleton has ever had

Appleton Council apologises to the people of the town for buying two strategic sites for a cut down price. We are sorry that this deal will allow us to develop the town centre in a way which the town would otherwise not have been able to afford. We apologise for being the first town council to actually get things done. Past Appleton councils have always talked a good talk, then never achieved anything. Those same people are now upset that the council is close to achieving its aims. We will continue to be the best council Appleton has ever had, but are sorry if that upsets people.

Signed

Appleton Council.

I clasped my hands together in delight – I had been wondering where page three would come from and there it was, gifted to me by the people that hated me the most. If only they knew what a favour they'd done me, I thought!

I had driven straight from The Ice House to work, so I had time to brew a cup of tea before Sheffield clattered through door into the news room. It was 8:58am and Katie had been waiting, watching.

"Look at this letter," I said, passing it over the partition after he'd slumped into his seat. He picked it out of my hands and read it quickly - a smile broadened across his face as he took it in.

"Did you write this?" he asked.

"Don't' be daft - and keep you voice down," I whispered, looking over at Tim. He was deeply engrossed in a book he was reviewing so I relaxed.

"Sorry boss," Sheffield said quietly. "But you can hardly blame me for thinking that after last week's splash."

He had a point, and I suspected he would question every decent story I had, now the cat was out of the bag.

"What were you up to last night then?" he added. "You smelled of bonfire when you got back."

"There was a fire at Ripley's industrial yard last night," I said hoping he'd be cool about it.

"A fire – you started a fire!" he hissed. "You could have killed someone!"

"Quietly," I said, noticing Tim's head bob out from the book. "No one's life was in danger. The building has been deserted for years and no one lives around there. I just lit a match and the whole place went up like a Christmas tree – let's call it revenge for what happened to the girl."

"Carrie?"

"Yes that's right. She would still be alive if she hadn't met me, you realise that?"

291

"You can't beat yourself up like that," he said. "She was dead long before you met her."

He scanned through the letter again, this time taking it all in. "This reads like something an angry school boy would write," he grinned.

"Exactly, and it will slot nicely onto page three."

Sofia loved it too, so I bashed it out after filing the page five story about Carrie:

"Best Ever' Council apologies for being too good

A south Somerset council apologised this week for being the 'best the town has ever had' after members were accused of profiting from property deals.

In a letter sent to The Sentinel, Appleton Council 'apologised' to townsfolk for buying two strategic sites 'for a cut down price'.

The council added:

- *"We are sorry that this saving will allow us to develop the town centre in a way which the town would otherwise not be able to afford.*
- *"We apologise for being the first town council to actually get things done.*
- *"Past Appleton councils have always talked a good talk, then never achieved anything.*
- *"Those same people are now upset that the council is close to achieving its aims."*

The council promised that it would "continue to be the best council Appleton has ever had, but are sorry if that upsets people."

Last week The Sentinel reported that the council had failed to renew special clauses when it sold properties to a development company part owned by Chairman Tom Ripley...

With page three filed by late afternoon and my splash in the bag, I was feeling pretty smug. But I should have guessed that Sofia would find a way of bringing me back down to earth. She had been chatting on the phone for nearly an hour, and made a beeline for me the moment she put the receiver down.

"A contact I have at the police has been onto us about The Ice House Fire," she said.

"That's great," I said nervously. "What did he say?"

"They have found DNA evidence at the crime scene indicating the arson was carried out by a white male," she said. "You can lead on that."

I felt prickles of heat bubble around my neck and ran a finger under my collar.

"Are you sure?" I asked. "I've never heard of that type of thing before."

"Neither have I," she said laughing. "But that's not the point. They might be trying to flush someone out of the woodwork, but it is a good line for a story."

My confidence was sapped - if they had my DNA, then it wouldn't take a genius to put two and two together and ask me to be tested. So I didn't rejoice when Peter told me that all eleven editions of the paper were going to carry the arson story on their front pages. "This business with the council is the biggest story we've ever had," he said to the whole newsroom. I blushed at the thought of the truth coming out.

"I think they're closing in on me," I said to Sheffield once Peter had left the room. "They must have my DNA!"

He burst out laughing. "Don't be daft," he said. "Who else is it going to be? In case you hadn't noticed, this county is full of white males. They are grasping at straws."

That calmed me down while I tapped out the story ready for filing the next morning:

Police seek 'white male' over arson attack

Detectives believe a 'white male' torched a building belonging to a council leader after an analysis of DNA evidence at the scene.

In a third attack on property owned by Appleton Council chairman Tom Ripley in recent weeks, The Ice House, at Ripley Industrial Estate, on Dark Lane, Appleton, is thought to have been torched by an arsonist on Monday night. The chairman's barometer shop was vandalised earlier this month and graffiti plastered over another building belonging to him a few days later.

Detectives believe the attacks were carried out by the same man.

A source close to the police said: "Forensics has found DNA from an unknown 'white male' at all three sites and pursuing that line. His DNA is not on police records so he is unlikely to have a criminal record."

Eight fire crews battled the fire on Saturday night….

Sheffield had been a great mate, so once I had finished the story I wanted to help him out. I hadn't bothered to ask how his front page was going, and expected another dismal story.

"How's your splash coming along this week?" I asked gently, hoping I could offer some advice.

"Fine thanks mate," he said. "I've just put it through to the newsdesk."

"Really?" I said. "You kept that quiet."

His cocky manner was unusual. It was like he was a new man.

"So what's the story?" I asked.

"Oh, someone plastered anti-council graffiti over the town hall last night," he said with a grin.

"You didn't?" I said utterly appalled.

"I did," he said poker faced.

I was shocked but could hardly complain. After all, it was me who'd inspired him.

"I guess we are in this together then," I said after a moment.

"Yes boss," he said.

"Will you come to London on Saturday then, I need to get the stuff for the sting?"

"Of course boss," he said. "Just let me know how I can help."

Chapter 40: National news

It all went pretty smoothly from then until we went to press, although there were a few grumbles from the other reporters about my story being on their front pages. But we settled down for drinks at the pub that night, and there were no hard feelings.

The next morning, Peter grabbed me as I walked into the newsroom with Sheffield.

"Great news," he said enthusiastically. "I've had a couple of national newspaper reporters on the telephone this morning wanting to interview you about the vendetta being waged against the council. They are linking it to the anonymous letter story and the council's apology. The guy from the Sun is calling them a bunch of fraudsters. He's going with the headline: Rotten Appletons."

"Wouldn't that be libel?" I asked, thinking I would never get away with it at The Sentinel.

"It's only libel if you can't prove it's true in court, Simon," he explained. "And the big papers have the best lawyers, so the council would be mad to sue them. Who would Appleton use against them – some provincial solicitor?"

I knew that newspapers rarely won libel cases because they were so unpopular with the public. But then again, politicians were pretty unpopular too, so they would probably cancel each other out.

"What's the other paper?" I asked hoping it wasn't another tabloid.

"It's The Times, which is not that surprising since they work in the same office at Wapping. Someone must have tipped them both off."

"Why don't they just share the story?" I asked.

"Oh they would never do that. There's huge rivalry between them - the editors would probably prefer another paper got hold of the story rather than be scooped by their stable mate. Watch what you say, though, because they may be at daggers drawn to get the best line "

If he was trying to relax me, it wasn't working. He gave me their numbers on a scrap of paper and told me to call them from his office right there and then, while the other reporters were gathering the bundles of papers from the basement.

"I'll leave you to it then," he said as he left the room, showing me a proud smile before he went. It was surreal, I was sitting at his desk feeling like the editor for a few moments.

I rang The Times reporter, Laurence Huntingdon, first, hoping he would give me an easier ride than the guy at the Sun. It soon became clear he wasn't particularly enthusiastic about the story, or at least hadn't bothered to read it properly.

"Any ideas who this white male is then?" he asked aimlessly.

"I wish I did," I said. "I'd have put it in the paper."

"Oh well, if you find out anything along those lines could you tip me off before you go to press?"

It was a sacking offence to give another paper a story before it was published your own. So he was either being ignorant or taking me for an idiot. "I'm afraid I can't do that because I'd be fired," I said "You'll have to wait until after my edition comes out. I'll give you a call if we print anything useful."

"It'll be too late by then," he reiterated. "I'll make sure you get a mention in the story if you give it to me beforehand. I'll even try to get you a joint byline if you like?"

"Okay I'll let you know if I can help," I said humouring him.

The exchange left me wondering if the standard of national newspaper reporters was sky high after all, and whether I should get myself up to London and try my luck.

"So what's your angle?" I asked trying get something from him.

"I'm thinking about going on the DNA angle," he said. "I've never heard of gender being identified before. It makes me wonder if they can determine eye colour or even hair."

"You'll need to ask the police about that," I said, "I really have no idea."

We carried on in that vein for a few minutes before he finally gave up. I put the phone down thinking he was unlikely to expose me.

The guy from the Sun, Matt Wakeford, was a totally different proposition. Impatient and aggressive, I got the feeling he was after something sensational.

"So your place gets trashed the week before," he said. "Then his industrial yard goes up in flames. That can't be a coincidence, don't you think?"

"That's probably one for the police," I said worrying he was on to me.

"It could be someone who has a grudge against you both, right?" he asked. "Maybe you wrote a story about how Ripley has done some guy over, so wants revenge against both of you! Him for what he did, and you for writing about it? Maybe it's something to do with those dodgy council deals?"

"Sounds like a long shot," I said hoping to throw him off the scent. "I mean, I can't think of anyone who had much to lose from those deals other than Ripley."

"There's something I'm missing," he said more to himself than me. "My instinct says there's a story here somewhere. I just can't see it. I'll have to think on it and get back to you. Okay?"

"Yes fine, you know where I'll be," I said thinking I would avoid him if I could. Hopefully he would move onto another story and forget about me.

Peter's face lit up when I told him about it all, delighted to hear about their line of questioning.

"It's fascinating that they are taking such different angles," he said. "But that's not surprising I suppose, given their readerships. Personally I think it's more of a 'mystery story.' You know, something along those lines – 'mystery surrounds a series of attacks against a council leader and a local reporter.' Maybe run with that this week?"

"I may well do that," I said. "If nothing else crops up by then."

"Good Simon," he said. "The national papers will be queuing up to hire you by the time you finish with this story."

He put the palm of his hand firmly on my shoulder as I left the room. "I've always said you young reporters should serve your time here, then move onto something better. I'll wish you the best when you go, Simon. I hope it's not too soon, but I really will wish you luck." I could only hope I would be leaving under the right circumstances, and not in the back of a police van.

I slipped back in the newsroom hoping no one would notice my absence. After all, people have been at the paper years and never had the ear of the editor.

Sheffield would normally have grilled me but he had gone on patch, hopefully finding real stories rather than more DIY stuff. So I found myself alone at my desk for a while. It was only a couple of days until the sting, and I came over with that feeling a kid gets before Christmas. I couldn't wait for the big day, but I still had the back pages to fill by end of play Friday.

I knuckled down to find something and fortunately old Tom Falding, the chairman of Bishopswood Council, gave me a story about a pile of human dung on a farmer's field which had 'residents kicking up a stink.' Then Longley Chairman, Ben Webster, rang with a tale about a family overlooking a cemetery who were complaining that a 'new headstone was spoiling their view.' Finally, late on Friday afternoon I filed my last nib and could relax.

Chapter 41: Spyware

It was during my time at the London Journalism School that I first became aware of The Spy Shop on the Edgware Road. Every aspiring reporter needs to a voice recorder and with my shorthand skills sorely lacking at less than 60 words a minute, I needed one more than most. So I had decided to buy the best recorder I could afford, which I imagined would allow me to replay interviews in the news room at my leisure. It was only later that I learned that local newspaper reporters don't have time to replay audio recordings - Teeline shorthand notes being a far more efficient way of getting quotes down on the page in time for deadline.

I had been mulling through a limited selection of old fashioned analogue recorders at one of the many electrical shops along the Tottenham Court Road, when a sympathetic journalist told me about The Spy Shop, which, he assured me, had a best selection of digital recorders in London.

I trooped down to the shop that afternoon before heading back to Ealing where I was living for the duration of my course. The shop itself was hidden amongst the eclectic mix of ethnic shops that punctuated the road. After scouting repeatedly up and down the street, and almost giving up hope of ever finding it, I spotted a small wooden sign directing prospective customers to the "personal security shop" down a narrow pathway called Pack and Prime Lane.

An antiquated bell, screwed to the door frame, twanged to attract the attention of the shopkeeper as I walked in. It proved to be an Aladdin's cave of surveillance equipment, offering everything from the simple digital recording devices to the most advanced wireless surveillance systems, presumably used by private detectives. I bought my recorder, which was no bigger than a match box, after a quick road test. It had an ear piece for recording telephone interviews, 24 hours of digital memory and clear playback sound quality. It hadn't occurred to me that I would be back in the shop less than a year later, to set up a major sting.

Sheffield offered to do the driving that Saturday morning. The idea was that we would split the cost of buying the surveillance equipment in exchange for adding his byline to the story. He wouldn't have any more involvement in the story after we got back to Yeovil, although he agreed to be contactable by phone to help in extreme circumstances, such as Ripley finding me in the house and threatening me with a butcher's knife. Quite what he would do then I wasn't sure. But it was good to have some moral support.

We set out at just before 10am, and were lucky enough to have a clear drive to London. There wasn't much conversation at first; instead we just bickered about directions and where to stop for some food. But the conversation eventually turned to our unique style of journalism.

"Do you think we are the only ones doing it?" Sheffield asked. "I mean, it's a great way of getting a scoop. We can't be the only people who have thought of it."

"I imagined I was the only person in the world who would want to do it, until you joined in," I said. "But I don't think we'd know if others were doing the same because they would hardly broadcast the fact. I suppose there could be hundreds of journalists out there doing it and we would be none the wiser."

It was a scary thought, but I'd been taught that nothing is new in journalism. So by that logic, we were not alone.

"I don't think there are," Sheffield said. "I mean, there must be plenty of Paddies out there - people who make up quotes. Everyone knows that's a temptation. But you are not going to get arrested for making up a quote. Whereas you could do a stretch in prison for what you've done - the shop, the graffiti, arson; they are becoming pretty big crimes."

It was true that things had escalated grotesquely, but the progression had been seamless, natural even. Like slowly boiling a frog in a beaker of water, I was getting in ever deeper trouble without noticing.

"I suppose we would have heard of someone being arrested if lots of reporters were up to it," I said. "It's too easy to get caught – all you need it some CCTV footage and that's that. I doubt the police would give you a slap on the wrist either for painting the town hall. You've probably ruined the place."

"I used water based paints so they should be able to wash it off," he said trying, and failing, to make a joke of it. "But being caught doesn't bare thinking about. Imagine the shame; we'd be 'door stepped' by television crews for sure. I'd probably move to Spain."

"I'd go to Australia," I said. "Have you ever been there?"

"No but it sounds like a great place to visit if things go wrong."

"The outback is so large that wanted criminals can disappear for decades. There's just one or two policemen for areas the size of Wales."

We arrived in west London at shortly after 1pm and parked at a free car parking spot I knew off the Finchley Road. From there it was just a few minutes by tube and bus to the Edgware Road, and we were soon walking past the little sign and down the alleyway to The Spy Shop.

The bell rang out as we entered just as it had the year before, and an elderly gentleman with a bushy white moustache came to the counter from the back office. He nodded politely and we said 'hello.' Then we started to browse the shelves.

Classical music was playing surreally in the background as we wandered through the forest of high tech gadgets. After scouting aimlessly for a few minutes, I asked the shopkeeper for help.

"We're looking for something to discreetly record a dinner party," I explained. "We are both journalists."

"I understand sir," he said poker faced.

"It's not a celebrity sting," I explained clumsily. "It's something in the public interest."

"Of course sir," he said with a hint of a smile.

Sheffield pointed to a 'Buttonhole microphone' on one of the shelves, which presumably could be sewed onto a jacket or shirt.

"What about using that boss?" he asked.

"We need something we can place in the room," I said. "Like a clock or a lamp with cameras embedded."

"I think I can help you sir," the shopkeeper said. He walked around the counter to join us and picked out several devices on a stand behind us. "They all have a camera embedded in them: clocks, pens, framed mirrors and paintings," he said.

I read an advert for a "mirror camera."

"High Quality Imaging: Lets you covertly record conversations using a one way mirror."

"If you tell me more about the setting, I may be able to recommend a device?" the shopkeeper continued.

"It will be in a manor house with eight people sitting around a dining room table," I said.

"Will you be attending?" he asked.

"I won't be at the table, so will need to start recording a couple of hours before the party starts and collect the equipment afterwards."

He scanned the shelf looking for something.

"This book has a camera hidden embedded into the spine," he said. "It has up to 16 hours of colour video memory."

"I don't think there is a book shelf," I said.

"How about this carriage clock?" he asked, opening up a glass cabinet and bringing out an antique style golden clock. "The lens is set in the middle of the dial."

I took a close look – the camera was virtually invisible to the naked eye.

"I'll take it," I said.

Sheffield pointed to what looked like a replica police speed gun. "Look at this radar recorder," he said. "You aim the beam at the outside of a building and record the conversation going on inside. I reckon you could use one of these next time the council holds a secret meeting?"

"But look at the price tag," I said - it was nearly twice our combined salaries.

"That technology was only available to the security services until very recently," the shopkeeper explained.

"Scary stuff," Sheffield said. "I wonder how many husbands have been caught having affairs with that."

The shopkeeper handed me another device. "You may find useful?" he said.

It read: *'Plug adapter recorder: Records hundreds of hours of high quality digital audio.'*

"It is very discrete," he explained. "The microphone is embedded inside the plug, which still works."

"I'll take it as a back-up," I said.

The bill came in at just over two weeks' pay, which Sheffield and I split down the middle. The shopkeeper placed the devices into a plain white plastic bag and we headed back to the car, well ahead of schedule.

We had another clear run to Yeovil, and played Sheffield's favourite game on the way. He was a genius speller, so the aim was to catch him out. He'd boasted that he could spell 'as well as a dictionary.'

"Spell Hart as in White Hart pub," I asked. I'd spelled it as 'heart' during my first week, much to Katie's amusement.

"Easy; H A R T," he said.

"What about source?"

"Chocolate sauce, a news source?" he said.

"Epitome?"

"With an 'e,' rather than a 'y,'" he said. "Come on, make them harder."

"Separate?"

"With an 'a'"

"Desperate?"

"With an 'e'"

"Principle?"

"School principle, a person's principals?" he said.

"Is council an 'are' or an 'is?'"

"Always an 'is,'" he said.

They were all mistakes I'd made at some point, although I didn't admit it.

The game kept us chatting for a while. But once we were back at Sheffield's place, he handed me the keys and wished me luck.

"Call me if anything kicks off," he said reassuringly as I left.

I parked a couple of hundred yards from the house and walked to the entrance. As soon as I got there, I sent Selina a text and waited for her to respond - hoping no one would spot me. She rang a few minutes later, telling me to walk to the back of the building, where she ushered me inside.

"Did you get everything you needed?" she asked.

"Yes everything went well. You still want to go ahead with it?" I said. I hadn't planned on asking but we were both taking a huge risk so it felt right to check.

"I've wanted to do this for years, so don't even think about pulling out," she said with a touch of frost. "Come on, let me show you the place."

She led me into the dining room where the table had been set with chintzy antique china. I wasn't going to say anything, but it looked old fashioned to me, like a scene out of the 19th century. There was solid silver cutlery and Royal Worcester plates with floral designs. A different rose painted on each one.

"Not my style dear," she explained. "It was bought on Tom's instructions."

Porcelain bonbon dishes decorated with peaches and plums with were placed between the plates and there was an ivory cruet in the middle of the table. Vintage crystal wine glasses glinted under a Victorian crystal chandelier. I was amazed at the effort Selina had gone to.

"This must have cost a fortune," I said checking the hallmark on one of the knives.

"Don't touch it, I've just polished them," she snapped. She looked stressed, as if the pressure was finally getting to her.

"Sorry," I said and polished the knife on my shirt, before placing it carefully back on its spot.

"Where are the girls?" I asked.

"They'll be arriving at the same time as the guests."

She glanced at the bag I was carrying. "Is that the surveillance equipment?"

"Yes, and it's all very discreet."

I pulled out the devices and placed them on the table next to a bronze figurine.

"This clock has a digital camera that can record continuously for up to 24 hours. We just need to angle it in the right direction. The plug adapter is an audio recorder, which I'm using as belt and braces."

"Looks like you've thought of everything," she said approvingly. "But will the paper run the story?"

"It will if we get everything recorded."

She picked up the plug adapter and examined it closely. "I can put this in the corner under the standing lamp. The clock can go on the mantel piece above the fireplace. They won't suspect anything."

"Where will Ripley sit?" I asked.

"At the head of the table, facing the camera," she said, walking to the mantelpiece and placing the clock there. "Are you still planning to lock yourself in the drawing room?"

"Yes I am. It'll give me a chance to see them arriving and leaving. And if anything goes wrong I'll be on hand to help you."

"Thanks but I don't need any help," she snapped. "Just make sure you're here at least an hour before the guests arrive. Otherwise Tiny Tom might spot you coming in."

Chapter 42: The Sting

Selina pulled into the manor house at 5:30pm with four pretty brunettes chattering in the passenger seats. Like some kind of Fifties television detective, I was peering at them through a gap in the velvet curtains of the drawing room. It was a bit creepy, but the escorts had no idea I was there, skulking in the darkness. The door was safety locked and the recording devices switched on.

Selina was wearing a tight red dress and the light from inside the house was casting subtle shadow across her figure, highlighting the glamour. The escorts also looked alluring in their little black numbers and high heels. They were every bit the high class companions Selina had been asked to provide. Ripley would be impressed.

The women were giggling as they entered the house and I could make out their conversation as they walked into the dining room. All good for the evening ahead, I thought. Someone switched on the chandelier, which caused a thin beam of light to shine through the keyhole, illuminating a patch on the drawing room floor.

I peered through the keyhole and got a good view of them all. It gave me sight of about half the room, including most of the table. I could watch and listen discreetly.

The smell of minted lamb wafted into the drawing room and I started to salivate because I had missed dinner. My stomach churned so loudly that I worried the guests might hear. I pressed down on my stomach to supress the rumbles.

Ripley was the next to arrive, the lights from his car blazing through the gap in the curtain and lighting up the painting on the drawing room wall. I backed away from the curtain for a moment, worried he might spot my silhouette. When I looked back, he was walking towards the front door. He was wearing a three piece suit and carrying a black walking stick. He bashed the door three times with its brass handle.

Selina scampered out of the dining room and welcomed him. Laughter filled the house as the women greeted his arrival like a returning king. It was a ridiculous charade, but one which pleased him greatly.

Pressing my ear against a wooden panel of the door again, I could clearly make out the conversation. Classical music was playing gently in the background, but Ripley's baritone voice easily cut through it.

"You have done a wonderful job my love," he said to Selina. "The table is beautifully set, the ladies look wonderful and the food smells delicious!"

He was being his most charming. Glasses clinked as vast amounts of bubbly were consumed. I could see them standing around the dining table, drinking and joking while they waited for other guests to arrive.

"Unfortunately tonight is not just about pleasure," Ripley said to Selina.

"Don't worry. The girls have been told keep quiet when the conversation turns business," she said.

He thanked her, reassured that everyone was aware of his plan. I was jotting everything down, just in case the recording equipment failed.

Cummings was the next to turn up, in a gleaming Chelsea tractor of some description. He was wearing a white dinner jacket, red tie and his cheeks were flushed with excitement as he flitted around the room greeting each of the girls.

Next was Inspector Lane, who had the temerity to arrive in a police car. He bear-hugged the two men, like comrades meeting up after a long break.

To my surprise, Joe Green then parked up. I recalled the letter he'd handed me on the day we'd met for lunch. If only I'd read it rather than stuffing it into the glove compartment of my car.

Finally, Selina's father rolled up in a Mercedes, popping a magnum of Champagne as he walked into the dining room.

They settled down at the table which was formed so each man had a woman sitting either side of him. Selina disappeared into the kitchen and came back with a trolley full of starters. The banter subsided while the guests tucked into their selection of prawn cocktails, wild mushroom soup or baked camembert.

It was a 'triumph!' according to Cummings. And to the uneducated eye, the party seemed full of joy. The men recounted their stories, the ladies listened patiently and laughed in delight at the punch lines. Selina was putting on a magnificent act, too. The men had no idea what fools they were.

She gathered all the empty dishes and disappeared to the kitchen for a second time before returning with a trolley full of main courses. The food was greeted with great enthusiasm - the lamb was 'the most succulent ever tasted,' and the roasted vegetables were 'an absolute delight.' And once the main course had been digested, the conversation turned to business.

What I didn't realise until I watched the video later, was that at this point Ripley pulled out a plastic pouch from his wallet, and proceeded to tap out a small pile of white powder onto the table.

"Would anyone like a go?" he said grinning and looking around at the table.

One of the escorts volunteered: "Yes sir!" she said. And they took turns to snort the powder using a rolled up note.

A few minutes passed and Ripley's seemed to lose all his inhibitions. "Do you mind if I take a sniff of this off you, my dear?" he said peering at the woman's breasts. She shook them playfully "Of course not," she giggled, and pulled down her top to reveal her full cleavage.

He tapped out a line on each breast, instructing her to keep still while he did so. Then he leaned down and he sniffed the substance into his right nostril, to a great cheer from the other guests.

"Anyone else," Ripley said triumphantly and holding the pouch in the air.

"I wouldn't mind having a go," said Cummings and he grabbed it.

The party descended into a near orgy at that point, with each of the men trying the same trick. Most of the powder ended on the floor, but enough went up their nostrils to ensure they were as high as a kite by the time Selina brought out the brandy.

Ripley warmed a glass in the palm of his hands, his cheeks flushed red from all the excitement. "If I might interrupt the fun for one moment, gentlemen," he said reclining in his chair and lighting a fat cigar. "I have to admit that I have an alternative motive for bringing you here this evening."

"We all assumed as much," said Cummings. "Is it to do with the press?"

"Exactly right, as always," Ripley said smiling. "And in particular The Sentinel."

"The latest headline was very damaging," said Cummings.

"It was, and it's not for the first time," Ripley said. "We need to review how we got where we are and what we can do to get out of the mess."

He turned towards Joe Green who had his nose in a glass of brandy.

"Joe, you gave him back his press card when he visited your restaurant?"

"I handed it to him myself, in an envelope with a note you gave me saying it was being returned by you," he said. "If ever there was a coded warning that was it. Any normal person would have taken the hint!"

"I agree wholeheartedly with that sentiment," said Ripley. "But it is evident that this is no normal person. The question I've been asking myself, is why doesn't he take the hint? I can only imagine he is very brave or very stupid?"

I pulled out my wallet and checked inside - sure enough the press card was missing. I hadn't used it for months so had no idea I'd lost it. I must have dropped it the night I smashed the shop window.

"If we'd followed my advice," said the Inspector, choosing his moment carefully, "we could have brought him in for questioning. Finding his press card puts him at the scene of the crime, but then you had to have it your own way as usual."

"I hold my hands up, I was greedy," said Ripley. "With hindsight it was a mistake to go for the insurance. But judging by what's happened since then, I doubt if it would have put him off the scent in any case."

315

"You may be right," the inspector conceded. "I assume you were behind the torching of his car, and the brick through his flat window?"

"How could you believe such a thing of me Inspector?" Ripley mocked. "But let's just say, I may know a man who did."

"Well I can't say I approve of that tactic," the Inspector said. "I've told you that before. It wouldn't take much for CID to get involved, and then what?"

"Well your plan to frighten him off with the DNA story fell well short of the mark too inspector," Ripley snapped. "He used it as the damn headline in the paper."

Inspector Lane brought his fist onto the table with a loud bang, causing the cutlery to jump and rattle. "He'll not make get the better of me, I promise you that," he shouted.

"Calm down Barry," Ripley said. "That's what we're here for tonight, to think of a way to stop him before he bankrupts us."

The table fell silent for a few moments while the men pondered.

"I am considering calling a lodge meeting to sort it out," Ripley said. "It's the only solution."

"There's no way they will back you over this, Tom," said Cummings. "You know that."

"So the oaths mean nothing?" Ripley sneered. "All the speeches and ceremonies, but when it comes to it, they won't act to help a brother in need?"

"Brother Malcolm won't break the law," the Inspector said. "They don't approve of the way you do things – you would be drummed out of the Masons."

"So what then, what can we do to stop this fellow?" said Ripley indignantly. "He's closed down The Lodge and ruined any chance we had of making something from Breakers Gate. And now The Ice House has gone up in flames. I don't believe in coincidences gentlemen."

The brandy was starting to run dry, so Ripley took a moment to snort another line of the white powder while Selina fetched a bottle from the kitchen.

"Perhaps we should try a honey trap?" said Cummings as she returned. He was staring at her intently, admiringly her figure.

"I think that may be our best bet. But how to do it?" asked Ripley, gazing towards Selina's father.

Mayor John Goodson, who had been quiet until that point, realised that was his cue to offer help. "Selina, my dear, I believe you know this reporter fellow we are talking about?"

"Yes father, I have spoken to him. You remember we met at the charity evening. And he has rung me a couple of times since. Calls unanswered naturally."

"Yes darling," he said, then looking round the table with a knowing smile. "Perhaps you could call him for us? Pamper his ego for a while. Every man has a weaknesses and mostly that includes the fairer sex."

Ripley clapped his hands in delight. "The solution was right here in front of us all the time," he said. "You could easily work yourself into a position of trust my dear."

"And then what?" asked the inspector.

"Poetic justice is what," Ripley said. "Let the reporter become the story for once. It would be easy enough, just get him to admit the shop vandalism, the arson etcetera."

"But why on earth would he say such a thing?" Selina asked indignantly.

"Well, if you promise him certain inducements my dear, he will probably admit to just about anything," Ripley grinned.

"There's no point," said the inspector. "It'll never stick in court. The judge would throw it out as 'entrapment'."

"But he would be out of our hair in the meantime!" Ripley roared, the cocktail of drugs making him even more ebullient than usual.

"I have another idea," said Cummings softly. "We have no proof that he was involved in the arson, but we suspect him, correct?"

"We do," said the inspector. "He has the motive and opportunity."

"Then we need to help justice a long a little. Get the odds in our favour."

"I'm listening," said the inspector.

"We need to plant some evidence inside his flat; something from The Ice House which would link him to the fire."

"Like what exactly?" asked the inspector. "People only need a match to commit arson."

"What about if the accelerant was found in his home, along with plans of the site and articles about arson?" said Cummings, "All hidden under a lifted floor board?"

"It could work," said the inspector. "The fire service says diesel was used to start it. So if evidence was found at his home it would probably be enough to prosecute."

"And regardless of whether he is convicted or not," said Mayor Goodson, "he would have to stand down at the paper. I could make sure of that."

The men nodded their approval and Ripley raised his glass.

"We have a plan then, gentlemen," he said and the four men chinked their glasses in unison.

"I will start drawing up the details later this week," said Ripley. "It should be simple enough."

He wrapped an arm around the narrow waists of the escorts either side of him, and hugged them tightly. "The bottom line is this," he added. "We cannot allow all good work we are doing for the community be undermined by one rogue reporter."

"He will never understand that we do everything for the wider public good," Cummings added. "If we look at this evening for instance, these delightful young ladies are given money to help pay the rent, feed their children. All because of the system. Without it, such costs would fall to the taxpayer."

"That's exactly my philosophy," said Ripley. "The community would be bankrupted if we let newspaper men run the world. More public funds would be needed for assets such as community halls, and folk would lose hundreds of affordable homes. We control vice, so criminals are driven out. All the drugs dealers have been run out of town thanks to us."

"There's no denying that," said the inspector. "We've closed down every supplier."

"A toast then," said Cummings. "To Chairman Ripley; for all his work in the community."

The guests staggering to their cars at 2am, each accompanied by an escort. Last to leave was Ripley who hugged Selina tightly before falling into his Jag.

After I was sure they'd all left, I unlocked the door and walked into the dining room. Selina rushed over and gave me a hug.

"It was horrible," she said. "They were worse than ever."

"But did you hear what they said?" I said. "They confessed to practically every dodgy deal that has ever been organised."

"You have enough for a story then?" she said.

"There must be enough material for ten front pages."

"But what about all the horrible things they were saying about you? How are you going to tell your editor?"

"Don't worry about that," I said. "I have a plan."

Chapter 43: All editions

The video flickered into life at the point where Ripley pulled out the bag of white powder. Peter's eyes bulged at the sight of him waving it in the air and then snorting the substance on camera.

I'd briefed Peter about the sting, and that there were various unfounded allegations against me, which I wanted to keep from Katie and Sofia. He suggested that we watch the video alone in his office.

He watched without saying a word as the story unfolded, the occasional guttural grunt being the only clue to his state of mind. After we'd watched the most incriminating parts, I switched the video off and waited for his reaction.

"You can't show this video to anyone else in the office," he said emphatically. "It would start rumours, which would be better avoided."

I was relieved at the sentiment, but surprised he wasn't more excited by the scoop.

"But are you happy to run the story?" I asked tentatively.

"Of course," he said, a smile returning to his face. "This is absolute dynamite. What sort of an editor would I be if I didn't run this? It's the biggest story the paper has ever run Simon."

Despite what I'd said to Selina, until that moment I hadn't quite let myself believe he would run it. But now I could see victory in sight and I was overcome with a sense of triumph.

"You'll need to give them all a right of reply to the story on press day," Peter added. "But the evidence is there on the screen, so you only need to contact them as a courtesy."

"Them? You mean I should run stories on all of them?" I asked.

"Of course - Ripley, the deputy, the police inspector, mayor – nail the lot," he said adamantly.

"You mean name them all in one splash?" I asked wondering if I could fit all the detail into one story.

"No, fill the paper with it – page seven onwards. I want every spit and cough. Run it across all the editions!"

Peter gave me his office for the rest of the week, so I could avoid the distraction of the gossiping in the news room. I spent half of Monday tapping out the quotes from the video. He brought in a round of sandwiches and gave me an update.

"I've cleared everything with Katie and Sofia," he assured me. "But make sure you meet the 4:30pm deadline because all the editions are banking on you."

A good story writes itself, so I had been told. And once I had worked out what page each story would go on, the writing flowed:

Page Seven: All Editions

Police chief admits colluding with council over illicit drugs

A police inspector confessed to closing down 'rival drugs dealers' so a criminal council could profit from the illegal trade

Inspector Barry Lane, of Yeovil Police, said the police had "closed down every supplier" to ensure Appleton Chairman Tom Ripley had a monopoly on dealing drugs in the district...

I texted Sheffield explaining I was working late so we were able to slip out of the building after the others had left. He updated me about the office gossip.

"Peter told everyone not to speak to you about the story even after work," he said. "Everyone knows about the sting. They are all talking about who was there and whether you are going to be made chief reporter. Katie and Sofia are furious they haven't been allowed to see the video. It's hilarious," he said smirking.

"Why would anyone think I was going to be the chief reporter?" I asked.

"Tim overheard Katie and Sofia talking about it, that's all I know."

"What about Colin?"

"Apparently he is leaving the paper to join the police because the pay is better."

Sheffield was as much in the dark as the others at that point. All I'd told him was that everything had gone well but he should wait to see how Peter reacted. I just didn't want to tempt fate. So I spent the evening explaining everything, much to his amazement. My only concern was that Selina had gone to ground after the party, saying she would be in touch after things "calmed down." So I didn't contact her even though I longed to see her.

323

As usual, Sheffield and I walked to the office on Tuesday, saying goodbye at the top of the stairs as I forked left into the editor's office. I'd tapped out the next two pages by lunchtime:

Page five: All editions

Masonic brotherhood link to council revealed

Appleton council chairman and his deputy have admitted being members of a secret order of free masons, the Sentinel sting has revealed....

Page three: All editions

Community hall project was 'a fraud' admits council leader

Plans to build a community centre at Alma Court, Breakers Gate and The Ice House were concocted to make Appleton Chairman Tom Ripley a huge profit, a Sentinel sting has revealed....

Sofia and Katie paid me a visit shortly after I'd put the pages through. They were full of compliments and waxing lyrical about the stories. It was quite surreal but I played along with it. They asked about the video, and if they could take a look more as a favour to me in case there were any legal issues to be avoided. I thanked them politely, but said they needn't worry because Peter was on top of things. They left with a slam of the door.

I'd filed the splash on Wednesday morning:

Pages one and two: All editions

Night of Shame for civic leaders

Civic leader, prominent businessmen and police were filmed snorting a white powder off prostitutes' breasts, a Sentinel sting can reveal.

Appleton chairman Tom Ripley and his deputy Pat Cummings were seen snorting the powder off the high class escorts at a party hosted by the chairman.

In a night of drugs and sex filmed by The Sentinel, other guests included Inspector Barry Lane of Yeovil Police, Yeovil mayor John Goodson and Appleton businessman Joe Green. They were recorded plotting to frame a Sentinel reporter for last week's arson at The Ice House.

The party was held on Saturday at Chairman Ripley's house near Appleton.

Four high class escorts attended the nine hour drink and apparent drugs binge….

With the story filed, there was just one task to be completed. I decided Ripley should be the first we called.

"I've told you to go through the clerk," he said gruffly after answering his mobile.

"I think you'll want to hear this one," I butted in before he could hang up. "We're running a story about the party you held on Saturday night."

"What party?" he said bluntly. "There was no party…"

"The drugs and sex orgy," I said. "And there's no point denying it, Tom. We are going to run the story anyway. We recorded the whole thing using surveillance cameras; you are seen snorting a white powder and fondling the escorts. We've also got you on the record admitting that the community hall was a fraud and your membership of the Freemasons. Plus your plan to frame me for the arson."

325

There was a long silent pause before the line went dead. I called back, but his phone went to voicemail.

I asked Sheffield to dial the others, after all he was getting a joint byline, which hadn't gone down well with Katie and Sofia. But my word was law by then, and they had to back down.

Unsurprisingly, none of the party guests was keen to talk. We got the anticipated threats of legal action, but that was never going to stop Peter running the story. Sheffield and I walked home on Wednesday evening happy in the knowledge that we'd done our jobs properly. The story was at the printers, ready to cause a sensation the next day.

Chapter 44: Murder story

Wetherspoon's was packed - as if every reporter and subeditor had turned up to celebrate Le Petit Weekend drinks after my splash. They'd come to hear gossip of course, but I did my best to deflect as much as I could onto Sheffield. He got a byline out of the story after all, and seemed to enjoy having the onus far more than me.

"It was a joint splash with Sheffield," I told Bob who was drilling me for information about how I got the story. "He can fill you in as much as me."

"Come on mate," he said sceptically. "He only got that byline because you are mates. You're doing him a favour to save him from the sack, we all know it. Has Ripley been in touch since you rang him?"

"I've not heard a peep out of any of them," I said as Colin joined the huddle, handing me another pint. I put it on the table in a neat row with three others.

"Something's brewing," Colin said. "He's not going to take that story lying down."

Just as he'd finished speaking, I felt my mobile ring. I pulled it out of my pocked fully expecting to see Ripley's name on the screen. But to my relief it was Matt, the Sun reporter. I let it ring to answerphone then walked outside so I could listen somewhere quiet.

"Hi it's Matt from the Sun," he said. "The police have tipped us off that you were behind the arson and two more criminal acts against the chairman. We are running a story about it in tomorrow's paper. Call me as soon as you get this."

I froze in fear, berating myself for not having seen it coming. How stupid was I for not predicting how Ripley would hit back? But when I'd thought it through, I realised that all was not lost. I even wondered whether I should reply. After all there was a good chance the editor wouldn't run the story unless they heard my side of things. I could keep quiet and hope it would blow over once my story was published the next day. Ripley's story would look like some kind of tawdry revenge if they ran it after that. Even a tabloid wouldn't publish it. But then I remembered what Peter had said about the tabloids having all the best lawyers. I couldn't take the chance of them publishing without hearing the facts.

I thought over my lines and dialled his number. "Matt, it's me," I said after he picked up. "I thought I'd better put my side before you commit a huge libel against me."

"Go on," he said indifferently.

"It's obvious - he's lashing out because we are running a massive story on him in tomorrow's paper."

"What story?" he asked.

"We hit them with a sting operation on Saturday night," I said. "There was a party - a drugs orgy - organised by Ripley. The police inspector was there, snorting white powder off a prostitute's breasts. And we got them on video planning to frame me for the fire. You run that story and you'll look stupid the next day. Plus I'll sue you for every penny you've got."

"Right," he said pausing to think. "What was the policeman's name then? The one at the party."

"Inspector Barry Lane," I said emphatically. "It's obvious they are lashing out because we've got them on video. They even admitted that they belong to the masons."

"Oh I see," he said. "You've got that on the record?"

"Right there on the screen in glorious technicolour."

"Okay, I'd better speak to my editor. Can we have the inside scoop if we go with your version?"

"Of course, as long as you don't run anything tomorrow. I'll give you an exclusive interview after that."

The phone clicked off and I breathed a huge sigh of relief. Surely I'd done enough? They couldn't run the story after that?

Sheffield had worked his way through half of my free drinks by the time I got back to the table.

"Who was that?" he bleated without a care in the world.

"It was the Sun," I said. "Ripley has accused me of the arson, but I think I talked the reporter around."

"How did you to do that?" he asked looking at me in astonishment. As if his world was about to implode.

"I just said they were making it all up because of tomorrow's sting. The actions of desperate men."

"Good thinking," he said, the smile returning to his face.

Things went quiet for a while, and copious amounts of alcohol were drunk by everyone but me. I was still too nervous.

Then I got a second call – but this time Ripley's name flashed up on the screen.

"Ripley," I said picking up.

"I suppose you think you've won?" he said coolly.

"It's not a game, Tom."

The phone went quiet for a few seconds, then Selina's terrified voice screamed down line. "Whatever he says don't come over!"

The phone went dead leaving me in a state of shock, helplessly wondering what I could do.

"What is it boss?" said Sheffield seeing the horror in my eyes.

"Ripley," I said. "He's got Selina!"

The phone rang again. "You'll have to do exactly what I say if you ever want to see this little traitor again," he said chillingly.

"Where are you?" I demanded to know.

"Come to The Lodge alone and we'll cut a deal," he said. "I'll wait for half an hour. If you are not there, then the deal is off and you won't see her again. Come alone."

"What's happening?" Sheffield asked.

"I have to get her."

"It's a trap," he said. "You know that don't you?"

"Of course, but I have no choice. He'll kill her if I don't."

"Let me come then," he begged.

"Not this time – it's too risky."

In a panic, I ran to my car and drove to The Lodge as quickly as I dared. Too fast in fact, because I misjudged the final bend and slid into a hedge. I ran the last few hundred meters to the gate, only slowing to a walk as I got there.

The front door had been left a few inches ajar so I pushed it gently, and I slipped into the darkness.

I couldn't make anything out at first, as my eyes adjusted. Then black shapes came into focus – I could see a flight of stairs.

Staying by the door, I phoned Ripley and could hear his phone ringing upstairs. Just three rings, then it went quiet.

Walking softly on the edges of my shoes, I started up the staircase to the bedrooms.

At the top was a hallway with three doors leading off it.

"Ripley," I called out softly into the darkness. But there was no reply.

Tip toeing to the nearest bedroom, I gently turned the brass handle and pushed the door open to peer inside.

Moonlight streaming through a thin lace curtain - it was empty.

A muffled cry came from the next room along, then a second.

I bolted out of the room and kicked the door open with the heel of my boot.

Ripley was sitting on a double bed, the moonlight lighting up one side of his face. He was holding a shotgun on his lap, and wore a demented grin. Selina was sitting next to him, her wrists and feet tied together. Duct tape was wound around her mouth and she was breathing heavily through her nose.

"I'm glad you could make it," Ripley said softly.

"You said you wanted a deal?" I said, my eyes drawn to his finger which was poised on the trigger. I'd thought about rushing him but I'd have no chance.

"I'm afraid it's too late for deals," he said, then slowly swung the gun barrel towards my head. "You see, I can't deny video evidence can I?" he said. "That was your biggest mistake."

"The copyright belongs to me," I said trying to think quickly. "I'll destroy it and your reputation will be saved."

"I'm not a fool, Simon," he said. "I know when I'm beaten."

"So why bring me here?" I asked in desperation.

"You and I are not so dissimilar you know." he said. "We both took a wrong turn at some point. And we are both motivated by revenge. I think you would do the same as I if you were in my position?"

"Do what exactly?" I asked.

He stroked Selina's face, letting go of the shotgun for a moment. "She's confessed her role, so it will be poetic justice that you both die," he said smiling. "We will go down in history you know. They will still be talking about us in 500 years' time. We'll be immortal! Wouldn't you like that Simon?"

The fleeting moment of opportunity came while he was waiting for my answer. His concentration broken by the need to humiliate me.

Selina rolled onto him, spinning madly and with elbows flying at his face. I flung myself at him, desperately grabbing for the gun as I got there. It dropped from his lap, bounced a few inches in the air and blasted into Selina.

He grabbed it and tried to swing it towards me, but I managed to clasp hold of the barrel with both hands, and we fell to the floor wrestling for control.

He was on top on me at first, pushing the steel barrel onto my neck, straining like a bodybuilder trying for a record weight. I made a grab for his throat, trying to hold his weight with one arm as I did so. And I squeezed.

He leapt backwards in horror grabbing his neck, coughing and the gun dropped to the floor. I grabbed it while he was still reeling, and aimed it towards his head.

"Let's do a deal," he gasped. But it was too late for him. I blasted off the final round into his temple, killing him instantly.

It was a scene of horror - Selina was lying on the bed, groaning in agony. Blood was gushing from her stomach and covering the white linen. I removed the tape from her mouth but she died before she had a chance to speak. Her eyes rolling into the back of her head as her spirit flew.

I held her for one moment, desperately willing her to live. It might seem callous, but then my survival instinct kicked in: first, I wiped my finger prints from all the surfaces, then I positioned the gun in Ripley's hands so as to make it look like a suicide. I took off his right shoe and sock and stuffed his big toe into the trigger mechanism in an attempt to make it look like he'd pulled the trigger with that digit. I didn't look back as I left, scared the image would haunt me forever.

Peter was standing over my shoulder as I finished typing up the splash next Wednesday morning. There had been massive press interest since news leaked out of Ripley's suicide. No one seemed to suspect me, not even the Sun reporter who was delighted when I gave him the exclusive. But then again, it helps when you write the news:

Splash: All Editions

Leader and hostess in suspected murder suicide

A Council chairman is thought to have taken his own life after murdering the daughter of Yeovil's mayor, according to sources close to The Sentinel.

Appleton chairman Tom Ripley was found dead from gunshot wounds next to the body of socialite Selina Goodson.

It followed a Sentinel sting last week in which Ripley was filmed snorting drugs and fondling prostitutes.

According to sources close to Yeovil police, Ripley was killed by a shot to the head. He is thought to have turned the gun on himself after he shot and killed Miss Goodson with a blast to the stomach. Police are not looking for anyone else in connection with the death...

Epilogue

They say we must reap what we sow but my many criminal actions have done me nothing but good; in terms of my career at least. Ripley's suicide story had 'legs' as journalists say - it ran and ran. Indeed, the story got bigger and more elaborate each day, until I was appearing on all manner of news and current affairs programmes waxing lyrical about the plot.

I became a household name in just a few weeks and was soon signed up as a crime correspondent by a major Sunday newspaper. I'm now a regular guest on national television whenever a major crime strikes. They ask me about motive, justice and the criminal mind, which is one thing I don't have to pretend to be an expert in.

From cub reporter television personality and household name was not a journey I envisaged, but perhaps it was always my destiny. I have been given a book contract, with my very own ghost writer, because I'd have no time to write it myself, you see. It's going to be about my time in Appleton, the folk there and how, if you scratch the surface, you may find something sinister lurking.

With the proceeds of the book, I'll buy a house in the country, ironically not too far from Ripley's party mansion. But despite all the trappings, I have this terrible fear, the stuff of nightmares; that one day a reporter will come calling who will tell the world what I have become: a fraudster, shammer, villain - the incidental murderer.

The End